HARLEY QUINN

MAD ♥ LOVE

ALSO AVAILABLE FROM TITAN BOOKS

BATMAN: THE KILLING JOKE by Christa Faust and Gary Phillips
BATMAN: THE COURT OF OWLS by Greg Cox

HARLEY QUINN

MAD ♥ LOVE

PAUL DINI AND PAT CADIGAN

Based on the comic book by Paul Dini and Bruce Timm

Harley Quinn created by Paul Dini and Bruce Timm

TITAN BOOKS

HARLEY QUINN: MAD LOVE
Hardback ISBN: 9781785658136
Ebook ISBN: 9781785658143

Published by Titan Books
A division of Titan Publishing Group Ltd
144 Southwark Street, London SE1 0UP
www.titanbooks.com

First edition: November 2018
10 9 8 7 6 5 4 3 2 1

A CIP catalogue record for this title is available from the British Library.

Designed by Crow Books.

Printed and bound in the United States.

This is for all the women
who met Mr. Wrong
and said,
This is the man for me!
(Hey, it coulda been worse—it coulda been forever.)
P.C.

♦

To Arleen Sorkin
for giving Harley Quinn
her voice, heart and soul on screen,
and to Pat Cadigan,
who gave her the same in this book.
P.D.

PROLOGUE

The story of Harley Quinn begins with a heist in a New York nightclub.

Given whom the world knows Harley Quinn to be, this may seem only fitting, perhaps expected. But as it happens, Harley Quinn wasn't involved. She wasn't even there at the time. Nonetheless, each life touches another. Nothing happens in a vacuum; the effects of every deed ripple outward.

The nightclub in question was called Pulsar and it was *the* place to be after dark on a Friday—noisy, crowded, jumping. Good music, good company, good feelings, good riddance to another work-week—it was all so good, nobody noticed the crew breaking into the owner's office. The owner herself was having a good time, not in the club but several floors up in her private apartment, with a particularly attractive gentleman caller. She didn't worry about being robbed; she had insurance.

Robbers, however, don't get insurance of any kind. Nor is there any compensation when a job goes wrong, as it did on this night. The robbers cracked the safe expecting it to be filled with money, bonds, and jewels; instead, they found the cupboard was bare.

The crew had had a solid plan drawn up for them by an experienced professional as payment for an outstanding debt. Said professional knew all about the safe, the office, and how to avoid Pulsar security. He also knew the owner would be more concerned with running her fingers through the long, silky hair of her gentleman caller than running the nightclub. On Friday nights, Pulsar ran itself anyway; you opened the doors and the wage-slaves came in to spend money on drinks and bar snacks till closing at three a.m. Other refreshments were also available—nothing says *We're having some fun now!* like Bolivian Marching Powder or super-X—but that was someone else's business, nothing to worry about on a usual night.

Unfortunately, the DEA and local law enforcement had picked this night to execute a raid. They swarmed in, killing the buzz along with the music just as the robbers discovered all their efforts had been for nothing.

Pointing at the empty safe and shrugging isn't a get-out-of-federal-custody-free card. The robbers had no choice but to shoot their way out, which was the last thing they wanted to do. Shooting cops was the best way to summon the wrath of the entire NYC police department in all its full, unrestrained glory. The feds could have whatever was left. If there *was* anything left.

But nobody wanted to go to jail, either. The robbers fled with nothing to show for their efforts but regret and some painful gunshot wounds for the mob doctor.

Harleen Quinzel played no part in this; she was seven years old and it was already past her bedtime when the robbers heard the police sirens. The following day, while everyone was lying low and Pulsar's owner was filling out insurance forms and letting her lawyer handle the cops, Harleen Quinzel was at Coney Island with her daddy.

1

This was the best day *ever*, and Harleen felt like she'd waited forever for it. She and her daddy had spent a lot more time together back when her parents had only had her. But then her baby brother had come along. The baby was cute but, boy, could he cry. Her daddy explained how he was totally helpless and needed a lot of attention, and he was sorry about that, but he and Mommy would make it up to her. She just had to be patient, be a good girl and help out.

So she was patient, she was a good girl and helped whenever Mommy needed her, and right around the time she thought Mommy and Daddy might make things up to her, they brought *another* baby brother home. Now there were *two* of them, and all she could do was go on being good and helping out. But Daddy said they were going to make it up to her. Daddy *promised*.

Then they went to the hospital and brought home yet *another* baby brother, for a grand total of three. *Three* baby brothers.

It was hard to believe that her parents really thought her having so many baby brothers was a good idea. But then, grown-ups could be so weird.

If they'd asked Harleen, she'd have suggested going to the movies or seeing the Ice Capades at Madison Square Garden. But what she really wanted was for Daddy to take her to Coney Island for the day, just the two of them. Daddy never got all bent out of shape about how many hot dogs and caramel apples she ate, and he wasn't afraid to go on the Wonder Wheel with her. When Mommy was there, she'd get after Harleen for dripping mustard on her shirt or having sticky hands from cotton candy or not wanting the rest of the apple after the caramel part was gone.

She knew Mommy couldn't help it; it was how mommies were. Daddy was different. But now that they had all those baby brothers, it seemed like he was always working and never got a day off. He would apologize to Harleen and tell her they'd have some fun together as soon as he could make the time, something really, really good. He usually said it as he was going out the door.

At least he and Mommy had quit giving her baby brothers. That was something to be glad about. But now Harleen was starting to think that Daddy was working so much, he'd forgotten how to do anything else. And worse, maybe he would rather work than be with her and Mommy and the three very loud baby brothers.

This morning she had been resigned to another Saturday changing diapers and pretending she didn't hear Mommy muttering about being trapped (which didn't make any sense because they didn't even have mousetraps), when suddenly Daddy told her to hurry up and get dressed or they wouldn't get to Coney Island until noon.

Harleen had actually wondered if it would really happen, afraid that as soon as they left the house, Daddy would get a call and he'd have to go to work after all and she'd be marooned on the dark side of disappointment, changing diapers.

But she and Daddy rode the Q Line on the subway all the way to Coney and got there *hours* before noon. Daddy told her if he got a work call, he wouldn't answer it. He wasn't even going to *say* the word "work" for the rest of the day.

And it was a *wonderful* day. Just her and Daddy, riding the carousel, the Wonder Wheel, and the roller coaster, and going through the Funhouse. The Funhouse had been completely repainted and done over. There was new stuff, too, like the big, fat cushioned rollers hanging vertically that pushed you through them like you were cookie dough, and a place where sections of the floor moved separately under your feet, going back and forth so you stumbled and staggered, and lots of funny mirrors that made you look short and squashed, or tall and stretched out, or warped and weird.

Even the long slides were new, bigger and longer. She was too afraid to go down one by herself so Daddy went with her, holding her tight as she screamed with the thrill of it.

For lunch, they had Nathan's hot dogs washed down with something called coconut champagne, which wasn't really champagne but it sure was *sweet*; she couldn't finish it. Daddy didn't mind—he couldn't finish his either. Later, when she had a caramel apple for a delayed dessert, he didn't mind her leaving the apple for the birds after all the caramel was gone. He said he didn't want to eat an apple without any caramel either, and they both laughed.

Daddy said he couldn't go on any rides right after eating so they played games—skee ball, ring toss, Lobster Pot Pyramid Smash, and Grab A Duck. Grab A Duck was best—she and Daddy both won stuffed animals. She won a funny monkey and Daddy won an ostrich. They were small but still wonderful because she and Daddy won them together. Daddy asked her to take care of his ostrich for him because he worked so much and he didn't want Ozzie to get lonely. Harleen loved that Daddy had already named him.

They were walking past the roller coaster when Daddy stopped and showed her the framework structure, the way the wood boards crisscrossed. It was called a lattice, he said, and it made a special pattern of light and shadow—if you stood inside and held very still, you'd be so well camouflaged that you'd be practically invisible to people passing by.

"Not that you'd ever need to do that," Daddy added as they walked on. "Not in a place like Coney Island."

Harleen nodded, holding his hand and looking back over her shoulder at the lattice.

When the shadows began to stretch and the sunshine turned

a soft gold, Harleen thought Daddy would say they should think about going home, but he didn't. Instead, they went to some of the sideshows, where Harleen saw a lady on an electrified throne with thousands and thousands of volts running through it and she never felt a thing, even though she lit a torch from her tongue.

Another lady was so flexible, she could twist herself into positions that made Harleen's eyes water. She'd never seen anyone so limber, not even her gymnastics teacher. Then there was a guy who hammered a nail right into his face and didn't even bleed.

Daddy took her back to the Funhouse after that and they went down the big slide five more times together. By the fifth time, she wasn't scared anymore and she was shrieking with laughter as she and Daddy sat on the little rug and slid down the long curve. Having his strong arms around her made her feel like nothing bad could ever happen to her.

On the way out, she and Daddy opened a door they thought was an exit and found themselves in a small, stuffy, and very messy room. There were cans of paint and varnish all over the place, like whoever had finished with them had just left them lying around for someone to trip over. Sheets of plywood leaned against one wall. Nearby were big bottles of carpenter's glue and pieces of blue chalk. A very large sheet of plywood lay over two sawhorses, with a power saw on top of it.

The air was dry and smelled heavily of sawdust, though there were other odors underneath it—wet paint, thinner, and something like rubber cement, only somehow more intense, like it had a lot more chemicals in it. Harleen felt her stomach turn.

"This isn't a nice place," she said unhappily.

"No, it's a work-room," Daddy said. "Somebody's got to make the fun stuff." He led her back out the door, shutting it behind them.

Harleen looked up at him. "I guess making fun stuff isn't much fun."

"You said a mouthful, kid," Daddy chuckled as she pulled him away from the door. That awful chemical smell was still in her nose; she needed fresh air to chase it away. When they did finally get outside, it was dark.

Harleen felt a thrill of excitement. It was so late! Mommy always said when the streetlights went on, it was time to go home. If Mommy had been there, Harleen would already have had her bath and be in her pajamas.

But Daddy still wasn't in any hurry to get home. Instead, he took Harleen to get something to eat—a real meal, he said, so when Mommy asked if they'd eaten anything besides hot dogs and candy all day, they could tell her they had. So they went to a funny little diner called En-Why, where all the waitresses had big bouffant hairdos, called everyone hon or sweetie, and popped their gum when they talked in heavy Brooklyn accents. Harleen thought it was almost as much fun as Coney Island.

Daddy let her order a bacon cheeseburger, curly fries, and onion rings while he had a meat loaf, mashed potatoes and gravy, and green beans. Mommy made that a lot, although sometimes Mommy's meat loaf seemed like it was a lot more bread crumbs than meat.

The diner meat loaf smelled awfully good; Harleen felt guilty just thinking it, as if she were being disloyal to Mommy. She thought it was kind of strange for Daddy to order something he could have at home, although she didn't say so. But Daddy seemed to know what she was thinking and said, "I'm just in the mood for meat loaf and I don't want Mommy to cook an extra meal so late."

Well, that made sense, Harleen thought, or as much sense as anything grown-ups did. The way Daddy ate, however, made her wonder. He ate slowly, like he wanted to remember how good it was. He offered her a bite but Harleen said no, thanks, she didn't feel like meat loaf, which made Daddy laugh. Secretly, she was afraid it might taste better than Mommy's.

When they were done—Harleen was too full for dessert—Daddy paid the bill and left a big tip for the waitress.

"Thanks, sweetie," the waitress said, popping her gum. Her name-tag said "Millie" and she had the biggest blonde bouffant of all, almost as large as a beach ball, Harleen thought. "Ya got a big heart, I can tell." Then she turned to Harleen and said, "You take care a him, okay, hon? Make sure he gets home safe."

"I sure will, hon, doncha worry about that," Harleen replied, imitating the woman's thick Brooklyn accent. Everybody around them burst out laughing, but it was good laughing, like for a comedian on TV.

Millie kissed the top of her head with a loud smack. "You got a precious little puddin' there," she told Daddy as they left the restaurant.

"You're full of surprises, Harleen," her daddy said as he picked her up and carried her toward the subway stop. "Thinking fast is a gift. Something tells me you'll go far."

Harleen put her arms around her daddy's neck and rested her head on his shoulder. She really *was* tired now. This was the perfect end to the best day ever, being carried home in her daddy's strong arms. She was barely aware of going into the subway and getting on the train. Her daddy kept holding her even after he sat down and the motion of the train rocked her to sleep.

◆

She didn't wake up until they were back on the street and only because she heard a man's voice growl, "So where'd you stash the haul, Nicky?"

"Yeah, Nicky, tell us," said another man, also growling. "Inquiring minds wanna know."

Rubbing her eyes, Harleen raised her head and saw two men standing in front of Daddy with their arms crossed, looking real mad.

Her daddy gave a big sigh. "Come on, guys, I've got my little girl here. Can't this wait till I take her home?"

"No can do, Nicky-boy," said the first guy. "We found out the hard way it's a bad idea to wait on anything where you're concerned."

"Like when you told us to wait till Friday," added the second guy. "You said we'd get in and out and no one would know? Well, guess what? Our big fat payday turned out to be a big fat goose egg."

Her daddy put her down then, even though she was so sleepy she could hardly keep her eyes open. Harleen hung onto his pant-leg, but Daddy gently pried her hands off and made her stand back a few feet.

"That safe was so bare, it was indecent," the first guy was saying. "Somebody beat us to the goodies. Only one person coulda done that—the only other person what knew about the job. So after we was done shooting our way out and running for our lives, we asked around. And son of a gun, we found out you were there on *Thursday*, having drinks with the broad what owns the joint."

"I told everyone we shoulda known better than to trust Slick Nick Quinzel," the second guy said. "But callin' in a police raid—that was low even for a worm like you."

"I had nothing to do with that," Daddy said urgently. "I didn't know the DEA was planning a raid—"

"You mean that was just a coinky-dink?" the first guy said. "Oh, well, that's *different*."

The second guy suddenly stepped forward and, before Harleen quite knew what was happening, he punched her daddy in the face, knocking him off-balance so he almost fell.

"Hey!" said the first guy. "Don't do that!"

"Why not?" the other guy asked.

"*I* got first dibs." Then *he* punched her daddy in the face, knocking him to the sidewalk.

Harleen screamed for them to stop. They ignored her as they hauled her daddy to his feet. The first guy held him with his arms behind his back so the second one could punch him again and again. She kept on screaming, but it was like they couldn't hear her, like she wasn't even there.

"I'm getting the cops!" she hollered at them and ran back toward the subway, where Mommy said you could find a cop if you needed help. But just as she got to the corner, she saw a patrol car and ran into the street, waving her arms and yelling.

Red and blue lights snapped on as it stopped. The cop who got out of the passenger side was a big guy, bigger than her daddy. Trying to pull him up the street was like trying to drag a tree out of the ground. The other one followed slowly in the car, the lights on the roof still flashing red and blue and red and blue.

The bad guys were gone by the time they got to her daddy; Harleen felt her heart break at the sight of him lying on the pavement like a heap of bloody rags. "Help him, *help him*," she begged as the other cop stopped the car and ran over. He was shorter and a little younger but he seemed just as solid as his partner. Their expressions were all concerned and worried, the way her mommy's was when Harleen skinned her knee or bumped her head. But when they saw her daddy's face, they changed completely.

"Well, if it isn't good old Slick Nick Quinzel," said the taller cop as he and his partner lifted her daddy to his feet.

"Be careful, don't hurt him!" Harleen shouted.

"Pipe down, kid, your old man's okay," the taller cop said. "Hey, Nick, you got any idea how many people are looking for you?" He pulled her daddy's arms behind him.

Thinking the cop was going to hold Daddy so the other cop could punch him, Harleen leaped at him, flailing her fists wildly.

"Take it easy, kid," the shorter cop said as he pulled her away. "We're just cuffing him so we can take him in. Nobody's gonna hurt him."

"But he's *already* hurt! You're supposed to *help* people!" Harleen sobbed.

The cops looked at each other, then at her daddy. "Are you hurt, sir?" the taller cop asked in a stiff, formal tone. "Do you require medical attention?"

Daddy spat blood and said, "It's just a scratch."

"He says it's just a scratch," the taller cop told Harleen.

They put her daddy in the back seat of the squad car and let her sit with him. She held him all the way to the police station. But he couldn't put his arms around her, and that was scary.

◆

At the police station, the cops handed her and Daddy over to a couple of detectives. One was older, with dark brown skin and watery eyes large behind the lenses of his black-framed glasses. Here and there in his short, curly black hair were single white ones, like someone had sprinkled little white threads all over his head. He introduced himself as Detective Jack Thibodeau. His partner, Brian Li, was Chinese. He had longer hair tied back in a ponytail and, under other circumstances, Harleen would have had a crush on him. He was kind to her but his face was so serious, she couldn't help being a little afraid of him.

Neither detective was dressed very well. Their clothes were so rumpled, Mommy would have said they must have slept in them. Maybe they didn't know about how to dress for an important job, like Harleen's teacher said you were supposed to, or maybe they just didn't care. If so, none of the other detectives did, either.

Worse, though, they said her daddy was a bad guy, and that couldn't possibly be true. A bad guy wouldn't take her to Coney Island for the day and ride all the rides and play all the games with her. Millie at the diner said her daddy had a big heart—no one would say that about a bad guy. And a bad guy wouldn't carry her all the way home. Bad guys never did that stuff; they were too busy doing bad things.

The detectives kept calling her daddy a "con man." Harleen had no idea what that was; she suspected it was something the cops had made up just to be mean. They claimed her daddy was behind a series of robberies and had planned one at a nightclub owned by a rich lady. But then he double-crossed the other bad guys and now everyone was looking for him, bad guys, good guys, *any* guys. *All* the guys.

Harleen tried to tell them her daddy couldn't have done anything wrong because he'd been having fun all day with her at Coney Island. She started to tell them for what seemed like the thousandth time about everything they'd done together. Her daddy was sitting on a chair next to Detective Thibodeau's desk and he suddenly pulled her onto his lap.

"Let me talk to her," he said to the detectives and swiveled so they were facing away from them. Harleen wrapped her arms around his neck again, glad he wasn't handcuffed anymore so he could hug her back. "Honey, these guys are just doing their job," he said, speaking barely above a whisper. "But they can't do anything if you keep interrupting."

"But—" Harleen started.

"But nothing." Daddy pressed his finger against her lips. "This is going to take a little while so you have to be my good girl and be patient, okay?"

"You want me to call your wife to come get her?" Detective Thibodeau asked.

Daddy turned back to him with Harleen still on his lap and shook his head. "No, Sharon needs her sleep. We've got three in diapers at home." He looked around, then pointed at an empty bench along the nearest wall. "Harleen, how about you sit over there and wait for me?"

She heaved an enormous sigh. "Okay."

"And maybe the detectives could find someone to sit with you?" Daddy added.

Detective Li took Harleen's hand and walked her over to the

bench. "I know you don't understand what's going on," he said as he sat down next to her.

"Yeah, I do," she said. "You're being mean to my daddy."

"That's not—" The detective stopped, hesitated. "We don't *want* to be mean to your daddy," he said. "But your daddy has been mean to people. A lot of people."

"*My* daddy's *never* mean," Harleen informed him, although she couldn't help squirming a little because that wasn't *quite* true. Sometimes he was mean to Mommy and Mommy was mean right back.

"Your daddy stole money that didn't belong to him," Detective Li told her. "He stole jewelry, too, and other very valuable things. Stealing is a *very* mean thing to do."

Harleen's urge to squirm vanished. The detective was trying to make her feel bad toward her daddy and that was *wrong*. He was her *daddy*. She looked up at him and she saw that he was waiting for her to agree with him that her daddy was mean. Well, he could wait forever; she'd *never* say that.

"It's wrong to steal, isn't it?" the detective prodded. "It's wrong and it's mean, isn't it? Your daddy was mean to steal, wasn't he?"

Harleen sat up a little straighter; something she'd overheard her mother say popped into her head. "They can spare it."

Detective Li's expression changed from serious to startled. He hadn't seen *that* coming, Harleen thought. Without another word, he got up and went back to his partner and her daddy, and she knew he was telling them what she'd said, like it was some great big deal. Detective Thibodeau gave her a sidelong look; maybe he was thinking about handcuffing her, too.

But her daddy only shrugged. "She's right—they can," he said and winked at her, a secret wink that made her feel better, but only for a few seconds. The detectives just kept *at* him, asking him the same questions over and over. Harleen wanted to ask *them* a few questions—like, was this really their job? How did it make them good guys? Daddy still had blood all over his face and his clothes and it was getting later and later and she felt like her eyeballs were coated with sand. And now she had to go to the bathroom.

She probably had to get special permission for that. Maybe they'd want to handcuff her, even though the Ladies' was really close—she could see it from where she was sitting.

Harleen tried to get someone's attention but everyone was too busy. Even her daddy was facing away from her, talking to a third detective. Finally, she just couldn't wait. It was probably a crime to pee your pants in a police station anyway. Nobody tried to stop her as she went into the bathroom, which smelled like it had just been hosed down with double-strength bleach.

Afterward, Harleen started to go back to the bench, then hesitated. No one seemed to have noticed she wasn't there anymore; they were all too busy. Detectives were bringing in other people in handcuffs and sitting them down next to desks. Once she would have taken it for granted people in handcuffs were bad guys, but now she knew better. Cops made mistakes. But they never owned up to being wrong; they just kept saying they were right until they forced everyone else to say they were right, too.

Harleen looked over at her father and the detectives. How many times would they ask him the same questions? Were they going for a world record?

This wasn't how the best day ever was supposed to end. Her daddy was supposed to take her home and put her to bed. She'd be so knocked out she'd sleep through the argument he and Mommy would have about his keeping her out so late.

Instead, her daddy got punched out by some bad guys and when she'd brought the police, they'd treated him like *he* was the bad guy. None of them cared her daddy was hurt. No one had said, *That was wrong. They shouldn't have done that to you.*

Everybody said cops were supposed to protect and help people. Harleen saw now that they only helped *some* people; whoever those people were, she and Daddy weren't included.

The swinging double doors marked "exit" weren't locked or even guarded. Cops and detectives were going in and out, sometimes with prisoners. Harleen remembered her daddy saying you could go anywhere you wanted as long as you looked like you knew what you were doing.

I'm supposed to do this, she said silently as she headed for the double doors. *I'm right where I should be, I'm official, don't worry. I'm not the droid you're looking for.*

No one gave her a second look as she went downstairs, out the front entrance, and onto the street. Harleen made herself walk at the same confident, unhurried pace until she was almost a block away from the station house. Then she broke into a run.

2

Years later, when Harley thought back to that night, she never wondered what had made her go back to Coney Island. She had found out the good guys weren't really as good as everybody thought and she was still afraid the bad guys would come back, so she'd hidden from all of them in the one place where only good things happened. Surely she would be safe where she'd just had the best day ever. In a perfect world, she would have been.

♦

Going back to Coney Island really wasn't a bad idea. It would never have occurred to the cops that she'd go there, not at that hour. The thugs who had tuned up her father wouldn't have thought to look for her there in a million years. Thinking was not their strong suit. But they were really good at following. They followed Harleen to Coney Island, one of them on the subway, the other in a car, because they were sure she would lead them to where Slick Nick had stashed the haul from the nightclub safe, the payoff they felt was rightfully theirs. It only made sense—now that Slick Nick was busted, he'd want to make sure the stash was safe. Naturally, he would send his daughter. His seven-year-old daughter. At three a.m.

Thinking *really* wasn't their long suit. They clearly weren't parents, either.

But even broken clocks are right twice a day, just as stupid adults have been making kids miserable since the dawn of mankind. Some things never change.

◆

Harleen knew Coney Island wasn't going to be all lit up and happy but she hadn't realized it would be *this* spooky.

The rides were all shut down and the games were shuttered, except for some, where shutters were stuck halfway, including the one with the milk bottles. Harleen and her daddy hadn't been able to win anything there.

She was thinking about crawling in and hiding there until morning (she could also check to see if all the bottles were glued to the shelves) when suddenly she heard a man laughing. She'd heard that laugh before. Automatically, she made a break for it, or tried to. Rough hands scooped her up under her armpits and held her off the ground.

"Well, whaddaya know—Slick Nick's pretty little girl decided to come back to the park when it's less crowded!" He turned her so she could see his face. "What a coinky-dink—so did we!" It was the shorter guy, the one who'd held her daddy so the tall one could punch him. The tall one was there, too, glowering at her.

"We never got properly introduced," the guy went on. "I'm Tony, and—" He turned her to face the tall guy. "This is my colleague, who goes by the colorful and highly appropriate moniker, Spike."

"She doesn't know what 'moniker' means," Spike growled.

"Do too!" Harleen said as Tony put her down. He kept hold of her shoulder. "Let *go*!" She put tears in her voice as she tried to twist away from him. "You're *hurting* me!"

"No, he's not," Spike said, still glowering.

"No, I'm not," Tony agreed. "See, Spike here is what you might call a pain expert. He'd know if I was hurting you, and if he says

I'm not, I'm not. But if you keep trying to get away from me, I'll have to. Like so." He tightened his grip on her shoulder, digging his fingers in hard.

"Ow!" This time, the tears in Harleen's voice weren't fake.

"Now I know Spike would say *that* hurts." Tony loosened his grip very slightly so it was uncomfortable rather than painful. "You see the diff, doncha? Thought so. You seem like a pretty bright little kid." He laughed a little. "Hey, it's too bad we don't have one of those kiddie-leashes, so we could hook you up like a dog. Any time you tried to get away, I could reel you in. But we don't, so you're gonna haveta hold still while we wait for the boss."

Spike let out a long, exasperated breath.

"What?" Tony said, sounding a little defensive.

"You never shut up, do you," Spike said.

"Aw, don't be like that," Tony said soothingly. "You'll scare little what's-her-name. Say, what *is* your name?" he added to Harleen.

"Why do you care?" Spike said, even more exasperated.

"It's good manners," Tony said reasonably. "And I go for the personal touch."

"Oh, yeah, me too," Harleen piped up suddenly, imitating Millie's sassy Brooklyn accent. "The poisonal touch is *so impawtant.*"

Both men stared at her in surprise. "Whadja say?" Tony asked her. His grip on her shoulder loosened a bit but Harleen didn't try to get away—yet.

"Yeah, ever since I started workin' my new job down on Toidy-Toid an' Toid, I been goin' for the poisonal touch," Harleen went on, pretending to chew gum. "People really appreciate that, ya know? Sure ya do!" She gave Tony an affectionate sock on his belly. "You got class, I knew the minute I saw ya. I says to my friend, Mabel, I says, 'Mabel, I'm just lookin' for a guy with class. He don't haveta be rich or handsome, he's just gotta be *classy!*'"

Tony laughed heartily and slapped his thigh with his free hand. His grip on her shoulder loosened a little more, just as Harleen hoped. Spike was a big sourpuss but he wasn't the one holding onto her. She had to get Tony laughing hard enough to put him off-guard.

"So you think I got class?" Tony said a bit breathlessly. "The feelin' is mutual. You're a classy kid."

"I'm glad it shows. I went to chahm school you know," Harleen went on, remembering a routine from TV. "They removed all my ahs. You know—Q, Ah, S, T? Now I drive a cah. It's just like a car except it costs more to fix. But I'm *woith* it!"

Tony was laughing even harder, and he was leaning on Harleen's shoulder more than actually holding it now. Spike looked like he wanted to slap her. If she could shift around so that when she pulled away from Tony he would lose his balance and fall into Spike—

"Thank God," Spike said suddenly, looking past her and Tony.

Harleen followed his gaze. At first, she could only make out a bulky shadow coming toward them. Then the shadow became a broad-shouldered man with thick arms and legs. Even his fingers were thick; Harleen caught a gold glint from a pinky ring. He walked with his head up and his chest out—like a man who expected trouble and didn't like to be kept waiting, her mother would have said.

She knew who he was; she had seen Bruno Delvecchio on the news and in the papers. Daddy said he was the boss of bad guys and everyone was so afraid of him, they did whatever he told them to.

Tony's grip on her shoulder tightened again as he straightened up. He stopped laughing and wiped his eyes with the back of his free hand. "Oh, hi, boss. How ya doin'?"

"What's so funny?" Delvecchio snapped. When a teacher asked this question at school, there was no good answer. Harleen knew this was the same thing.

"It's the kid here," Tony said cheerfully. "You shoulda heard her just now—"

"I don't want to hear *her*," the boss replied with even more of a bite. "I want to hear *you're* taking care of business."

Delvecchio was taller than either Tony or Spike, and Harleen could tell he didn't just look down *at* someone, he looked down *on* them. His suit was like the ones she'd seen in the window of the tailor shop she passed on her way to and from school—handmade and very expensive. Daddy had told her the only people who could afford suits like that were *connected*. He would have looked classy, except his tacky pinky ring ruined the effect.

"The cops still have Quinzel, I take it?" Delvecchio said, his tone lofty now, as if he considered them far beneath him.

To remind them how important he is, Harleen thought, *and they'd better not forget it.* She looked up at Tony. He had a strong grip on her shoulder again but he was standing with his head slightly lowered and his shoulders hunched, like he thought Delvecchio might hit him. Spike was standing up straight, looking belligerent; he didn't like taking orders.

And Delvecchio knew it, she realized, her gaze moving to him from Spike. Delvecchio knew how Spike felt and he made a point of bossing him around. It was all so obvious when you knew what you were looking at. These guys would never think she could understand stuff like this because she was a kid.

God, adults were so *stupid*!

◆

"Well, don't just *stand* there," Delvecchio said to Spike in a put-upon voice. "Make the call. Unless by some miracle you've done that already?"

Spike looked super-sour as he held up his phone and took her photo, then walked off to lean against one of the shuttered games. The flash startled Harleen and she had to force herself not to cry. She *hated* having her picture taken with a flash because it hurt her eyes—hurt *physically*. Harleen had told her daddy always to warn her if he was using a flash so she could look away.

Daddy had said it was smart to look away from *any* camera flash.

Now all she could see were big colored blotches in the dark. She got so distracted trying to blink them away and readjust her eyes to the night that she forgot to pay attention. Then something Tony was saying caught her ear: "…that Sharon'll pay up, whether Slick Nick wants to or not."

"You sound pretty sure about that," Delvecchio replied in his lofty boss-voice. "I hope you're right."

"Oh, I *know* I am," Tony assured him. "She only looks like a mousy little hausfrau, all shy and everything. But she used to be a doctor. In a *hospital.*"

"Did she?" Delvecchio tried to sound bored but Harleen heard the interest in his voice. Like maybe he hadn't known that but he didn't want Tony to think he'd told him something.

"Oh, yeah," Tony said. "She passed all the tests, did her internship and residency like they do, got her license to practice. Then Slick Nick came along and *bam!*"

"'Bam'?" Delvecchio said, as if it were a bad word from a foreign language.

"Yeah, bam! Now she's got four kids and the bail-bondsman on speed dial." Tony gave a short laugh. "Hey, she could be useful. She could be your personal physician."

"If anyone's gonna need a personal physician tonight, it won't be me," Delvecchio said darkly, just as Spike came back.

"She's on her way," Spike said, looking pleased with his own efficiency. "I told her to call when she gets here and we'll tell her where to drop the, uh, package off."

"The 'package'?" Tony laughed. "What are you, a spy or something?"

Harleen's vision had cleared enough to let her see the look Delvecchio and Spike gave Tony. "Always good to be circumspect," he said. He patted Spike on the shoulder and added, "Good boy." Spike's sour face returned. "As long as she thinks it's a straight trade—the kid for the package."

Spike's eyes swiveled from Delvecchio to Harleen and back again.

"I can't just let this go," Delvecchio went on. "Otherwise everyone'll think they can get away pulling all kinds of shit on me. People gotta remember the golden rule: you make *my* life difficult, I make *your* life hell." Delvecchio glanced down at Harleen and his nose wrinkled slightly, like he was looking at a dog turd someone hadn't pooper-scooped. "The cops'll hold onto Nick for a while. One of you drop by holding later and tell him why nobody's coming to bail him out this time."

"Will do, boss," Tony said cheerfully, as if Delvecchio had asked him to water his plants while he was on vacation. It probably meant about that much to them. Harleen knew she had to do something fast.

At the same moment, Tony actually let go of her to reach into his pocket for something. Harleen didn't even think about it—the moment his hand was gone, so was she.

"*Get her!*" Delvecchio bellowed.

♦

This was like playing hide-and-seek backward, Harleen thought as she pelted through the park; she was It and everyone was trying to find her. Her chest was starting to tighten and burn and her legs were getting heavy but she pushed herself to go faster, faster than she ever had before. Because this wasn't just a silly game. It was nothing like a game.

She hadn't thought about where to go when she had taken off at warp speed, only that she had to get away. The bad guys hadn't seen that coming. They must have thought she was too scared to move.

Well, she *was* scared, more than she'd ever been in her life. She hadn't understood everything Delvecchio had said, just enough to know something bad was going to happen to her and her mommy.

Which had made her too scared *not* to run.

Harleen could hear Delvecchio hollering somewhere behind her, ordering Tony and Spike not to let her get away. She was breathing hard now but she didn't dare slow down. If it had just been Tony chasing her, she could have outrun him easily; he had a belly on him that showed he liked pizza and beer, not gym workouts. Spike was skinny but he stank like cigarettes—*yuck*! He'd have been coughing and wheezing and puking before he could even get near her. And Delvecchio probably didn't even walk fast; he hired people to run for him.

But all three of them were after her. They could split up, surround her, trap her, unless she could find a way to get around them or under them or something. The problem was, she didn't know the park very well anymore. She wasn't even sure where she was right now; nothing looked familiar. Her heart was pounding so hard and loud, it almost drowned out the sound of her gasping for breath. Worse, it seemed to be getting even darker and there were fuzzy colored patches in her vision, like she saw when her eyes were closed.

But she couldn't close her eyes and she couldn't stop. Harleen tried to push herself to run even faster but her legs felt awful heavy, like they had after she'd proved to Benny who lived on the ground floor that she could run up and down the stairs half a dozen times when he'd bet her a dollar she couldn't (and then the crumb-bum had refused to pay up).

Despite her efforts, Harleen felt herself slowing down. If she couldn't run, she had to think. The park was big but it didn't go on forever; if she kept going, she was bound to come to a fence or something. She was good at climbing fences. She might get over the fence and out before those guys even knew it. They'd be running around searching the park, never knowing she wasn't even there anymore—

Except Mommy wouldn't know, either.

Mommy was on her way and they were going to do something

bad to her. She had to find Mommy first so they could both get away. How was Mommy going to get into the park? Would she go to the front gate and call those guys to tell them she was there? Harleen couldn't picture her mommy crawling under the barrier to get in the way she had.

Should she find a hiding place near the main entrance, Harleen wondered? Or get out the way she had come in, and hope she found Mommy there? The surge of hope Harleen felt lasted barely a second before she realized she had no idea where the entrance was.

"Over here! This way!"

Spike. Harleen's heartbeat doubled as she ran faster through the shadows, past big, dark structures, low buildings, and weird shapes that could have been trash cans or sleeping robots or other unearthly creatures. All at once, she saw a tall skinny thing she recognized as the strong-man test. Daddy called it the high striker. You hit the base with a big mallet to make the striker go up. If you rang the bell at the top, you won a prize. Her daddy had only made the striker go halfway up—no prize for that. Harleen had told her daddy it didn't matter, he was really the strongest man in the world. Besides, no one else got the striker as high as he did.

The strong-man test was right in front of the Funhouse; and there was the word FUNHOUSE glittering in the moonlight. It was near the wooden roller coaster, she remembered, slowing down a little. She and Daddy had ridden it three times in a row before Daddy said he needed to take a break. On the best day ever. That was just today—well, yesterday, Harleen supposed, although it felt like a hundred years ago. How could everything go so bad after going so good?

Harleen remembered what her daddy had said about the roller coaster lattice being good camouflage. That probably worked even better at night, she thought, and headed toward it. She wasn't sure how to get inside the lattice. There had to be a way, though—

maintenance people had to get in, didn't they? Daddy said everything had an entrance for maintenance. Most people simply didn't notice.

Harleen was trying to remember what else her daddy had said about maintenance when the world exploded in a blinding white flash.

Before she could even cry out, something caught her ankle and she fell forward, scraping her hands and knees on the pavement.

"Damn, Spike," Tony said. "You're, like, a genius."

"If by 'genius' you mean 'not a moron,' you're right," Delvecchio chuckled.

Harleen felt a familiar large, rough hand clamp onto her left arm and drag her up to her feet.

"Don't!" she yelled, more angry than scared for the moment. She was going to get Spike for flashing the light in her eyes, she promised herself, she really was. It was like red-hot needles stabbing her eyes. And she seemed to be even blinder than she was the last time—she couldn't see anything but great big purple blotches, no matter how much she blinked.

"If she'd gotten away, I dunno what we woulda done," Tony was saying, holding her arm too tight. "Sharon woulda never given us the loot."

There was a brief silence. Then Delvecchio said, "Perhaps you really *are* a genius, Spike."

"Perhaps I am," Spike said, but he sounded sulky, not like he thought it was a compliment.

"Hey, my hat is off to anyone with smarts—" Tony began.

"Shut *up!*" Delvecchio snapped.

"You got it, boss," Tony assured him. He started dragging Harleen back the way she had come.

Fresh tears sprang into her eyes. Tony had to know he was hurting her now. How could he do that to her when she'd made him laugh? When you made people laugh, they felt good and they liked you— they didn't want to hurt you. How could Tony be so mean to her?

She was going to get him for that, him and Spike both.

"…an errand to run," Delvecchio was saying. "If I leave you two here, can I count on you to take care of Dr. Quinzel, Medicine Woman, or whoever the hell she is?"

"Hey, we *always* take care of business," Tony said proudly.

But Spike was talking over him. "Consider her dead, boss. You want us to take care of the brat, too?"

"Absolutely *not*," Delvecchio replied. "I want her alive and in good condition when I get back." Harleen still couldn't see but she felt him examine her knees, then her hands. "The man I'm bringing with me is what you might call a connoisseur of the beauty of youth, particularly in those magic, single-digit years. He'll pay top dollar for merchandise in good condition." Delvecchio chuckled. "He can afford it."

Harleen felt her stomach turn over. She would get Delvecchio, too.

"It's too bad about the scrapes," Delvecchio added, "but I'm sure that in every other way, she's, ah, pristine."

"Whatever you say, boss," Tony said cheerfully.

Harleen's vision cleared in time for her to see Delvecchio walking away in a boss-man strut. *I* will *get you*, she thought at his back. *Even if it takes twenty years, I'll pay you back for ruining my best day ever.*

"Boy, am I glad *he's* gone!" she said in her tough-Brooklyn-cookie voice. "Talk about a buzz-kill—that guy just doesn't know how to have a good time, am I right?" She poked Tony's middle with her free hand; she was starting to lose all feeling in the arm he was holding. "Right? Right? You know I'm right, doncha?"

Tony laughed but not as much as before. She needed better material.

"Hey, you think maybe he was raised by a family of eggs?" Harleen went on. "And that's why he's not crackin' up?"

Tony sat her down on a bench near the strong-man test but kept a tight grip on her arm. She couldn't even feel her hand anymore.

"Hey, siddown, why doncha," she told him. "Take a load off." Tony plumped down next to her, laughing a little. She turned to Spike, who was looming over her. Inspiration struck and she tried a slightly different voice. "Can we talk?"

"Shut up, you little brat, or I'll shut you up!" Spike shouted at her with a ferocity that shocked her.

"Jeez, take it easy," Tony said, taken aback. "I'm startin' to think you got some serious anger issues."

"You can shut up, too!" Spike snapped at him. "Compared to you, I really *am* freakin' Einstein. I don't know why Delvecchio makes me work with you."

"What the hell's bitin' *you?*" Tony asked him.

"We're gonna take out her mother and give her to a pervert buddy of Delvecchio's," Spike said, putting one foot up on the bench and leaning over Tony. "And you're telling me I've got anger issues?"

"*Serious* anger issues," Tony corrected him. "Maybe you should talk to someone."

"Hey, we all need to talk sometimes," Harleen said, being the tough cookie.

Both Tony and Spike turned to her. "Shut up," they said in unison.

"Don't interrupt when the adults are talking," Tony added firmly. "It's not polite."

Turning away from them, Spike threw his hands up. "Why is God punishing me?" he said, looking up at the sky.

Harleen couldn't help herself. "'Cause *you* ain't got no class," she said promptly and looked at Tony. "*Somebody* hadda tell him. Am I right?"

"That's it!" Spike yelled. All at once, he was pulling a gun out of his jacket. Tony's laughter cut off as he jumped up and tried to grab it.

As soon as he let go of her, Harleen sprinted for the Funhouse.

3

There wasn't much fun in the Funhouse now; in fact, it was downright creepy. Except for the faint glow from an exit sign here and there, the place was completely dark. Harleen wasn't afraid of the dark, not really, but she wasn't that crazy about it even when there *weren't* a couple of bad guys after her.

She felt her way along a wall and came to a door. Immediately, she knew this was the door she and Daddy had mistaken for the way out. She had no idea *how* she knew—maybe it was just the way the knob felt in her hand. She slipped inside and closed it silently behind her.

The smell of sawdust and chemicals was heavier than ever; Harleen felt as if she were stifling. Maybe this hadn't been such a good idea after all, she thought, feeling her way along another wall. This was a small room with no place to hide and it would probably be the first place Tony and Spike would look, using the light on Spike's phone—

Abruptly she tripped over something and fell on a bunch of paint cans and plastic bottles. If Tony and Spike were in the Funhouse already, they must have heard that, Harleen thought, biting her lips together to hold the tears in. She kept very still, listening for their voices, but all she heard was her own heart pounding like a big bass drum.

After a bit, she got to her feet and, keeping close to the wall, moved more carefully, feeling ahead with her foot for any more obstacles. She tried to remember what the place had looked like with the lights on.

Suddenly, she came to another door. Her heart leaped—she didn't remember seeing another door when she and Daddy had been there earlier. It was unlocked but, to her dismay, it wasn't a way out, just a closet. There were lots of shelves on one wall; another had tools hanging from pegs. But the wall opposite the door was bare, except for something like a metal cabinet set right into it. Harleen pulled it open; there were lots and lots of switches—the circuit breaker. Well, this *was* a house, after all.

Daddy had taught her all about the circuit breaker at the tenement. It was enormous but he had showed her the switches for their apartment. When the power failed, sometimes it was because a circuit had become overloaded. When that happened, a switch would flip and you had to flip it back to get the power back on. Daddy showed her how to do it and warned her to leave all the other switches alone, especially the ones for other people's apartments.

Mommy hadn't liked Daddy showing her the circuit breaker; she said Harleen was too young. But Daddy said that there might be a power cut when he wasn't home and Mommy couldn't leave the apartment—like, if one or two, or even all three, of the boys were sick. Then she'd be glad she could send Harleen down to the basement.

Abruptly the muffled sound of Tony and Spike's voices brought her back to the present. They were sure to find this room—unless something distracted them. Impulsively, she reached up and flipped the main switches. The lights went on and there was a cacophony of silly music and recorded laughter as the Funhouse came to life. With all the noise, Tony and Spike would be so confused, they wouldn't know where to look first. With any luck, she could sneak out the back door and they'd never know.

Or, she thought as she stepped out of the closet and looked around the work-room, she could *get* them before she left.

Harleen found a tool-belt lying on the floor near several cans of spray paint, bags of glitter in every color, and several bottles of glue of various kinds, including—she smiled—super. The belt was too big for her but she discovered she could wear it slung over one shoulder, like a Miss America sash, and stuff would stay in the pockets. She stuffed them full of glitter bags, some spray cans, and lots of super-glue.

She meant to open the work-room door just a crack to see if Tony and Spike were nearby, but she froze with her hand on the knob. She couldn't just stay there until they cornered her—they'd do something to make sure she couldn't get away. And when Delvecchio came back, everything would get worse.

Plus, they were going to kill her mommy. She had to help Mommy. Harleen pulled the door open a tiny crack and put her eye to it.

"I'm gonna *cripple* that little brat," she heard Spike yell over the music and crazy laughing. "And whoever's in here helping her!"

In spite of everything, Harleen couldn't help grinning.

♦

Crouched behind one of the funny mirrors, Harleen listened for the men's voices over the silly music and recorded laughter, trying to figure out where they were. If she held very still and strained her ears, sometimes she could catch Spike cursing and saying he was going to blow her head off.

"Just make sure you don't accidentally blow *my* head off," Tony told him. Harleen was pretty sure if that happened, it wouldn't be an accident. Tony probably wasn't any safer from his hothead partner than she was.

Not that Tony was any better than Spike. Spike hated her

personally, but she wasn't even a person to Tony, just a thing to hang onto until his boss came back with his pervo friend. Harleen had heard pervos did things to kids but no one had ever told her what, which probably meant it was a sex thing. She knew sex was how babies were made although she didn't know the details, and with three baby brothers, she didn't want to. But it seemed obvious that if sex was how grown-ups *had* kids, they weren't supposed to feel sexy *about* kids.

Which meant she had to escape before Delvecchio came back with his—*ew*—friend.

Harleen peered around the side of the mirror again, then ran to the vertical rollers. Just as she reached them, she heard Tony holler, "I got her! Over here!"

Reaching into one of the belt pockets, she grabbed a handful of glitter and turned around to find Tony was frighteningly close. He lunged at her and she blew gold glitter into his face.

Tony yelped, stumbled, tripped over his own feet and fell to his knees, spitting and rubbing his eyes. Harleen laughed as she let the rollers pull her through backward, splashing them with glue as she went, even though the chemical smell almost knocked her over. The label on the bottle said it was strong and quick-drying. She hoped it didn't dry before Tony and Spike could test how strong it was.

Harleen turned to hop across the moving floor. She and Daddy had figured out how to cross it without falling down. She spread more glue on the shifting sections, giggling. This really was funny. Once Tony and Spike got through the rollers to the floor, it was going to be hilarious—like watching two of The Three Stooges.

"Take off your jacket!" Spike yelled.

"But it's new—" Tony whined.

"*Just leave it!*" Spike roared. He sounded like an animal.

"Gimme a little help here," said Tony, still whining. "I can't get my arm out."

Harleen heard the sound of thick cloth ripping. The padding on the rollers was nice and soft but the rollers were really strong. Tony's head appeared—he still had gold glitter in his hair and all over his face.

"Hey, I see her!" Tony yelled. "She's right there. You, kid, what's-your-name—stay there!"

Was he really *that* stupid, Harleen wondered, shaking her head and laughing.

"I mean it, kid! Stay right where you are!" Tony struggled mightily for a few seconds and finally came through without his suit coat and with his hairy man-boobs showing because he'd lost half the buttons on his shirt.

Spike was right behind him and he'd lost his suit coat, too, along with his tie. His shoulder holster was all twisted around and his weaselly face was red with fury. "I'm gonna kill you, you little brat," he promised her.

"Ya gotta catch me foist, big boy," she said in her tough-cookie voice.

They were so mad, they didn't even notice the floor was moving, Harleen marveled; they just came at her and down they went on top of each other. She burst into loud, hearty giggles as they tried to extricate themselves from the floor and each other. Could they really be *that* stupid, she wondered, that they wouldn't stop to think after what she'd done with the rollers?

No, she realized—they thought *she* was stupid. Which made them *twice* as stupid, and a riot to watch. While they went on trying to pull themselves off the constantly moving floorboards, she leaned forward and spray-painted their faces a bright blue.

Both of them started howling and cursing and trying to rub their eyes except their hands were stuck to the floor or to each other. Tony suddenly let out a cry that was very close to a scream; he'd finally pulled his hand free but left a lot of skin on the floor. That was gonna hurt for *weeks*.

"You little shit," Spike snarled at her as paint ran down his cheeks like electric-blue tears. "I'm gonna *kill* you, I swear to God." He had only one hand stuck to the floor and he was trying to pry it off without skinning his palm. His legs were stuck across three boards moving in different directions at different speeds. Tony was actually *crying* with pain now.

"I need something to wrap around my hand," Tony sniveled and started pulling at Spike's shirt with his other hand. "Tear off your sleeve so I can use it as a bandage."

"Get away from me!" Spike swatted his hand away but Tony kept tugging at him and somehow Spike's gun fell out of his shoulder holster.

Tony reached for it but Spike grabbed it first. "Put that away," Tony ordered him, sobbing now, "before you—"

The explosion knocked Harleen flat on her back and made her ears ring painfully. At first, she thought the Funhouse had blown up—she could smell something harsh and burnt, like a whole bunch of fireworks had gone off right in her face.

But it wasn't fireworks, she saw, sitting up and clutching the belt with both hands. Spike's gun had gone off in *Tony's* face. Which didn't exist anymore.

Even with the floor moving back and forth under him, Tony was still up on his knees, one hand clutching Spike's sleeve at the shoulder as if he were about to rip it off Spike's arm and wrap it around his hand. Without a face he had no expression, but Harleen half-expected to hear him whine, "See? I *toldja* this was gonna happen!"

And Spike was just staring at him, like this was one more of Tony's stupid mistakes. After another second or two, Tony crumpled in a way that was absurdly graceful, like a ballet dancer doing the dying swan.

It was the last deranged straw in a night gone stark raving mad. Harleen burst out laughing.

She laughed so hard and so loud it drowned out the ringing in her ears. When she tried to get up, she collapsed holding her middle. The belt slipped off her shoulder, spilling glue bottles, spray cans, and glitter everywhere and she was laughing too much to do anything about it. Far from the shifting boards, she rolled on the floor kicking her legs and pounding her fists.

"You cold-blooded little *shit!*" Spike shouted at her. "You think that's *funny*, you sick little *freak?*"

The sound of his angry voice made Harleen's laughter cut off as she jumped up. Spike was still stuck to the floor; so was his gun. He tried to pull himself free and couldn't.

"You want funny? I'll show you funny." Spike's face was so twisted with rage, the blue paint looked scary, not silly. "When I get loose, I'll make you laugh your head off, you little monster."

Harleen looked around, spotted an exit sign, and ran for it.

◆

Maybe this would have been a hilarious cartoon, Harleen thought; a grown man chasing a little kid around Coney Island after dark, yelling about how he was going to make her laugh.

Or maybe not. She didn't know if Spike had managed to get his gun off the floor and didn't want to find out. But the way he was running, she was afraid he might actually catch up with her.

A grown-up smoker shouldn't have been able to run like this. Harleen should have left him panting and puking without the breath to curse at her. But he kept coming. She couldn't get far enough ahead to lose him and when she looked over her shoulder, he seemed to be gaining on her.

Harleen tried to go faster as she ran through the park into the food area and finally beyond that to the stretch along the beach.

The games booths—maybe she could get into one of them—

Or she could jump into the water. Maybe Spike couldn't swim.

No, all adults could swim. Well, most. But a lot of them didn't swim very well and they never wanted to go in with all their clothes on.

But Spike didn't have all his clothes on. Just his underpants, his shirt, and his shoes; the rest was stuck to the Funhouse floor. She was hoping he'd hesitate to jump into the water long enough for her to get away. He wouldn't be able to hold his breath as long as she could, not after running for so long. She wasn't nearly as out of breath—gymnastics had built up her stamina.

When she got to the pier, she made a sharp right turn. It was high tide, she saw with a surge of hope. She could launch herself off the end of the pier like a flying fish—

Abruptly, she was face down on the rough splintery wood with an enormous weight pressing down on her back, squashing her so she couldn't breathe.

"How about this?" Spike panted. "How's *this* for funny?"

He was kneeling on her with all his weight; he was going to squash her like a bug, and she couldn't even get enough air into her lungs to scream.

Then suddenly he was dragging her upright by the back of her neck. "You know what's even funnier than that?" He sounded vicious even though he was out of breath. "Delvecchio's pal who pervs on kids. If you thought a guy with his face blown off was a hoot, that guy'll have you trippin'!" Spike threw her down on the pier again and knelt over her. "Lemme give you an idea of what he's got in store for you—"

"Get away from her, you son of a bitch!"

There was a loud *crack!* and a splash of blood as Spike's head bent sideways so sharply his ear hit his shoulder. He keeled over and Harleen found herself staring up at a woman holding the great big strong-man hammer in her hands.

"Mommy!" Harleen threw herself into her mother's arms and buried her face in her neck.

♦

Mommy hugged her tight for a long time. Harleen almost broke down in tears but Mommy wasn't crying, she was too brave and strong; she still had the mallet in one hand. If Mommy could be brave and strong, she could, too.

She did come very close to breaking down when she told Mommy what had happened, how the bad guys had beaten Daddy up and the cops hadn't even cared. Mommy looked very serious as she listened but her eyes stayed dry, so Harleen forced her own tears back.

After a while, Mommy let go of her and looked at Spike lying on the pier. "Here, take this," she said, holding out the hammer to Harleen. Wide-eyed, Harleen took it from her and hefted it. The hammer was heavy, but to her surprise, not as heavy as it looked—not so heavy that she couldn't have used it herself if she'd had to. She looked it over from one end to the other. The handle was smooth from the thousands of hands that had swung it, trying to ring the bell. She hadn't seen a single person who was strong enough to do that—even her daddy had only got it to the halfway mark.

Because it wasn't all about the hammer, Harleen thought. It was heavy, but you really had to be strong if you were going to ring any bells with it. Not just strong enough but good enough. You had to be *worthy*.

The sound of a splash brought Harleen out of her reverie. Spike was gone; Mommy had rolled him off the pier.

"So, you ready to go home now?" her mother asked in a light voice, like this was the end of a day out, not the middle of the night.

Harleen nodded and held up the hammer. "Can we keep this?"

"Sure," her mother said, "but I think we'd better wash it off first."

"Oh, yeah," Harleen said. "It's kinda icky. I'll do it!"

4

Daddy was waiting for them when they got home. The sun had come up by then. Mommy told her to go straight to bed; she'd wake her later. Harleen stayed awake just long enough to hear Daddy tell her that one of his friends bailed him out, but she fell asleep when Mommy started saying what she thought of his friends. It was all stuff Harleen had heard before anyway.

Harleen slept much more deeply than usual, the way she did when her gymnastics teacher worked her extra hard and made her stretch for an hour afterward. Only this was more intense. Her fatigue was emotional as well as physical. Like how she felt when Mommy and Daddy had an especially bad fight, the kind when Mommy would drag out suitcases and start throwing clothes into them, saying she'd had enough and so had the kids.

Harleen dreamed practically from the moment she shut her eyes, and though they weren't horrible nightmares, they hadn't been pleasant. They were filled with unhappy, angry people who didn't know what to do about their problems except to blame someone else for them. She kept looking for Mommy and Daddy and although they were nearby—in the next room or across the street or upstairs—she couldn't get to them. Sometimes they were too busy arguing with each other to see her; other times they did see her but they wouldn't come to help.

When she woke all on her own at midday, her head felt like a balloon full of cotton balls and her eyes were so heavy it was hard to keep them open. She shuffled out to the kitchen and found her parents sitting across from each other at the table. They looked startled, like they'd forgotten she was home. Maybe they'd thought she'd sleep longer.

Mommy fixed Harleen a baloney and cheese sandwich and a big mug of tomato soup and set it up on a tray table in front of the TV. Things had to be pretty bad if Mommy was letting her eat in front of the TV, Harleen thought. Her baby brothers were either upstairs with Mrs. DiAngeli or down the hall with Paula, who'd gotten laid off again.

That was *extra* bad.

Mommy had turned the TV up a little louder than usual, enough to make it hard for Harleen to catch anything of what she and Daddy were saying in the kitchen. They were talking to each other in low, tense voices, and that was *super*-extra-bad. The longer they used their low, tense voices, the more super-extra-bad it got.

It was better when they shouted at each other; when they did that, Harleen knew everything was going to be all right eventually. She didn't like it—they could say such mean things to each other— but it was like they both had built up a lot of pressure inside and when they shouted, a safety valve opened to let it out. Then they could find their way back to okay.

Harleen wished they had some other way to do that. They might feel better after one of their knock-down-drag-outs—that was what they called them, even though no one got knocked down or dragged out—but Harleen would cry into her pillow. How could people who loved each other—who loved her and her baby brothers—be so cruel to each other? Why didn't Mommy and Daddy know how awful it made her feel? Sometimes they sounded so mean, she couldn't believe there was any love in them even for her and her brothers.

She wanted to talk to her parents about all of this but she didn't know how to explain her feelings without making it sound like she thought they were horrible people and she didn't love them. Sometimes, though, they *were* horrible, and sometimes when they were at their most horrible, she felt like maybe she *didn't* love them.

But that wasn't a bit true. Harleen knew she loved her parents with all her heart and soul because the idea of being without them was too unbearable to think about. She felt the same way about her baby brothers; all she wanted to get rid of was their dirty diapers.

Hey, she thought, what if she toilet-trained them? Diapers cost money and if Mommy and Daddy didn't have that expense to worry about, they would be happy—happy enough to stop fighting. Especially in those low, tense voices.

◆

All day Harleen waited for her parents to blow up at each other but they didn't. For a while, they shut up altogether. The atmosphere was awful; it was like being inside a house made of pain. Harleen tried to work up the nerve to ask if she could go to the playground around the corner but, after last night, she didn't think Mommy and Daddy would let her go out by herself for a long time. She considered asking if she could go help Mrs. DiAngeli or Paula take care of her brothers but then she remembered they both charged extra for her, no matter how helpful she was. Bringing her brothers back here was no-go—in this atmosphere, they'd never stop crying and she wouldn't blame them.

Harleen curled up on the couch, hugging her knees and staring through whatever was on TV. Was it a DVD? She couldn't remember if she'd put one on or not. Yesterday had been the best day ever, and it was like it had never even happened. Her heart had been full of joy; now she felt empty and alone. She wondered if this was how it felt to be in prison; when her parents were like this, it was even worse than being punished for doing something wrong. She felt as if she couldn't take another moment, but somehow she did, one after another, after another, after another.

This was all the cops' fault.

If they had treated her daddy the way they were supposed to, if they'd made a report about him getting punched out and then given them a ride home, everything would be okay now. It wouldn't have been the perfect end to the day, but she'd have slept in her own bed last night and woke up in the morning instead of feeling like a zombie in a house of pain.

But the cops had acted like her daddy had done something wrong and while they were doing that, the *real* bad guys captured her and tried to trick Mommy into coming to get her so they could hurt her—*kill* her! And did they know about Delvecchio and his pervo pal? Did they even *care*?

◆

The day lasted forever, like the hours were crawling by on hands and knees. No one went to get her brothers from the sitter and Harleen began to worry even more. The low, tense voices started again, stopped for a bit, then resumed. Harleen wanted to cry but she wouldn't let herself. Her daddy always told her, when she got nervous or worried, she should try to imagine what she'd be doing next week, how this would all be in the past. But she couldn't—it felt more like she'd be trapped in this horrible time forever.

Near the end of the afternoon, Mommy got out the suitcases. Harleen ran to her room, got into bed, and pulled the covers over her head. Sometime after that, Mommy brought her brothers in and told her to watch them. They all should have been cranky and restless but they just looked spooked. Even Ezzie, who was the youngest, didn't fuss.

After a while Mommy came in with food for Barry and Frankie

and a bottle of formula for Ezzie and left again. Harleen fed everyone as the tense voices got louder.

"Almost over," Harleen whispered to Ezzie, rocking him gently. "It's almost over."

Barry and Frankie curled up on the floor with their blankets and went to sleep. Ezzie was quiet but his eyes were still wide open. He didn't cry until the shouting started. Then he wailed and wailed and wailed. Barry and Frankie never stirred. Harleen sang all the songs she knew and recited silly rhymes but nothing she did would comfort him. She could barely hear her parents over his crying. After a while, she wondered if *that* was why Ezzie was crying—to drown out Mommy and Daddy sounding so hateful.

If Mommy and Daddy asked me right now, I'd say I hate them both, Harleen thought, and for the first time, she didn't feel a smidgen of guilt. If anyone should feel guilty about anything, it was her parents. But they probably didn't. Grown-ups did anything they wanted and kids could just lump it.

After what seemed like forever, the shouting stopped and the apologizing began. Ezzie quieted down and went to sleep. Harleen couldn't, so she was stuck listening to them.

I'm sorry.

No, I'm sorry.

No, I'm to blame, I know how hard things are. I promise I'll be more understanding, you'll see.

No, I promise I'll do better, I'll work harder—

Rotten cops, Harleen thought, wide awake, wishing she could doze off like a baby. They'd ruined *everything*.

She tiptoed to the door, opened it and peeked out. In the kitchen, Mommy was sitting on Daddy's lap and Daddy was promising what happened yesterday would never, *ever* happen again and they had to stick together. Together they were going places.

Daddy was half right. He went to prison.

5

Today, seventeen-year-old Harleen Quinzel was exactly where she wanted to be: in the zone. She was so much in the zone, she felt as if she were glowing. Good thing—this was it. Today was the day. The gymnastics lessons her mother had scrimped and saved to give her, the hours she had spent training and practicing, pushing herself and never settling for "good enough," all the studying, developing her mind as well as her body, never blowing off her schoolwork to hang out at the mall, and today was the day it all came together, just the way she planned, just like her mother had said it would. Her mother had been so sure—sometimes she had even been surer than Harleen herself was. The way her mother believed in her, it was like she'd already seen proof, like she knew for a fact that Harleen was going to get the gymnastics scholarship to college—full ride, four years.

No doubt that was why her mother didn't feel the need to be here, Harleen thought. She scanned the people in the bleachers anyway, but she hadn't been there when Harleen had looked thirty seconds ago, and she still wouldn't be there thirty seconds from now. But all of Harleen's friends were; that was something at least.

"Next up," said the voice on the gymnasium loudspeaker, "Harleen Quinzel!"

Her friends cheered loudly, waving at her, calling out, *Go, Harleen, go! You got this, girl!*

Harleen stood and walked gracefully to the corner of the spring floor. She gave her friends a nod to show she was glad they were there. Still no Mom.

No Dad either, but he was months away from parole. He'd probably get it, too—he'd been a model prisoner. If only he'd been a model citizen, he wouldn't have been in there in the first place and both her parents would be here today.

Dream on; that was somebody else's life, not hers, never hers. She was on her own and she should be used to that by now.

Harleen raised her arms and her music began. *Scheherazade* by Rimsky-Korsakov—she felt her heart lift and she took flight. Two full tumbles one after another, then an aerial cartwheel. She stood for a fraction of a second facing away from everyone before she bent gracefully backward and went into a handstand. She held it for a few seconds, then folded herself in half, keeping her legs perfectly straight in a V-shape, as she swept them just a few inches off the floor. She held it for a few seconds without touching down, then went back into a handstand, followed by a walkover.

Then she was flying across the floor again, flinging herself into a pike, a split, and a straddle in rapid succession before rolling into a pose with her chest on the floor and the rest of her body bent up and over, her pointed toes barely touching her head.

Her legs flowed forward into another back bend as she let the music carry her up into three aerial cartwheels, hitting the floor progressively harder on each one to build up enough lift for the double twist.

She heard everyone in the gym gasp as she came down perfectly, finishing without a wobble. The applause was heartier this time and it wasn't only from her friends.

Harleen felt her throat tighten. *Don't cry—no tears!* she thought as she walked gracefully back to her seat. She had told herself she wouldn't look at her scores until she sat down again, but just as she reached the chair, she heard her friends scream and the rest of the audience break into wild applause, and she couldn't help herself.

Harleen felt her jaw drop. Every judge had given her a ten, every single one of them, even that old stick-in-the-mud Anna Carrera. Getting a seven from her was like a nine point five from anyone else. But even she had given Harleen a ten, making it a perfect score. Her friends were still screaming and whistling; everyone in the bleachers was smiling and cheering for her.

And her mother still wasn't there.

"*Malenki zirka!* Little star! You did it!" Harleen's coach, Liliana Lewenchuk, hugged her tightly and gave her a loud smacking kiss on each cheek. Liliana's eyes were bright with happy tears; she looked at Harleen with so much affection that Harleen had to look away. Liliana didn't notice—she was already hugging Harleen again, squeezing her tightly.

"I can't breathe!" Harleen said, laughing to cover how awkward she felt. Liliana let go of her for all of a second, then immediately hugged her again.

◆

"Of course you did," said her mother when Harleen told her she'd gotten the gymnastics scholarship. "I knew you would. I never doubted it for a second."

They were sitting on the shabby sofa in the employee lounge at the cafe where her mother worked her second job, waiting table. Harleen had had to wait ten minutes before her mother could get a break. It was only part-time—thirty hours a week. So was the job at the charity clinic. The clinic didn't have the budget to put her on full-time. Two part-time jobs added up to sixty hours a week— time and a half at the regular rate. Her mother was a real bargain.

Harleen knew she wasn't being fair, but she couldn't help feeling angry that her mother hadn't told her boss that, just this one time, she needed a couple of hours for her daughter's important gymnastics competition. She'd missed all the others but this one she had to be there for. Just this one time and she'd never ask again, because this was Harleen's last high-school competition ever.

She told her mother all about it, only there wasn't much to tell, seeing as how her mother knew all along that she'd come out with the top score and the scholarship. Somehow that made the post-competition letdown even worse.

"I'm glad *you* knew it," Harleen said. "I didn't."

Her mother laughed.

"Well, I *didn't*," Harleen insisted.

Her mother laughed harder.

Harleen went into tough-Brooklyn-cookie mode. "So I guess it's true what they say—Muddah knows best, right? Ya knew it all along so ya didn't haveta bothah showin' up, didja? Cuz ya already knew, right?"

Her mother's laughter cut off instantly as her expression went cold and stony. "Yeah, I was having so much fun here serving crappy coffee for quarter tips that I couldn't tear myself away to watch you do your gymnastics thing."

"My gymnastics *thing* is going to put me through college," Harleen said. "Not you."

Her mother's hardened expression intensified. "No, not me. Just because I paid for all those gymnastics lessons, went without so you could have the best trainer—whose house I cleaned to make up the shortfall when there wasn't enough money—that doesn't mean I contributed to your going to college at all. The only thing I can do is make sure you and your brothers get enough to eat and keep a roof over your head. And in my spare time, I chillax by visiting your father in the pen—*by myself*, not because *I* don't want to take you with me but because *your father* asked me not to, because *he* doesn't want you to see him like that. My life is such a whirlwind of fun and games that, occasionally, I have to let something go by.

Suck it up, buttercup." Pause. "And don't talk like that, people'll think you're a ditz."

"The more fool them, because I'm not," Harleen said. "I just don't understand. All the things you've done—all the trouble you've faced, that we've faced together—and you can't tell your boss you want a couple hours off to watch your daughter's gymnastics competition. Why? Just tell me that at least."

Her mother's expression didn't change. "Because I'm not allowed to bring a giant hammer to work."

Harleen gaped at her, shocked. "Is that supposed to be some kind of joke?"

Her mother gave her a sidelong look. "You hear anyone laughing?"

6

College set Harleen Quinzel free.

Going away to college is, for many kids, their first taste of freedom, when they can finally make their own decisions—some good, others unfortunate. But for Harleen Quinzel, it was so much more than a rite of passage. It was like being released from prison after an eighteen-year sentence.

As much as she loved her family, she had chafed under limitations that were unavoidable when one parent had to work two jobs to support four kids while the other parent was... *away*. Once her brothers were all in school, they didn't need the same degree of attention. But it still fell to Harleen to make sure they had clean clothes, did their homework, ate their vegetables, and stayed out of trouble.

It wasn't a whole lot of fun being stand-in Mom, but Harleen knew she had to be a good girl and help out. When things were especially hard on her, she reminded herself she had college to look forward to, provided she could get a scholarship. Gymnastics was her ticket out, but only if her grades were equally good—colleges didn't give a full four-year ride to a C-student, or at least not one whose father was doing time in the state pen.

Her father had been paroled in time to see her graduate from high school. Both he and her mother had been in the auditorium that day with her brothers. It was the only time she could remember the whole family being present for something other than the reading of a verdict.

◆

The freedom of being at Gotham University was positively intoxicating.

For one thing, she could go by Harley without having to listen to her mother object. Mom wouldn't tolerate Harley; it always, always, *always* had to be Harleen. Harleen was an English name that meant "meadow of the hares." Harley was the masculine form. *You are neither a boy nor a motorcycle*, her mother would tell her in a that's-final tone of voice. As she got older, Harley came to understand how seldom her mother got anything her way, so she hadn't fought her. But once she was out of the house, she decided there were now three kinds of Harley: the masculine form of Harleen, the motorcycle, and the tough Brooklyn cookie with the gymnastics scholarship.

Welcome to the new world order, everyone—hope you like what I've done with the place.

◆

Of course, renaming herself was the easiest part of going to college. Even for someone who had learned to study with three noisy brothers bouncing off the walls; or sitting in a laundromat with a dozen women gossiping loudly around her while their kids were tear-assing through the place; or occasionally in an emergency room, waiting to find out if Barry or Frankie or Ezzie had a break or a sprain after falling off the monkey-bars; college was more demanding than anything she had ever faced. It could even be more exhausting than gymnastics.

And even with a full scholarship, Harley found she needed a work-study job for incidentals like food, clothing, and those books not officially required but strongly recommended by her professors. S.T.A.R. Labs had an animal research facility on campus and they were only too happy to have a pre-med student.

Harley's grades were good—but, to her dismay, not great. The first semester of her freshman year, she had been mortified when she got a D on her logic mid-term instead of the A or A- she had expected. This, too, was a common experience among freshmen. It was a rude awakening when kids who were ranked in the ninety-ninth percentile in high school discovered they didn't measure up quite so well in a setting where everyone else had also been in the ninety-ninth percentile. Students who had hardly ever studied found themselves having to hit the books for the first time in their lives.

Harley thought about calling her mother—Sharon Quinzel had been through college and med school; she knew what it was like—but she just couldn't. Her mother was still working two jobs to pay her father's legal bills, while her father was having trouble getting any kind of legit work. Jobs were so scarce, even a crappy fast-food joint paying minimum wage could afford to be picky about who they hired, and they weren't looking for ex-cons. Plus, there were lots of jobs convicted felons weren't allowed to do, no matter how qualified they were. Harley's problems paled in comparison.

Calling to tell her mother she was having a hard time keeping up with the reading for her course-work sounded ridiculous even to her—like a rich guy telling a homeless person that he'd had a bad day because his show horse pooped in his car elevator. This was what she had signed up for, Harley told herself, and vowed to do better.

But like so many students—again—Harley learned this was something more easily vowed than done. She did improve but not as much as she'd hoped. She decided to talk to her professors. It only made sense—if you had trouble with a subject, you talked to the teacher about it.

Which was how Harley Quinzel came to the next rude awakening for college students: unlike teachers in public education, college professors didn't have to care. They didn't even have to pretend to care. College was a choice, not required by law. Anyone who wasn't up to college-level work didn't belong there.

The epitome of this attitude was Dr. Eugene Farrow in the psychology department. Among the many classes he taught was Statistics in Psychology, which Harley had been told was crucial if she planned to go into psychiatry. Harley had studied statistics in high school but this course was exhausting from day one. When she went to see Dr. Farrow, he gave her a slew of extra assignments, telling her the only way out was through.

"Good thing I've got a gymnastics scholarship," she told him with a weak laugh. "I can just cartwheel through."

Dr. Farrow surprised her by bursting into hearty guffaws. When he caught his breath, he told her to cartwheel on back to his office at the same time next week to pick up more work.

Harley left with mixed feelings. She seemed to have won over a professor not known to be sympathetic to students, especially undergrads. But she'd done it by making tons more work for herself, and she'd already been struggling to keep up with what she'd had before.

Her part-time job in the small animal lab began to feel like a refuge. All she had to do was make sure they were fed and watered and their cages were clean. Oh, and sometimes chase down the ferrets that had escaped. Harley was pretty sure the other student working there had been letting them out and playing with them. Gabriela Matias had some kind of weird weasel fixation. She and Harley never worked the same hours, which suited Harley just fine. There was something creepy about Gabriela and it wasn't just the weasel thing; the girl could have been obsessed with unicorns and rainbows and Harley still would have thought there was something unsettling about her.

Harley didn't want to feel that way about her or anyone else—

her own background didn't fit the standard American middle-class mould. But Gabriela was just too… icky.

The only thing Harley found more disturbing than Gabriela was Batman.

Growing up in Brooklyn, Harleen hadn't heard much about Batman. But when she enrolled at Gotham State University, she never *stopped* hearing about him. It was like everybody was tuned to the all-Batman channel—or Bat-channel—and they never shut it off. She learned more about Batman than she ever wanted to know. Anyone would have thought the guy had cured cancer, ended poverty, and brought about world peace. But as Harley saw it, nothing could have been further from the truth.

Batman was a self-appointed crimefighter who took down the worst criminals—but only by being a criminal himself. Vigilantism was against the law, and Batman, whoever he was, had actually made it into a lifestyle, with clever accessories! Besides the outfit, complete with cape, mask, and utility belt, he had a special car and a panoply of custom-made equipment, all festooned with bat designs. Obsessive much?

But the truly astonishing thing to Harley was that no one in Gotham City seemed to think there was anything weird or abnormal about this. Because Batman was a good guy and everybody knew that good guys weren't weird or abnormal, they weren't criminals—they were on *our* side. Good guys were okay.

And how did everybody know Batman was a good guy? Because everybody said so! If it weren't true, everybody wouldn't say it. Nothing like a little circular logic to keep things lively.

When Harley tried to question this, she was brushed off with what was apparently Gotham City's official mantra: *You don't understand because you're not from around here.*

She might have tried to argue more about that but Gotham's local TV news changed her mind. As outré as Batman was, he had nothing on Gotham's hometown criminals. They all wore crazy costumes as if crime were just a form of cosplay to them. They even went by wacky personas with names like the Riddler or the Penguin or the Joker, whom Harley thought was even freakier than Batman. She had watched the viral video of his being loaded into a van bound for Arkham Asylum after his recapture—by Batman, of course—and wondered if it were real or just a reality show trying to kick things up a notch. No, her friends told her, the tall skinny guy dressed like a clown's nightmare really did have green hair and a permanent clown-white complexion and he always put on a spectacle when they sent him back to Arkham.

The sight of him thrusting his face into the camera and urging people to steal cream pies and hit cops with them made her rethink her position on Batman. The Joker called himself the Clown Prince of Crime but his humor came with a body count. If this was how the criminal element rolled in Gotham, maybe Batman really *was* a hero.

Harley decided Gotham City had to be a psychiatric gold mine.

◆

While Harley never gave up trying to do better academically, gymnastics was where she shone most brightly. Liliana Lewenchuk's little star became a great big nova, throwing herself into every competition and coming away with top marks. Harley never again achieved a perfect score like she had that day in her high-school gym, but then, she never expected to. That had been a once-in-a-lifetime achievement, and something most people would never experience. The only thing that bothered her were the comments about the Olympics.

What an incredible talent—she's so brilliant. Too bad she never competed in the Olympics.

It rankled Harley; as if all the years of practice and training, all her ability, all her championships and medals counted for nothing.

She herself had no regrets. Every four years, she watched another group of little girls on the floor or the balance beam or the uneven parallel bars, their faces hard with concentration, showing none of the joy she herself felt when she took flight, and she wasn't sorry she hadn't been one of them. Her mother had never been able to afford an Olympic-class training program but Harley felt more like she'd dodged a bullet than missed the boat. What was so great about being washed up in your twenties? She pushed herself as hard in the gym as she did in her classes, not for a medal but because it felt good.

Why did so many people seem to think that you were either an Olympian or you were a zero? It simply wasn't true. But people would believe whatever they chose to, even when evidence to the contrary was staring them right in the face. Harley didn't know why that was and it gave her one more reason to go into psychiatry, to see if she could find out.

♦

As Harley's college education progressed, she became adept at reading people. It was a skill she had inherited from her father— con men had to be good at reading people and sizing up a situation at short notice. Not that it occurred to Harley to think of it in that way. Harley made use of her gift for people-reading mostly without realizing what she was doing, and when she did, she associated it with all the psychology she'd learned.

Harley found that sometimes it wasn't enough to be a conscientious student. Sometimes engaging emotionally with a subject, whether it was eighteenth-century English literature, twentieth-century world history, organic chemistry, abnormal psychology, or even principles of physics, could make the professor grade a bit more generously. Or even a lot more. Professors found less fault with students who seemed to be personally invested.

It was impossible to do this with every subject, of course, but it *was* possible to bluff—you just had to know the right keywords. This was why listening was so important, and Harley was positively adept at that. Being a lovely young woman didn't hurt, either. Professors loved having the attention of an attractive young woman, and not just the men. Women enjoyed her company just as much. Harley liked being liked, and it seemed to make her even more likeable. She hadn't thought life could ever get this good for someone like her.

Oh, once in a while, she got a not-so-good vibe from a professor and immediately understood they'd have happily traded sex for a grade. After a couple of unfortunate experiences, she learned what signals to watch for and how to stay several steps ahead, steering the situation—she used the term "manipulate." They required more effort but she eventually came away with an A without even taking her shoes off. Which seemed to confirm the commonly held wisdom that the more attractive a person was, the more they could get away with.

After exposure to the larger world beyond Brooklyn, Harley came to the conclusion that most people weren't so much bad, as they were simply at the mercy of their own weaknesses, which could produce at worst a whole lot of evil, and at the very least, mediocrity and tedium. And it seemed like so many people let themselves get used to mediocrity and tedium; instead of living, they just... *faded*, like old photographs. At times, Harley wanted to jump up and down and scream, just to interrupt the continuous march toward entropy.

Someday she was going to meet someone larger than life, someone who was all bright colors at maximum volume, who was a lot more than just the sum of their weaknesses.

She hoped so, anyway.

♦

Med school was so challenging that Harley finally gave in and called her mother. Her mother sounded overjoyed to hear from her; before long they were chattering and comparing notes. Harley found herself getting to know her mother in a new and deeper way.

At the same time, however, Harley made sure she didn't call too often. She was *from* Brooklyn—she was *out*. She wasn't going to get sucked back into the old neighborhood and the old life, where mob bosses and thugs and fathers going to prison were nothing out of the ordinary.

Her mother was concerned about her going into psychiatry. It was a specialty that wasn't quantifiable in the same way as cardiology or orthopedics, she told Harley. Sometimes it was hard to know if you were actually doing a patient any good; worse, continuous contact with neurotics could take you to a dark place it was hard to escape from.

But Harley was determined. The mind was an adventure, and Harley was very much interested in adventure.

Which brings us to the present…

…almost.

7

A mere two years ago…

Dr. Joan Leland had been at Arkham Asylum for fifteen years, and the Head of Psychiatry for the last six. She was the first woman to serve in the position and, barring unforeseen circumstances, she planned to be there until she retired twenty years from now. It was what she wanted, but her predecessor Dr. Antonio Lopez had told her it was just as well. After you'd been at Arkham for an extended period of time, changing jobs could be difficult. Other doctors tended to be nervous around you, as if you might be as dangerous as the inmates.

She had to admit, albeit reluctantly, there was something to that. When she attended medical conferences, her colleagues looked at her apprehensively, as if they had no idea what she would do next. Once, after a long day of lectures and panel discussions, she'd joined a few other psychiatrists in the bar for drinks and tried breaking the ice with a joke about the voices in her head taking the night off. Within five minutes, her colleagues had decided to go to bed early.

But it was Joan Leland's innate sense of duty that had made her decide to stay at Arkham. It wasn't easy to find doctors and nurses willing to work in a place that housed the most dangerous psychotics and psychopaths in the country. It wasn't just the fact that the job could be dangerous—everyone on the staff had been through several unpleasant incidents, and even the minor ones could be hard to shake off. Despite security measures tighter than any other hospital (and even a few prisons), inmates sometimes escaped; the staff and their families became targets, for payback, for sadistic compulsions, or simply for the hell of it.

There was a team of burly "orderlies" as well as a state-of-the-art security system to deal with the job's inherent dangers. They had nothing comparable for the larger problem—viz., many of the patients were broken beyond repair.

This was antithetical to the whole concept of the practice of medicine. The conscientious doctor was supposed to find some way to treat a patient, or if all else failed, administer palliative care to relieve their suffering. Treating mental illness wasn't the same as treating a disease like cancer or emphysema or COPD. But advances in pharmacology had produced better psychotropic drugs. Many patients who in an earlier time would have been institutionalized and forgotten now had a chance at some kind of life. But these weren't the kind of patients who usually ended up at Arkham.

The vast majority of mentally ill people were more likely to be victims of crime than perpetrators. Many patients in Arkham, however, were dangerous not simply because they were insane but because they were psychopaths. Psychopathy was incurable and difficult to treat or just manage even in sane criminals; prison therapists had learned to their horror that therapy only taught psychopaths how to fool a parole board.

A psychotic psychopath was the patient from hell. For one thing, you couldn't be absolutely sure they *were* psychotic; thus, medication might be pointless. Worse, the patient might hoard pills to sell to other patients or unscrupulous staff members, usually orderlies—but not always.

It was hard to fill staff vacancies at all, let alone find someone with an unwavering moral compass, flawless ethics, and nerves of steel to withstand the ambience of a place full of crazy, dangerous people, for what the state considered a decent, even competitive salary.

In Arkham Asylum, nothing was what it seemed. Things could change from moment to moment. You had to second-guess everything, even third- or fourth-guess it, and do it fast. This was not what most people who became doctors or nurses really wanted to do.

Most doctors wanted to heal, or at least help. They had come to the profession with ideals, planning to follow the noble tradition of Hippocrates. A lot of them were surprised to find, when they finally became real, live physicians, that Hippocrates' instruction to "First, do no harm" wasn't actually included in the formal oath. Nonetheless, Dr. Leland knew as well as anyone this sentiment was foremost in all doctors' minds and hearts when they began their careers.

There was a lot more to the Hippocratic Oath than *Primum non nocere*: it included, among other things, the art of medicine as well as the science, compassion, and the willingness to share knowledge, as well as the admonition to avoid both over-treatment and therapeutic nihilism.

◆

There had been six full-time psychiatrists at Arkham until Dr. Vincenzo had retired. Dr. Leland had prepared herself for a long, arduous search for someone to replace him but, to her astonishment, an application came in the day after Vincenzo left. And *mirabile dictu*, not from someone who had graduated last in their med-school class and barely got through residency but from the accomplished young woman Dr. Leland was about to show around the facility.

Dr. Harleen Quinzel arrived for her first day on the job in the same kind of seriously professional outfit she'd worn for her interview. The tailored navy blue suit, cream-colored silk blouse, straight skirt, and conservative black pumps made her look like she always knew exactly what to do. The no-nonsense black-framed glasses added to the effect, as did her neat French roll hairdo. Her appearance projected confident competence, but if you looked twice, you'd notice she was also gorgeous, which had been why Dr. Leland had hesitated to hire her, even with her amazing med-school transcript and the many glowing references, all of which had checked out. So here she was, about to give this young, unwary woman a tour of what Dr. Lopez had called Hell's waiting room.

They had just come up the short flight of stairs from the mezzanine level where all the doctors' offices were located and started down the main corridor in Long-Term Wing A when the red and yellow ceiling lights began to flash and the alarms went off. Even after fifteen years, Joan Leland always jumped when this happened, but lovely, young Dr. Quinzel didn't even flinch—she only looked around, eyebrows raised in an expression of mild curiosity.

"Code Croc!" yelled Armand LaDue over the PA system. "I repeat, *Code Croc*! This is *not a drill*!"

Dr. Leland felt a flash of irritation. Only Armand felt compelled to say *not a drill*, even though everyone would know it wasn't. Arkham didn't have drills, only emergencies.

"All personnel clear the halls and common spaces! Security only!" Armand went on. "I repeat, *security only*!"

Dr. Leland turned to Dr. Quinzel and took her elbow. "We need to go back to my office—" she began. But Dr. Quinzel wasn't listening. She was looking at the end of the hall where Killer Croc had just appeared in all his hideous, scaly glory.

The Croc was definitely one of the more eye-catching Arkham inmates, as big as their biggest orderlies, with scaly green skin, a mouth full of nasty, sharp teeth, and hungry, reptilian eyes. Dr. Leland didn't know if normal crocodiles ever made growling noises but Killer Croc certainly did, and it was one of the most frightening things Joan Leland had ever heard, the sound of an inhuman beast that had burst out of a nightmare to attack the real world. He had been a man once and technically he still was—his DNA, though mutated, wasn't purely reptilian and his brain waves were human. But none of that mattered when he was bounding toward you with a murderous roar.

The inmates in the rooms lining the corridor began howling and jeering. The lights were still flashing, the alarms were still whooping, and Armand LaDue was still yelling on the PA. Joan Leland's world suddenly started tilting sideways; she ordered herself to get a grip. This was no time to feel dizzy. But the world went on tilting as Killer Croc came at them, his brutish gaze fixed on the tasty morsel that was Dr. Harleen Quinzel.

Dr. Quinzel casually reached out and took a fire extinguisher off the wall beside her. Dr. Leland had just enough time to wonder if the woman thought the place was on fire before Killer Croc leaped. With a smooth, practically casual motion, Arkham's newest staff psychiatrist swung the extinguisher forward and up, hitting Killer Croc squarely in his most sensitive spot.

The Croc's roar went up three octaves as he collapsed on the floor a few feet from the round toes of Dr. Quinzel's tasteful black pumps, holding his crotch and rolling from side to side. A second later, the orderlies pounced on him with sedatives and wrapped him up in a canvas cocoon.

"You okay, Doc?" one of them asked Dr. Leland, looking as boggled as she felt.

She nodded. As they carried the still-whimpering Croc away, she turned to Dr. Quinzel, who was busily inspecting the extinguisher.

"No damage," Dr. Quinzel said cheerfully, "but it'll have to be recharged next month." She put it back on the wall, then smiled brightly at Dr. Leland. "You were saying?"

"I was?" Dr. Leland said.

Dr. Quinzel's smile became even brighter. "About the new neuroleptics?"

"Oh, yes." Dr. Leland still felt a bit shaky but at least the world wasn't tilting anymore. "We have new neuroleptics."

"How new?" asked Dr. Quinzel chattily.

"Some are recent releases," Dr. Leland said. "But a couple aren't on the market yet."

Dr. Quinzel's eyes widened behind her no-nonsense glasses. "Tell me about *those*."

♦

Within thirty minutes, everyone on the premises had heard how the utterly unflappable new doctor had taken down the Croc in full attack mode, then stood over him chatting with Dr. Leland until the orderlies hauled him away. Oh, and she was also a knockout.

Sitting in his room at the very bottom of criminally insane hell, the Joker was fascinated. He listened to several different accounts from both staff and patients. They all told the same story—a hot young blonde clocked the Croc in the family jewels without flinching, like he *wasn't* the most grotesque thing she'd ever seen. She was described variously as Helen of Troy, the goddess Athena, a Valkyrie, and the reincarnation of an actress who was actually still alive.

This was the woman he'd been waiting for, the Joker thought. Someone who wasn't going to bore him to death. Who might actually be worth whatever time and effort it would take to destroy her.

He couldn't wait.

8

Harleen had been prepared to share an office with one or two other people. At Arkham, however, there was plenty of office space to go around. Her office was big, too—not enormous, but you could open the door without it hitting the desk. There was even a window. This was Harleen's office, not Harley's.

No one would have called the view scenic—Arkham Asylum was out in the middle of nowhere, in an area where the landscape wasn't inspiring even in summer. Just outside her window was a very old, twisted tree. She wasn't sure what kind of tree it was; no one else seemed to know, either. Dr. Leland had warned her not to touch the weird, misshapen leaves; the inmate who had been taking care of it had done something to it and now the leaves produced a highly toxic substance, worse than poison ivy.

When the wind blew from just the right direction, the long, skinny branches at the end of one of the gnarled boughs would tap on her window like someone trying to get her attention. Harleen thought she could probably have climbed out onto it if she were ever trapped in her office and needed a quick getaway. Which was a rather silly idea. Arkham Asylum was pretty outré and, as she'd seen on her first day, it could even be dangerous. But thinking she might need to use the tree outside her office to escape—that wasn't even crazy, only childish. It was more like something that would occur to a seven-year-old, not a woman twenty years older with a medical degree.

On the other hand, it wouldn't have been a silly kid's fantasy for seven-year-old Harleen. That little girl hadn't been given to idle make-believe; she hadn't even believed in Santa Claus. When she had stared down a mobster's hired muscle on a pier at Coney Island in the middle of the night, it hadn't been Santa who had come to her rescue.

There was a tap at the door and Dr. Leland poked her head in. "I thought we'd continue introducing you to the schizophrenics today."

Harleen smiled. Ever since the Killer Croc incident, Dr. Leland had been her new best friend. Yesterday the woman had taken her through the ward housing the least dangerous patients, those thought to have some chance of leaving Arkham. Harleen was far more interested in meeting patients closer to the Killer Croc end of the spectrum. But she was the new kid; she had to be patient.

◆

Three weeks later, Harleen was running out of patience.

Dr. Leland still hadn't taken her down to Arkham's lowest levels, where the most difficult and dangerous inmates were kept. One of the other psychiatrists, a balding forty-ish man named Reginald Percival (Harley knew he wasn't from Brooklyn—he'd never have survived his childhood with that name), referred to those wards as storage. Dr. Percival kept his head down, did what was required to get through the day, then went home and drank.

Drinking was the most common coping strategy for Arkham Asylum staff overall. It wasn't a great solution, Dr. Leland said, but it was legal without a prescription.

Harleen thought the hardest thing about the job wasn't how dangerous the inmates were or that most of them would never be well enough to leave. It was the fact that, unlike other hospitals where she had interned or been resident at, Arkham had no overall rhythm.

There was routine—meals, medication, therapy, recreation,

bedtime—but each ward had its own; nothing connected all the different areas of Arkham into a unified whole. The most dangerous patients might as well have been in another hospital. It certainly seemed that way from what Harleen read in their files. They all lived in worlds of their own without much in common save the fact that they'd never leave.

Arkham had no set visiting hours—anyone wishing to see a patient had to make an appointment twenty-four hours in advance. "Nobody at Arkham has regular visitors," Dr. Leland told her over a late lunch in her office. "Their friends and family feel they've all suffered enough."

Harleen nodded knowingly. "As my abnormal psych prof used to say, people with antisocial personality disorder don't suffer from it—everyone around them does."

"Good one," Dr. Leland said with a short, humorless laugh.

"Still, there seem to be a fair number of visitors," Harleen went on. "Mostly at night."

"Sometimes doctors bring in specialists for consultation," Dr. Leland said. "Others are scientists doing research on certain kinds of pathology and their effects on the brain." She spoke in a brisk way and Harleen knew she wanted to change the subject. "Whenever possible, they make their findings available to us." She nodded at the black filing cabinet against the nearest wall. "You can find them in the third drawer down. The folders are toward the back, in the section marked 'New Data.'"

"Why *wouldn't* they make their findings available to us?" Harleen asked, honestly curious.

"If they're working on a new drug or trying to improve an existing medication," Dr. Leland said, "information about work-product is confidential."

"Even when they're beta-testing on our patients?" Harleen asked.

"No one beta-tests anything on our patients," Dr. Leland said sharply. "Our patients are either too atypical or too unstable."

Harleen's impatience spurred her on. "What about clinical trials?"

"The last clinical trial we ever participated in was thirty years ago, before my time. There's a report on it in the bottom drawer of the same filing cabinet. It's not pleasant reading." Dr. Leland put down her fork and pushed her salad to one side. "Is there something on your mind you want to discuss?"

I was just wondering about some of those "scientists" who come in around midnight with great big cases on wheels, Harleen thought. *What's in them? What are they doing to the patients, which patients are they doing it to, and who said it was okay?*

"I'm just curious," Harleen said. "Especially if they're patients I'll be treating."

"Arkham Asylum is where criminals bottom out," Dr. Leland said. "The people who end up here are truly lost souls. The whole world has washed its hands of them. Even those patients who have a genuine chance at rehabilitation and release. That's a *chance*, not a sure thing.

"But even if they actually make it, even if we send them out of the gates to catch the bus to Gotham with new clothes, a shine on their shoes, and a certificate declaring them legally sane, it wouldn't change the fact that they'd been in Arkham. In the view of so-called respectable society, anyone bad enough to be sent here is too damaged ever to be fixed. They might look like all the king's horses and all the king's men put them together again, but it's only a matter of time before they blow up real good. Then it's back to Arkham where they belong, post-haste, *tout suite*, and good riddance."

"Does that happen a lot?" Harleen asked.

"Not as much as it used to," Dr. Leland said. "But only because we don't discharge most patients anymore. When we do, we send them to a halfway house in Gotham City. Which I personally think is the exact wrong thing to do, but I don't have any say in the matter."

Harleen frowned. "You think it's wrong to send them to a halfway house?"

"No," said Dr. Leland, "I think it's wrong to send them to Gotham City. There's something about Gotham that's no good for them."

◆

Harleen threw herself into her work, while trying to figure out if there was anything she could do to make Arkham less disjointed. The problem may simply have been that Arkham was so understaffed.

In Harleen's opinion, there should have been at least ten full-time shrinks, and a dozen would have been better. But the board of directors held the purse strings, Dr. Leland told her, and the board said they couldn't afford more staff.

The board must have been made up of rich people, Harleen thought. Only rich people were so stingy. And they wondered why people wanted to rob them. She'd have bet good money that if every board member threw in what they spent on a week of fancy dinners, they could probably have built a whole new wing with an indoor swimming pool.

Well, okay, maybe the pool would have to wait till the next fiscal year.

◆

After a while, Harleen realized she was starting to drift. Worrying over all of the problems here kept her from focusing properly. She was getting to be like Dr. Percival—just doing whatever she had to do for the day, then going home, except she wasn't drinking herself into a stupor. The upside of her scrimping through college and med school on scholarship and loans was that she'd never been able to afford to go out drinking—or even stay in with a six-pack—so she'd never got into the habit of drowning her sorrows. If she kept on like this, however, she'd probably start. The last thing she needed was a drinking problem.

Harleen went back and reread a lot of patient files, with the idea of constructing a three-dimensional picture of Arkham. This time, however, she paid more attention to the patients designated as unusually high risks to themselves and everyone around them. They comprised a relatively small number of patients, and yet a great deal of Arkham's resources were committed just to keeping them contained. Even so, some of them managed to break out. The Joker in particular was especially skilled at engineering escapes, although for the life of her, she couldn't see how. They kept him in solitary in the sub-sub-sub-sub-basement with at least one orderly stationed outside, and more if he seemed to be getting hyperactive.

According to his file, the Joker had absolutely no regard for anyone's safety, including his own; he risked his life in terrifying ways, jumping out windows or off rooftops to what should have been sure death and survived by crazy-dumb luck, finding something to land on or, in one case, actually having his clothes catch on a second-story gargoyle before he could hit the street.

Of course, being a daredevil and a thrill-seeker went along with being a psychopath; as impressive as his split-second survival might be, other people *didn't* survive. Humor with a body count, Harleen reminded herself. Even so, she couldn't help being impressed. If only he could turn his energy toward something constructive and worthwhile, instead of acting out just for attention.

That was what it was—attention-seeking; Harleen was sure of it. He was like a great big kid yelling *Look at me! Look at me! Look at me!*

Well, a great big kid with a body count.

But if you overlooked the homicides, you were left with a great big spoiled five-year-old in clown white—which, she remembered, didn't come off. She couldn't recall what had happened, just that he blamed Batman for it. But that was no distinction—he blamed Batman for everything.

Still, if she'd been stuck with a face like that, Harleen thought, maybe she'd have taken it out not just on Batman but the rest of the world, too.

In any case, this was a mind she really wanted to delve into. Harleen let herself fantasize for a minute or two before reluctantly setting the idea aside. Dr. Leland would never go for it; she'd say Harleen was too new and it was too risky.

◆

All things considered, Dr. Leland was doing the best she could with too little funding from an uncaring board, Harleen thought, but if she disappeared tomorrow (like some of the consulting doctors), she wouldn't leave much of a legacy. None of the doctors would. That wasn't how Harleen wanted her own career to go. She'd never settled for "good enough" and she wasn't going to start now. So how could she do more?

Harleen reviewed the notes she'd made and it suddenly hit her: In all the time Arkham Asylum had been protecting polite society from the forces of chaos and evil, very little consideration had ever been given to the special problems of being criminally insane and female.

Time to make a difference, Harleen thought, and began work on a project she hoped would impress Dr. Leland.

◆

Harleen sweated over writing up her project, trying to get every detail exactly right. This wasn't like writing a dissertation or a research proposal; she wasn't even sure what Dr. Leland would expect to see. All she could do was make it clear that she wanted to help these women if it was at all possible.

But would the decision be up to Dr. Leland, Harleen wondered, or would she have to show it to the board of directors—whoever they were—and get their approval? If they were anything like academic committees, they might keep sending it back with requested changes, and—oh God help her—that could go on for months. The possibility of a long delay made her seriously consider scrapping the whole thing rather than deal with bureaucracy. Bureaucracy was like kudzu—it took over and choked the life out of everything. But opting to do nothing just because of that was hardly productive.

When she finally delivered the proposal, however, Dr. Leland told her to wait while she skimmed the ten pages—Harleen had also put together a PowerPoint version, just in case—then dropped it on her desk and told her to go ahead. "The only thing I insist on is that there be an armed guard in the room and another right outside the door."

This was a win; common sense told Harleen to take it and run, but she couldn't help herself. "Really?" she said. "I thought this would be harder."

Dr. Leland smiled. "As long as it doesn't require special shoes, human sacrifice, or extra funding, you can do almost anything, as long as you let me know about it. I must say, I quite liked getting a formal written proposal."

I had no idea it was this *bad.* Harleen barely managed not to say it aloud.

"If there's nothing else you need," Dr. Leland went on, "you can go ahead and convene your first meeting of the Female Inmates Support Group, or whatever you want to call it."

"Thank you, Dr. Leland," Harleen said with a mix of confidence and apprehension. "I won't let you down. Should I come by and tell you how it went?"

Dr. Leland dipped her head noncommittally. "Or if you need a good cry."

Harleen laughed, then realized Dr. Leland hadn't been making a joke.

9

Two days later, Harleen looked at the women seated in a small semicircle in front of her and wondered, *What have I done?*

Well, she had asked Dr. Leland for Arkham Asylum's most egregious female patients and Dr. Leland had obliged. Not that there had been a large pool to choose from—the criminal justice system sent fewer women to Arkham. The files for these women described their behavior as bizarre, grotesque, and seemingly irrational, with the emphasis on *seemingly*. It varied; sometimes it was *supposedly* or *appears to be*, depending perhaps on how bad the evaluating physician's day had been.

This was usually followed by a warning that the patient, though irrational, was capable of acting with purpose and intent. Staff were advised to be on their guard at all times and cautioned against being alone with them, even while restrained.

Dr. Leland had come by Harleen's office a few hours earlier to tell her to stay safe. "Don't let the armed guard leave you alone in the room with them, don't turn your back on them, and for God's sake, don't let any of them touch you."

"Their *touch* is dangerous?" Harleen had said, incredulous.

"Or at the very least disgusting." Dr. Leland looked worried. "The female of the species is far more dangerous than the male. *All* species. That's not a double standard, Dr. Quinzel, it's a fact."

"I'll keep it in mind," Harleen told her. "As it happens, I'm a female of the species, myself."

"More power to you, and Godspeed," Dr. Leland replied and left. Harleen began to wonder if Arkham's female patients couldn't get proper treatment because their problems had been blown completely out of proportion.

Now she was also wondering if she was in over her head.

All the women had arrived in full restraints accompanied by two orderlies, who proceeded to chain them to the heavy wooden chairs in the room. One of the orderlies saw the dismayed look on Harleen's face and told her Dr. Leland had insisted the women be restrained throughout the session; he had mistaken Harleen's growing anxiety for compassion. Unfortunately, patients weren't as easily fooled. She tried to project an air of professional concern, detached but not cold, open but untouchable.

The woman in the chair to the left was going to be her toughest customer. Pamela Isley, who preferred to be called Poison Ivy, was the patient who looked after the tree outside Harley's window. Or rather, she had been; her gardening privileges had been curtailed after she'd made the leaves toxic. She was still allowed time in the greenhouse where she was supposedly working on a way to reverse this. So far, she hadn't had any success, although she had managed to reduce the toxicity so the leaves no longer ruined the paint job of any cars they fell on.

She was also permitted to have a small number of potted plants in her room, although "permitted" wasn't quite the right word. Things just *grew* around Pamela Isley, and there was nothing anyone could do about it. Arkham's board of directors in concert with Dr. Leland came to a compromise with her: they would "let" her maintain a small indoor garden, and she would keep it small and non-toxic. It was better than having to send in a hazmat team twice a week to rip out rogue vegetation, or suffer with a local pollen count of ten thousand even when it wasn't hay-fever season.

Harleen wondered how Arkham managed to keep her confined.

Either Pamela Isley wasn't as powerful as she wanted everyone to believe, or she was just biding her time while she waited for... well, whatever.

Or maybe Pamela Isley was just crazy.

She was a beautiful woman. But what would have turned heads on the street more than her good looks were the vines snaking through her gorgeous red hair. On anyone else, it would have seemed like a cheap, silly affectation—*Hey, world, check me out. I'm so crazy!* But on Pamela Isley/Poison Ivy, they looked—well—not normal, but not out of place. Natural, even.

The way she cooed and whispered to them, however, wasn't natural, and the way the vines seemed to move in response to her was downright unsettling. Harleen decided she would always address her as Pamela or Ms. Isley. Openly refusing to participate in Isley's delusion would be a much-needed reality check, even if only for the duration of the session. The patient needed to know she wasn't the only tough customer in the house.

At that moment, Isley was making a big show of ignoring Harleen, turning away from her as much as her chains would allow, which wasn't a lot. That was actually a good sign; the more effort it took for Isley to snub her, the more important she considered Harleen to be. It wouldn't be easy getting through Isley's jungle of defenses to reach the real her, but Harleen had hope. Which was more than she could say for the other three women.

The woman to Isley's left was Harriet Pratt. Like Isley, she had a nom de guerre—March Harriet—but that was all they had in common. Isley was independent, single, and proud of it. Pratt had willingly latched onto the Mad Hatter, a foul and caustic character that even other criminals couldn't stand.

Harleen was baffled as to what the woman saw in him. There was nothing gentle about him, nothing that suggested he might be affectionate. If Alice had met him at the Mad Tea Party, Harleen thought, she'd have woken up screaming. And if Harriet Pratt had been there with him, poor Alice might never have slept again.

At the bottom of the first page in Pratt's file, someone had scrawled *Crazier than a shithouse rat!!* Dr. Leland strongly discouraged profanity or terms like "crazy" as unprofessional and grounds for a disciplinary note in the employee's record. Despite that, the notation remained untouched, although it could have been blacked out easily. Apparently what it lacked in professionalism it made up for in accuracy.

Harriet Pratt's time in Arkham had taken a toll on her. Poor diet had dulled her complexion and thinned her blonde hair. Her clothing was loose and shapeless; Harleen wasn't sure if she was carrying extra weight or just had poor muscle tone from inactivity. Her file put her age at thirty-five but she looked fifteen years older.

Or that might have been the effect of her scratchy speaking voice and the cringe-inducing Cockney accent she put on, calling everyone "ducks" or "ducky" or "luv." A little bit of that went a long way, Harleen thought unhappily; somewhere in London's East End, a Pearly Queen was having nightmares. Pratt's accent and her exclamations of "Crikey!", "Blimey, mate!", and "Oo-*er*!" were as abrasive as the Mad Hatter's ugly laugh.

"Shiny! Shiny!" piped up the woman in the next chair over. Margaret Pye was definitely going to be Harriet Pratt's stiffest competition for Most Annoying Patient, Harleen thought. Everyone called her Magpie and she was very much like her namesake. Anything that glinted, sparkled, or shone drew her eye and once she fixated on something, there was no distracting her. She would go through anyone or anything to get her hands on it, and she was a lot tougher (and meaner) than she looked.

Dr. Leland had insisted Margaret Pye be included, and Harleen hadn't argued for fear of being shut down. But after reading Margaret's file, Harleen was sorry she hadn't at least questioned Dr. Leland's decision. Several doctors had diagnosed Margaret Pye with inadequate personality disorder complicated by OCD. In

Harleen's professional opinion, what Margaret Pye needed was a carefully structured program of therapy with goals and periodic rewards. That, and medication for her obsessive-compulsive disorder, would do her more good than group sessions.

Unfortunately, Arkham's threadbare budget couldn't provide this kind of treatment for an indigent patient. If Margaret Pye had been high-profile as well as dangerous, the board would have looked for a researcher with a grant to cover expenses. If she'd had a wealthy, prominent family making demands, the board would have hit them up for a hefty donation.

But Magpie had been dumped at Arkham by another mental hospital after an unfortunate incident that had left three people dead. It had been somewhat shocking at the time but not particularly memorable. The news had given her name as Poe and no one, not even the hospital, had tried to correct it. She had no family of any kind and apparently no friends. A scrap of paper clipped to her file folder noted her birth certificate was missing and a replacement was "on the way." But the note had obviously been there for a long time; no one knew whom to query as to why it was taking so long.

Harleen felt for the woman. If she had an inadequate personality, it was only because she lived in an inadequate world that had failed her at every turn. Perhaps Dr. Leland had thought being around other women would somehow stimulate her mind and get her interested in things that weren't just *Shiny! Shiny!*

Well, it wasn't impossible. Stranger things had happened, Harleen thought, and the last woman in the group was one of them.

Mary Louise Dahl had enjoyed a successful career in cinema as a famous and much-loved child star. Unlike other child stars, however, her career hadn't been scuttled when she'd grown up, because she hadn't, and never would. Something called Turner's Syndrome, a rare disease exclusive to females, had sentenced Mary Louise to life in a child's body without possibility of parole.

At first glance, most people might think she was seven or eight, maybe a little young for her age because of the doll she always carried. But she would never grow any taller, never experience puberty, never achieve physical maturity. She'd been lucky not to have the serious health problems that often came with Turner's like heart and kidney trouble. Her worst misfortune was having a family who colluded with her agents and the studios to hide the whole truth about her condition from her for the sake of her career—i.e., for the sake of all the money she made. By the time she found out, it was too late for the hormone therapy that might have let her be a grown woman.

But while Mary Louise's childhood was endless, her movie career was not. The adult trapped in the child's body couldn't remain hidden forever. What audiences saw was a non-child trying to ape the real thing, and the effect was similar to the uncanny valley phenomenon produced by human-like robots or realistic CGI animation—except, as many moviegoers put it, "a whole lot creepier."

If there had been an award for Most-Royally-Screwed-Over-Person-Of-The-Century, Harleen thought Mary Louise would have owned it forever, and if there was any justice in the world, her family and agents and every other person complicit in her ruin should have been locked up for as long as Mary Louise was. Harleen wasn't sure there was any path out of the dark place where Mary Louise lived; despite that, Harleen found herself hoping she might somehow benefit from the group. She communicated only in pseudo-baby-talk, but Harleen was sure it was habit, not an impairment. Being locked up in Arkham hadn't given Mary Louise much incentive to increase her word power. But maybe after a couple of sessions she'd have more to say than, "I *did*-unt *mean* to *do* it!" or "Nasty-wasty asywum!"

Harleen figured today's auspicious achievement was just having the women there at all, even if it wasn't by choice. Harleen watched

Mary Louise rock back and forth in her restraints and Mary Louise stared back at her over the top of her doll's head, her eyes bright.

She's watching *me,* Harleen thought uneasily. *Not just watching—she's watching me watch her. Sizing me up.*

Something one of the nurses had said came back to her then. Esther Netanyahu had been at Arkham even longer than Dr. Leland. Harleen liked her because she didn't seem jaded and cynical but she was nobody's fool either. *Keep your guard up,* she'd told Harleen. *They've got a lot more experience being them than you have being you, and they know it.*

Mary Louise suddenly began blubbering loudly. "I *did*-unt *mean* to *do* it!" she wailed as tears ran down her face. "It's not *my* fault! It *is*-unt! I wanna go *home*—why can't I go *home?*"

"Here we go with the waterworks already," Pamela Isley said, sounding world-weary and bored. "I hate being near that brat. Can't somebody shut her up? Or aren't there any grown-ups in the room *not* chained to a chair?"

"Now, now, ducks," said Harriet Pratt in her exaggerated accent. "She's just a little girl."

"Like hell." Pamela Isley caressed one of the vines in her hair. Harleen blinked; had she actually just seen that vine curl itself around her finger? A real vine couldn't do that. (Could it?)

"Tsk, language, luv!" Harriet Pratt waggled her finger at the other woman. "There's children and ladies present, you know."

Now everyone except Pamela Isley was staring at her expectantly. Isley was absorbed in a close examination of the ends of a lock of her hair.

Harleen put on a bright, professional smile. "Since this is our first meeting," she said, hoping she sounded assertive rather than unnerved, "I thought we'd keep things light and just get acquainted. Each of us can say who we are and mention one or two things about ourselves or that are important to us—"

Pamela Isley never looked up: "Is there anyone in this room, chained or unchained, who doesn't know who I am? Didn't think so. I need no introduction."

A smart therapist never lets the patient drop the mic. A doctor at the hospital where she'd done her residency had told her that. "You could tell us a couple of interesting things about yourself," Harleen said, defiantly cheerful. "Or that are important to you."

Isley let out a long, put-upon sigh. "I prefer plants to people. Also, I don't like people anywhere nearly as much as plants. If you were expecting something about long walks on the beach or my favorite food or how I make it through every day here without slashing someone's throat, including my own, tough stuff."

"Aren't *you* a cheeky bit of rough," Harriet Pratt said, waggling her finger again.

Harleen ignored her. "Well? Don't keep us in suspense," she said to Isley. "How *do* you get through every day without slashing someone's throat, including your own?"

The woman kept pretending to be focused on her hair but Harleen caught the small movement of her eyes swiveling in her direction under half-closed lids. Pamela Isley had glanced at her. It was a very brief glance and she probably thought Harleen didn't know. But she did, and it counted.

"It's just that you brought it up," Harleen added. "Now I'm curious."

Pamela Isley continued scrutinizing her hair in silence. Harleen was about to give up and introduce herself when Isley said, "I can't give it all up today, Doc. What'll we talk about next time?"

Gotcha, Harleen thought gleefully, hiding her smile behind the file folder.

"It's not my *fault!*" Mary Louise insisted loudly, as if someone had claimed it was. Her tear-stained face was red and angry, and she was glaring at Harleen now. Resenting the loss of attention, Harleen thought. The ex-movie star was still a diva.

"We was *all* framed, ducky," Harriet Pratt said in cheerful agreement. "Me, I was just mindin' my own business, not hurtin' a soul, goin' for a ruby down me local. Next thing I know, two John 'Ops are feelin' my collar. They drag me in front of a judge who tells me *I'm* Radio Rental and there's a flowering dell waitin' for me in Arkham. Blimey!"

"Shiny! Shiny! *Shiny!*" Magpie yelled over her, staring hard at Harleen's throat, and Harleen finally realized she'd forgotten to take off her necklace. It was a simple disk with a caduceus on one side and the words *Primum Non Nocere* engraved on the other; her mother had given it to her when she had graduated from med school.

Hurriedly, she buttoned the very top button of her blouse, hoping if the woman couldn't see it, she'd lose interest. But Magpie kept staring at her throat as if she had X-ray vision. Harleen supposed a real magpie probably wouldn't have been fooled, either, and made a note to take the necklace off before the next session.

◆

"You don't look like you've been sobbing your heart out," Dr. Leland said when Harleen dropped by her office afterward. "Don't tell me it went well?"

"It wasn't great." Harleen sat down on the leather sofa instead of the chair in front of Dr. Leland's desk. "It was hard to get a word in edgeways between all the *Shiny! Shiny!* and the sobbing denials. But it wasn't an extinction-level event. Pamela Isley spoke to me. *On purpose.*"

Dr. Leland's eyebrows strained toward her hairline. "Really?"

"God's honest truth," Harleen said, raising her right hand. "She wouldn't sully her eyeballs by looking at me, but she did address me directly."

"Never mind Poison Ivy, how'd you escape with your necklace?"

Harleen grinned. "I buttoned the top button to hide it. Thought

I was gonna choke to death. Next time, I'll take it off beforehand. I'll have a written report for you tomorrow. Spoilers: Mary Louise still protests her innocence. And thanks to Harriet Pratt, I'm so tired of Cockney rhyming slang, I could scream. I was tempted to tell her how we roll in Brooklyn. Down on Toidy-Toid and Toid, ya know?"

Instantly Dr. Leland's expression turned serious. *"Never* do that, Dr. Quinzel. I'm *not* kidding," she added as Harleen smiled. *"Never* play with them. It makes you look weak, and in Arkham, if you *look* weak, you *are* weak. If you need a rodeo clown, call an orderly. I mean it."

"Okay, okay, no goofing around," Harleen said, shifting on the sofa. She'd felt pretty good about the session and all of a sudden Dr. Leland was chewing her out for something she hadn't even done.

It's because she's the boss, Harleen thought, suppressing a sigh. People in authority were always reminding you they were in charge. If they couldn't get you for screwing up, they'd make you feel like you had. And there was never a rodeo clown around when you really needed one.

"I got Pamela Isley to talk to me without doing anything reckless or stupid," Harley said, hoping she didn't sound as defensive as she felt. "I feel like that's something."

Dr. Leland's severe expression softened. "Just don't get too sure of yourself. This was only the first session. Patients here'll try anything once. They wanted to see how you handled yourself. And believe me, they learned more about you than vice versa. When's your next session?"

"I wanted to talk to you about that." Harleen sat up straighter. "Originally, it was scheduled for next week but I'd like to move it up to the day after tomorrow. If that's all right with you, of course."

Dr. Leland grimaced. "You can binge-watch a TV series but there's no such thing as binge-therapy."

"It's not binge-therapy," Harleen said, not entirely truthfully.

"We need to build up momentum. Seven days from now is a long time. It'll be like starting all over again, because we'll all be trying to remember where we were last time."

"Maybe that's not a bad thing," Dr. Leland said, but Harleen could see her wavering. "However, I understand what you're saying. Reschedule for *two* days after tomorrow. Momentum's good but so is getting a little distance on the previous meeting."

"Okay, two days after tomorrow," Harleen said, trying not to grin from ear to ear.

Dr. Leland hesitated, gazing at Harleen with her head tilted to one side. "Didn't your mother ever warn you to be careful what you wished for?"

"Well... no." Harleen's smile was wry. "At our house, we learned early on we couldn't get much of anything by wishing."

Dr. Leland was unmoved. "All the more reason she should have warned you."

10

The optimism Harleen had been coasting on after the first group session began to fade slightly when she saw Harriet Pratt's sour expression before the second even started.

Looks like the gloves are coming off, Harleen thought, although she held out a faint hope that Harriet's bad mood had nothing to do with her. She pretended to go through her notes while she waited for the orderlies to transfer all the patients from the wheelchairs, sneaking surreptitious glances from under her brows.

If Harriet was bent out of shape over the wheelchair, Harleen didn't blame her. It was standard practice for transferring high-risk/dangerous patients within Arkham but Harleen didn't like it. The chairs had restraints for every part of a patient's body, head included; it was clamped to the high back of the chair. At a staff meeting, she had questioned the necessity of immobilizing patients to the point where they couldn't even look around; a nurse named Frieda Vance said she'd obviously never been head-butted by a psycho in a bad mood.

Harleen still didn't like it. Not allowing patients to walk even a short distance on their two feet seemed like a bullying tactic. Surely a show of force wasn't *always* necessary. If the staff always acted like they expected trouble, then the patients would simply live up—or down—to their expectations. If, on the other hand, the patients were treated with a modicum of respect, they'd be more inclined to civilized behavior.

Granted, there were some very dangerous inmates who couldn't be allowed to move about freely—Killer Croc, for example, who probably remembered their first and so far only meeting as vividly as she did. She didn't know how they moved him around; an ordinary wheelchair wouldn't have held him for two seconds. But there was only one of him. Harleen had familiarized herself with the files of all Arkham's current residents and if she had listed them by how dangerous they were in descending order, these four women wouldn't have made the top ten.

Not that they wouldn't have been extremely dangerous in the outside world, especially Pamela Isley. But they weren't outside and they knew they never would be—assuming Magpie even knew where she was. But treating Margaret Pye as if she were one of the most dangerous patients in the place couldn't possibly be therapeutic and gave her no reason to say anything except *Shiny! Shiny!*

"Need us for anything else?" an orderly asked Harleen. His name-tag said Kevin; it seemed incongruously boyish for a man who was six-foot-five and had had a career as a linebacker on Gotham's pro football team.

"No, we'll be fine," Harleen replied.

He started to leave, then paused to lean down and whisper, "Watch out for Harriet, she's loaded for bear today."

The armed guard at the door let the orderlies out and assumed his usual parade-rest stance. Harleen winced inwardly. *If Harriet's loaded for bear, so are we. And we always shoot first.*

She turned back to the group. Pamela Isley was still ignoring her. They'd chained her up differently today, curtailing her range so she could only reach the longest strands of her hair. That was kind of mean, Harleen thought. Maybe she should call the orderlies back in and make them change it.

Harriet was glaring at her as if her eyes could beam death rays. Magpie was muttering *Shiny! Shiny!* under her breath and staring at Harley's bare throat with a mix of hurt and suspicion, as if the absence of Harleen's necklace was a personal affront. While Mary Louise Dahl *did-*unt *do* it but had yet to work herself into a crying jag.

"All right," Harleen said, hoping her cheerful tone didn't sound forced. "I thought today we could talk about what we hope to get out of these sessions. I'll give you a little time to think—"

"I can tell you that right 'ere and now, miss," Harriet said.

So that's what high dudgeon looks like, Harleen thought. "It's Doctor. Not miss, Doctor. Or Doc for short."

"'Ave it your way, but then you always do, don't you, *Doc*." Pink spots appeared on Harriet's cheeks. "You *all* do. And us, we has to take it, we does. 'Cause we're just scum to you. It's your world; we just live in it. If you call *this* living." She rattled her chains.

Harleen wondered if someone had forgotten to tell her Harriet Pratt was a meta-human with telepathy.

"All right, Doc," Harriet went on, "'Ere's what *I* want outa these *sessions*, as you call 'em." She drew herself up as much as she could. "Tea."

Harleen blinked at her. "Say again?"

Harriet looked heavenward for a moment. "Blimey, Doc, did the Lord strike you Mutt and Jeff? 'Cause you can't be *that* Tom Thumb. Tea! I want tea! Kiki Dee! Bruce Lee! You and me!"

Harleen was looking through the folder for information on Harriet's medications, thinking someone had forgotten to give them to her when Pamela Isley said, "She means the drink. Like, cup o' tea. Earl Grey, English Breakfast. Lipton, Tetley." She sounded even more bored and jaded than she had in the last session, but Harleen was sure she detected the barest hint of amusement. Which also counted.

Mary Louise burst into tears. "It's not *my* fault!" she sobbed. "It's *yours*! *You* did it!"

"She's right, Harriet," Pamela Isley said, still tired of it all. She'd given up trying to reach her hair and was now studying her manicure. "It's your fault for being deliberately obtuse. *I* knew what you meant, but I've been stuck in here with you long enough to grow a redwood. I know Kiki Dee and the rest of it is supposed to be Cockney rhyming slang—"

"It's not *supposed* to be, it *is*," Harriet snapped. "'Ave a butcher's on the web, see if I'm right!"

"—but the doc probably thought you were having a stroke," Pamela Isley finished with a long, heavy sigh. "If I had a time machine, I'd go back to the days when I couldn't understand a word you said. Made it so much easier to block you out."

The tension in the room was all but electric. Behind her, Harleen heard the guard open the door and beckon a few orderlies in. She twisted around in her chair briefly and held up one hand to tell them to stay back. They were ready to swarm over the women and subdue them, and she couldn't let that happen. She had to show all of them she didn't need a goon squad to rush in with restraints and tranquilizers every time someone had an emotion. Especially when they were already in restraints.

"Time out, everybody," Harleen said, making the hand-signal. "There's only one thing we need right now—a nice cup of tea."

Instantly Harriet's demeanor went from belligerent to delighted. "Don't mind if I do, ducks. Earl Grey, if you please."

"Herbal," said Pamela Isley, more jaded than ever.

Harley turned to Magpie and Mary Louise. "Shiny," Magpie said sulkily, her eyes fixed on Harley's throat.

"Pop," Mary Louise demanded. "Not nasty-wasty tea. *Pop*."

Harleen turned to the orderlies. "Is anyone writing this down?" she asked. "Harriet wants Earl Grey tea, herbal for Pamela—" she hesitated for a moment. "Water with lots of shiny ice cubes for Margaret Pye, and soda for Mary Louise, something without caffeine—ginger ale or grape or something. And green tea for me.

Bring enough for more than one cup or glass, please."

"We'll probably have to take a couple of them to the bathroom," an orderly named Oscar said.

"That's what they pay you for," Harleen said archly. "Though you should have a female nurse to chaperone. And cookies."

The orderly stared at her, baffled. "Cookies?"

"Bring a plate of cookies with our beverages," Harleen told him. "Refreshments aren't complete without cookies."

♦

"Now this is what I call *civilized*, ducky," Harriet said as the orderlies wheeled in a cart. None of the other patients argued; even Pamela Isley sat quietly as an orderly set a cup of herbal tea on the wide arm of her chair. She removed the teabag, set it in the saucer, and picked up the cup. Unfortunately, the chain attached to the cuff on her wrist didn't allow her to bring it all the way to her lips. If she wanted to drink, she had to bend her head awkwardly. It was the same for the others.

Harleen was appalled. "Could we *please* adjust these restraints to give everyone a better range of movement?" she demanded, not hiding her irritation. "These women should be allowed to eat and drink without contorting themselves!"

The orderlies hesitated and Harleen turned to look at the armed guard. "Do as she says," the guard told them. The orderlies looked dubious but they obeyed.

"Thank you. I'll call if I need anything else," Harleen said when they were done and jerked her head toward the door.

"As I was sayin'," Harriet Pratt purred when the orderlies were gone. "Civilized. Ain't I right now, ducks?"

The question seemed to be addressed to Pamela Isley; it looked like one of the vines had fallen into her cup. Harleen wondered if she should tell her not to do that. But why? She wasn't dipping her vine in someone else's drink and she didn't seem to be doing herself any harm.

Sipping her green tea, Harleen let them have a few minutes to enjoy their respective drinks. In truth, she needed a minute to get over feeling stupid and guilty. She should have thought of this without Harriet Pratt's histrionics. All her self-righteousness about treating patients with respect and it had never occurred to her it would be nice to serve refreshments in the middle of the afternoon. It was the way they did things in the outside world—the *civilized* world.

From now on, their sessions would always include a refreshment cart, Harleen decided. She would try to make these meetings more like an oasis of calm and dignity—or as much as they could be with the patients chained to their chairs.

◆

"I almost intervened and shut you down for good," Dr. Leland said later when she dropped by Harleen's office. "But the way you took charge of the room—not just the patients but the staff, too—gave me a good feeling. I'm inclined to let these sessions continue and see where they go. *With* the refreshment cart," she added.

"The orderlies told you all that?" Harleen said, surprised.

Dr. Leland shook her head. "Security showed me the video. Most rooms in Arkham are monitored. You know that."

Harleen looked around nervously. There had been a few times she'd changed her pantyhose here, and once she'd had to staple a broken bra strap. Had she been giving Security a peep show? She was about to say something but Dr. Leland was still talking.

"...keep your guard up. It's okay for the patients to relax but don't give them the idea that they can get familiar. Never forget they're criminally insane. Make sure they're clear about your boundaries and they don't overstep."

Harleen wanted to ask whose boundaries Security respected but Dr. Leland received a text and hurried back to her office. Disappointed, Harleen made a note to do all her pantyhose changing and bra repair in a stall in the doctors' lavatory, although for all she knew the stalls were monitored, too. If they were, there was probably a horror story behind it. Arkham was a very bizarre place to work.

Maybe this was why Dr. Leland was so caught up in structure and convention. She was so concerned with Harleen's maintaining proper boundaries with the group but never considered how the women felt about being forced to participate in restraints, in actual *chains*. Women in chains—metal, not metaphorical. No doubt the rattle and clink kept boundary issues from slipping their minds.

Even if there was no chance these women would leave Arkham, Harleen saw no reason not to try getting them out of their chains. If she helped them enough that they would be allowed to walk from one place to another and to sit in ordinary chairs like regular people rather than being chained up like animals, how much better their lives would be. Maybe they'd be more receptive to therapy rather than fighting it.

Just because they were permanently incarcerated didn't mean they shouldn't be helped.

♦

Harleen was nervous about the third session. Dr. Percival had made a stupid joke in the staff meeting comparing it to a third date. Danielle Duval, the head nurse for the lighter-security ward on the fifth floor, asked him with a straight face if he'd ever had a third date himself, and if so, how long ago. More people had laughed at that one, which had put Dr. Percival's nose out of joint and made Harleen feel a little better.

But it was Dr. Leland who had really put her on edge.

Sometimes she thought Dr. Leland made a point of doing that right before a session. She had stopped in at Harleen's office half an hour before the session to repeat herself about maintaining proper boundaries, staying alert and observant, and remembering that Magpie and Mary Louise could be as cunning as Poison Ivy. Harleen had very nearly corrected her with the patient's real name as an example of a boundary issue, but she resisted. Having an argument with her boss wouldn't put her in an ideal frame of mind to meet with her patients.

The session proceeded without incident, although it seemed to Harleen that everyone, including the orderlies and the armed guard at the door, were on edge to some degree. Emotions could be contagious, especially negative ones like anxiety and apprehension; Harleen made a lengthy note in her personal journal that this was what she really had to be careful of. Boundaries be damned— projecting a confident, positive attitude was far more important, and she should be more mindful about that.

Despite her determination, Harleen came away from the fourth session more dismayed. The conversation had been more aimless and unfocused than in their first session. She had tried to facilitate a discussion but no one had responded to any of her openers. Instead of blubbering, Mary Louise had spent the time mimicking Poison Ivy, pretending she was bored, and saying nothing other than *Nasty-wasty Arkham*. But at least it proved her baby act really was a put-on.

Even Magpie had been quieter than usual, only saying *Shiny!* a few times in a sulky voice, as if making an accusation. And Harriet had been almost mute, responding to whatever Harleen said to her with a grunt or an emphatic shrug that rattled her chains.

It pained Harleen to admit it but she had to take a page from Dr. Leland's playbook and add more structure after all. The women had to understand that the sessions weren't merely something to break up the afternoon routine, but a purposeful, therapeutic program. As such, there were goals that the women were expected to achieve. So starting with the fifth session she would have an agenda for every meeting. The women might not like being pushed, but she couldn't let them get away with doing nothing. That wasn't therapy; that was entropy.

◆

"I'd like to do something new today," Harleen said when they were all settled with their various drinks.

"There's a new way to sit around in chains and talk about nothing?" Pamela Isley said in her standard, tired-of-life voice. "Oh, joy. I never dared dream."

Harleen told herself to be positive. "At our second session, we talked about what we wanted to get out of these sessions—"

"Well, ducky, that's what *I* want," Harriet said, laughing. "I want to get out of these bloody sessions!"

"If that's true," Harleen said, refusing to be discouraged, "you have to have a plan—"

"I *have* a plan," Pamela Isley said languidly. "I'm going to put Batman's head on a pike."

"Me, too!" said the other three in unison. Harleen's jaw dropped. She hadn't thought Magpie would ever say anything other than *Shiny!*

"It's Batman what put most of us in this dungeon," Harriet added to Harleen, as if in a confidential aside. "If it weren't for bloody Batman, we'd all be—"

"Shiny!" proclaimed Magpie.

Harriet chuckled. "Right you are, ducks. We'd all be shiny 'n' happy 'n' runnin' free with the wind in our 'air—"

"Nasty-wasty Batty-man!" Mary Louise began to cry. "*I* did-unt do it, I *did*-unt! It was-unt *my* fault but *he* did-unt *care*! Hate, hate, *hate*!"

Instead of complaining about Mary Louise, Pamela Isley launched into a story about her last encounter with Batman, the one that had put her in Arkham. Harleen's first impulse was to try to steer them back to the topic of setting goals, then she caught herself. Pamela Isley was *talking*—not taking shots, but talking about something that had happened to her. And *without* acting like she was so bored she could barely stay awake. Magpie had uttered a different word—no, *two* of them. And Mary Louise's blubbering had subsided; like the other two, she was *listening* to what Pamela Isley was saying.

The hell with structure, Harleen thought. If she cut this off now, Pamela Isley would shut down and the rest would follow suit. She might never get any of them to open up again. Maybe they'd just needed the right subject. It was like they'd all been wandering around lost in their respective darknesses and then suddenly they'd all found the North Star simultaneously.

That would make a fascinating article, Harleen thought. Or a chapter in a book.

She started making notes as she sipped her tea. Batman was the key to breaking down the walls they had put up. So what if their feelings weren't terribly positive? Getting through to them was what mattered, and if she could only do that by way of something they all hated, so what? It united them, made them a real group—

"Except for the nasal filters," Pamela Isley said, and looked directly at Harleen for the first time.

"Nasal filters," Harleen said, nodding as if she'd heard every word.

"Of all things." Pamela Isley shook her head. "Nasal filters never occurred to me."

"Why do you think that is?" Harleen asked. The question sounded inane even to her but it was the only one she could think of. How could she have let her mind wander when Pamela Isley had actually been saying something?

"They just *didn't*." Pamela gave her a contemptuous look and turned back to the other women. "If Batman hadn't been wearing them, my special strain of night-blooming jasmine would have knocked him flat on his bat ass, and he'd be fertilizing my garden even as we speak. Instead, he got me committed to this place, where you can't get decent sunlight even from a southern exposure."

"Shiny," Magpie said, her voice mournful.

Harleen wished she'd paid closer attention. But even as she thought it, her mind was trying to wander again. This was a hell of a time to lose her psychiatry mojo, she thought. Then she wondered when she had started saying things like *mojo*.

"Now, Pammie-luv, I can tell you *exactly* where you went Pete Tong," Harriet was saying in a know-it-all tone.

"Oh, do tell." Pamela's voice dripped with sarcasm.

"You took the blighter on by yourself! You can't go up against the big bad Bat alone! You need a *gang* backin' you up, along with a partner you can trust with your very *life*." Harriet's smugness was so intense Harleen could have sworn the air shimmered around her. "Takin' on Batman without anyone else—well, that's just *mad*."

"Oh, right." Pamela looked down her nose at Harriet. "A woman is nothing without a man. How did I forget that?"

"Now, now, luv, everybody needs a best mate, someone who's got your back," Harriet went on. "No man is an island, and no woman, either. You can't be workin' without a net. Me old china, we make a perfect set, we do, him bein' the Mad Hatter and me bein'—"

"Shiny," Magpie declared.

"March 'Arriet," she corrected.

"And yet, in the end, you didn't do any better." Pamela waved one hand and the vines seemed to copy the gesture. Only they couldn't have, Harleen thought; they were plants, not snakes. Although right now, they looked like plant–snake hybrids. "You're in here with us and your best buddy is where? At someone else's tea party, I guess—he certainly isn't at this one. That's what you get for being some man's appendage. When it's crunch time, they always throw you under the bus to save themselves. *Always.*"

"It wasn't like *that*," Harriet snapped.

"Really?" Pamela gave a short, scornful laugh. "Can't tell just by looking."

"Shiny!" Magpie put in.

All the woman turned to Harleen, their faces expectant.

"Well, this subject is—is difficult," Harleen said, speaking slowly, trying to gather her thoughts. The cup in her hand was suddenly so heavy, hard to hold up. Like her eyelids.

Meanwhile, the vines in Pamela's hair were getting longer, flowing over her shoulders and down her arms… except they couldn't have been. They couldn't have grown all the way down to the chains. And they certainly couldn't be breaking the links as if they were flimsy plastic right before her eyes.

I did not just see that, Harleen thought as the vines moved on to free Harriet, then Magpie, and Mary Louise. *I'm hallucinating. It didn't happen.*

"Oh, but it did happen," Pamela Isley said, no longer bored. "You're *not* hallucinating."

How did I speak aloud and not know it, Harleen wondered, watching as Pamela got up from her chair.

Pamela was smiling as she came toward her. "Did you know that roots can break through metal pipes buried in the ground? Even crack the foundation of a house?"

All the women were getting up now. Then Pamela was looming over her, with more vines growing out of her hair. Harleen's cup slipped out of her fingers and fell on the carpet with a distant thump.

The tea, Harleen realized.

"What's the matter, ducks?" asked Harriet from somewhere

behind Pamela. "Something amiss with your tea?" Her hand reached over Pamela's shoulder to dangle a teabag in Harleen's face.

"You know, I'm a doctor, too, even if it's not the kind you are," Pamela said. Her low voice was practically a purr but there was nothing soft about her expression. "Brand new Dr. Harleen Quinzel. It's so obvious this is your first job." She gave a short laugh. "What did you tell yourself you were doing—trying to make a difference? Striking a blow for the looney sisterhood? Or can you actually admit you want to use us Looney Ladies of Arkham to get famous by writing a trashy true-crime book?"

"Shiny! Shiny!" Magpie said shrilly.

Where was the guard? Where was Security? Wasn't this room monitored?

"Don't worry, ducks, we took care of the guard." Harriet crowded in next to Pamela, still dangling the teabag from two fingers. It looked homemade and smelled all wrong. "And all anybody's seein' on the closed-circuit TV is us sittin' nice 'n' quiet like the good little Looney Ladies we are."

How? Harleen thought. *How?*

"How what, luv?" Harriet cackled. "Be specific!"

"I *did*-unt *mean* to!" wailed Mary Louise and began hitting Harleen with her doll, hard, over and over. It was a lot heavier than any doll Harleen had ever had and squeaked *Mama!* on every blow.

"No! Stop!" Harleen pleaded. It was an enormous effort to speak but she had to get through to them. "I didn't want to *use* you—I wanted to show how you've all *been used!* By the police! By the justice system! And most of all by Batman!"

"More tea, luv?" Harriet shoved Pamela aside and brandished a broken mug. "Just half a cup!"

Harleen turned her face away and saw the guard on the floor, tightly wrapped in vines from head to foot, unable to move or call out.

Eager hands grabbed at her throat and she realized belatedly she had forgotten to take her necklace off. Harleen felt the chain cutting into her neck as Magpie yanked on it. "Shiny! Shiny!"

"*I did-unt mean to!*" sobbed Mary Louise.

Harleen saw Pamela Isley push herself in front of the other women just as everything went black.

11

Harleen opened her eyes, then sat up with a start.

"Relax," said Dr. Leland. "You're safe."

By some miracle she was on the leather sofa in Dr. Leland's office and, as far as she could tell, only slightly the worse for wear. Strands of hair hung in her face, her neat French roll was one big snarl, and her clothing was rumpled, but she wasn't hurt. Even the glasses in her blazer pocket were unbroken.

"The guard didn't come out quite as well," Dr. Leland added.

"Will he be all right?" Harleen asked.

"He'll probably suffer from a green plant phobia for the rest of his life but he'll live." Dr. Leland gave her a glass of water.

Harleen suddenly realized she was dry-mouthed and thirsty and gulped it down. "How did I get out of there in one piece?" she asked.

"Pamela Isley," Dr. Leland replied, refilling the glass for her. "She saved you."

Harleen shook her head, thinking she hadn't heard right. "No, Isley was the ringleader," she said, sipping the water more slowly this time. There was still a funny taste in her mouth from the tea, or whatever it had been. "She freed the others so they could all attack me." She felt for her necklace and discovered it was still around her neck: another miracle. "Mary Louise was hitting me with this incredibly heavy doll when I passed out." She gave a short, humorless laugh. "I'm sure she did-unt *mean* to."

"The doll's head was stuffed with rocks," said Dr. Leland. "Pamela Isley loathes and despises all of humanity, singly and as a species. But apparently she loathes and despises you less than everyone else. Quite a lot less. She held off the others and called for help. All four are confined to their cells indefinitely. And, needless to say, they won't be participating in any more group sessions. Nor will any other patients."

Harleen nodded glumly. "I've learned my lesson—no more therapy sessions where I'm outnumbered."

"And while we're exercising hindsight," Dr. Leland went on, "I should never have allowed a meta-human inmate to participate without a whole lot more security. And better personnel watching the monitors, people smart enough to notice when a pre-recorded loop has replaced the live feed."

"But it wasn't recreation, it was therapy," Harleen said. "Or it was supposed to be."

Dr. Leland sat down on the sofa beside her. "I bear all the responsibility for what happened. But I confess, I wanted you to be right—that treating them like patients rather than the characters they pretend to be would force them out of their role-playing and give us a way to counter their illness."

"That *was* the idea." In spite of everything, Harleen felt pleased that Dr. Leland understood. "I thought all I had to do was persist and I'd get through to them."

Dr. Leland sighed. "Well, we can dream."

They sat together in silence for a few seconds. Then Harleen said, "You knew, didn't you? That it wouldn't work."

"Like I said, I wanted you to be right," the other woman told her sadly. "I thought maybe your being a new face with new ideas could make it happen. I hoped that having a new staff member work with them would remind them that, as much as Arkham might feel like limbo, time passes and things change and maybe they'd start thinking they didn't have to just be dangerous criminals in permanent lockup. That they might actually *want* something better."

"Sometimes Arkham does feel like limbo," Harleen said. "It's out in the middle of nowhere. The patients have no human contact except with the staff and each other. There's no internet or social media—"

A small line appeared between Dr. Leland's eyebrows as she frowned. "People sent here are too dangerous for a maximum security penitentiary, and too sick for a locked ward. They've been declared too toxic for even the most polluted environment, as if they poison the air just by breathing it."

Harleen blinked at her. She could barely believe this woman had just been talking about wanting to improve the inmates' lives.

Dr. Leland gave her a sidelong look. "That's me on a *bad* day," she said.

"Not *everyone* here is hopeless," Harleen said. "*Some* people get better and leave."

"Sometimes," Dr. Leland said. "It's an increasingly rare occurrence. Perhaps because the world is getting crazier, not saner, and Thomas Szasz was right."

"You mean about insanity being the only sane reaction to an insane world?" Harleen asked.

"Got it in one." Dr. Leland rose and went to her desk. "And, no, he's no relation to Victor Zsasz. That I know of, anyway."

Harleen moved from the couch to the chair in front of Dr. Leland's desk. "But if that were true," she said slowly, "it would mean there's no point in trying to help patients recover their sanity. And I ain't buyin' that for a minnit, hon," she added in her tough-Brooklyn-cookie voice.

Dr. Leland laughed a little. "Good for you. Take the rest of the day off and tomorrow as well, just to make sure whatever they put in the tea is completely out of your system. Rest up and come back the day after. There'll still be windmills to tilt at."

"I can't understand how they managed to drug me," Harleen said. "They were all in restraints until Pamela's vines—" she cut off. Was that really what she had seen or had it been a hallucination?

Dr. Leland shrugged. "It's not the first time inmates have done the impossible here. They're a clever bunch, even the ones without, ah, *abilities*."

Harleen got up from the chair. Suddenly she felt very tired. "I really thought I was doing something for them," she said.

"Now do something for yourself for a change and stay home tomorrow."

"But I don't want to look weak," Harleen said. "I won't have any credibility with the patients if they think Pamela Isley can knock me on my butt whenever she wants."

"Don't worry about Poison Ivy," Dr. Leland told her. "Remember, she hates you less than the rest of us. That'll work in your favor. A lot of inmates follow her lead, and they're not all women."

◆

Harleen went back to her office to pick up her things, including a few patient files. If she was going to stay home, she might as well be productive. She was trying to decide which files to take and whether to focus on personality disorders rather than diseases as she struggled with the stubborn lock on her office door.

When she finally got the door open, the first thing she saw was the rose in the bud vase on her desk.

Harleen stood in the doorway, transfixed. The rose was a rich dark red, in full perfect bloom, its elegance underscored by the simple, clear vase. The idea that someone would want to give her something so lovely made her heart lift, the way it did when she launched herself into a gymnastics routine to her favorite music. This was meant to bring her joy. It seemed like forever since anyone had done something like that for her.

Get a grip, girlfriend, said a small, sensible voice in her head. *It's a flower, not a pile of gold bullion or the Hope Diamond or even a pay-raise. Did you notice that's a* plant? *Remind you of anyone?*

All the little hairs on the back of Harleen's neck stood up. Would Pamela Isley—Poison Ivy—try something else so soon? Or was it a peace offering? *Sorry we tried to kill you. I won't let it happen again.*

Oh, God, what if Poison Ivy didn't merely not hate her but wanted to be friends? What would *that* be like?

No, Poison Ivy didn't cut flowers—to her, it was like killing them. She wouldn't do that for anyone.

Then who *had* sent it?

Maybe it was booby-trapped.

She felt silly. How could anyone booby-trap a rose?

Ask the inmates, she thought; *they can probably booby-trap air. They're experts.*

It could be electrified. Or maybe it shot poisoned thorns. Maybe when she bent to smell its fragrance, it would squirt her in the face with vinegar. Or something a lot worse.

She reached her desk without anything blowing up or crashing down on her and saw there was something else on the desk—a playing card, turned face down. Without giving herself time to catastrophize, she picked it up.

Harleen stared at it for a long moment; then she laughed, feeling all the tension drain out of her. She should have known. This wasn't from Poison Ivy or any other woman.

The card was a Joker. Under the grinning cartoon face was the message:

Welcome! Why don't you come down & see me sometime?—J

"Well played, Mr. J," Harleen said aloud in her tough-Brooklyn-cookie voice. "Pun definitely intended."

The single perfect rose was a male thing. Only a man would think that one perfect rose would make a woman so blissfully weak in the knees she wouldn't miss the other eleven. Someone had to disabuse Mr. J of that notion, and she was just the woman for the job.

Tomorrow.

She didn't want him to think she'd come running at the drop of a rose.

12

Dr. Leland looked surprised and disappointed when Harleen came into work the next morning.

"I thought we agreed you were going to take another day to recover," she said.

"I *have* recovered," Harleen assured her. "I feel too good to justify taking time off work."

"I still think you should," Dr. Leland said, her concerned expression deepening.

"But I really don't need to," Harleen said. "If I did, I'd be home right now. But I'm fine! No after-effects from drugged tea, and I'm not traumatized." It was an effort to keep the impatience out of her voice. Sometimes Dr. Leland seemed more controlling than concerned. "I just want to get on with my work."

Dr. Leland looked doubtful. "All right. You win. But if you get shaky—"

"I'll go straight home," Harleen said. "I promise. But I won't. There's no reason to leave you shorthanded when I'm not sick."

Her remark about being shorthanded had probably persuaded Dr. Leland to give up and go off to her rounds, Harleen thought as she settled down behind her desk. The rose and the card were untouched; she moved them to one side so she could spread out her planner and see what her schedule looked like. She had patients to see, medication regimens to review, reports to write. And somewhere in her busy schedule, she would deal with the Joker.

Early in the day was best, when she had more energy. And she couldn't just wing it—she had to think carefully about what to say, the points she wanted to make. This wasn't just some two-bit smoothy who thought a grand, inappropriate gesture would get the pretty lady-doctor's attention, even though she wasn't his doctor. How cheesy!

The more she thought about it, the angrier she felt. How stupid did this clown think she was? And how stuck on himself was he to think she'd take one look at this pathetic overture and fall into a swoon?

She would definitely do this right away, while she was fresh. The boost she'd get from putting him in his place would make the whole day a win. Nothing succeeded like success.

Harleen jotted down a few ideas in a small notebook—writing things down always helped her remember them better. She read them over, added a couple of things, and tucked it away in her blazer pocket.

She put on her no-nonsense glasses, made sure every hair in her tidy French roll was in place, and, armed with the status, professionalism, and fortitude characteristic of competent women, she marched out of her office and down to the sub-sub-sub-sub-basement where the Joker was waiting for her with all his fully weaponized charm on display.

◆

There was nothing the Joker enjoyed more than a great trick. A great trick was a rare thing. There were plenty of good tricks, and even more that were so-so. A great trick was a work of art, elegant and irrefutable.

According to many people, the greatest trick of all time had been achieved by no less than the Devil himself by convincing the entire world he didn't exist. What made this trick truly great was the fact that everyone knew about it and they *still* didn't believe he existed! The Joker thought it rated first place in the Hall of Fame. It made perfect use of human nature's most enduring features—the tendency to believe something despite there being either evidence to the contrary, or no evidence at all.

The Joker had yet to pull off something that perfect. Nonetheless, he had some moves and they weren't too shabby. He had something very special in mind for the heady mix of brains and beauty that was Harleen Quinzel. It wasn't new or innovative, but it *was* a classic.

It wouldn't be easy. He was going to have to work hard to put this one over, but when he did, it would be a masterpiece. He could call it: "The Greatest Trick The Joker Ever Pulled Was Convincing Harleen Quinzel He Was Worth It."

Not short and pithy, but it wasn't that kind of joke.

◆

His beautiful target marched—literally marched—into his cell and told the guard who followed her in to get lost. And buddy-boy didn't argue; she glared him out the door through black-framed hard-ass spectacles. The doctor knew how to take charge—pick the biggest guy in the room and cut him down to size. The guard was an enormous brute who made the Joker seem positively dainty by comparison, but one look from Dr. Quinzel and he gave like a wet paper bag. The Joker hadn't seen such an effective display of dominance in a very long time.

Even better, she'd done it wearing a tailored suit with a kick-pleat and sensible shoes, not a leather corset and thigh-high boots with five-inch heels. Perhaps this was a sign of things to come. Was Certified Public Accountant the new sexy?

◆

"So glad you've finally come to visit me down here in my lonely cell," the Joker said in a cordial purr.

"It's only fair," said the formidable presence that was Dr. Quinzel. Her straight posture made her seem taller than she was. Anyone would have thought she was in full command of all she surveyed.

He made to get off the bed but she raised one hand sharply. "Don't bother—I'm not staying."

"Whatever you say, Doctor." Smiling, he stretched out on his side, propping his head up on his fist. "How can *I* help *you*?"

Dr. Quinzel produced the playing card he'd left on her desk, making it snap. "Care to tell me how this got into my office? My *locked* office?"

"Well, *I* put it there, of course." His smile widened.

"You did?" She made the card disappear. "You *personally*?"

"I never do anything *impersonally*. I think it's rude."

Of course, the beautiful lady shrink didn't crack a smile. "I'm sure Dr. Leland and Security would love to know how you escaped from your cell, procured a rose in a vase, left it in my office, and returned to your cell without anyone knowing."

"I'm sure they would," the Joker said. He sat up and put a pillow between his back and the wall, then patted a spot on the bed, inviting her to sit. She pretended not to notice. "But *I'm* certainly not going to tell them! And if you were going to rat me out, you already would have. So I guess they'll never know."

Dr. Quinzel's expression didn't change, and he knew she'd never snitch on him about anything.

"You've made quite a name for yourself around here already, you know," he went on.

"Oh?" She looked down her perfect nose at him. "What have you heard?"

"That you're mighty handy with a fire extinguisher," he said cheerfully. "Though less good at tea parties."

Her face went a little pink but her expression didn't change.

"However, at least one Looney Lady of Gotham admires your nerve—your *pluck*," he went on. "As do I. In fact, all your patients give you high marks. I'd say your true strength is in one-on-one treatment, not groups. Never had much use for group therapy myself, especially here. Get a group together in Arkham and they all start one-upping each other, trying to be the biggest badass. Which is pointless."

"Because *you're* the biggest badass?" Dr. Quinzel said.

"Well, I don't like to brag." He looked down for a moment in ersatz modesty.

"No," Dr. Quinzel said, "you *love* it."

"Ooh, ya got me, doll-face," the Joker said, clapping a hand over his heart.

She bristled immediately. "My name is *Dr. Quinzel*, not doll-face."

"I beg your pardon," the Joker said. "I have a tendency to be inappropriate. That and my *penchant* for braggadocio have made me bad at winning friends, good at influencing enemies, and very difficult to talk to. I'm not so much a person anymore as I am a cross to bear, which few care to do. Thus I sit in my lonely cell on the bottom-most level of an institution that is itself rock-bottom."

"Which is where you should stay," Dr. Quinzel said. "In your cell, that is. No more illicit jaunts."

The Joker pretended to think this over. "All right, Dr. Quinzel, I'll be a good boy, as a personal favor to *you*. I ask only one thing in return."

"You're in no position to ask anything of me," Dr. Quinzel told him loftily. "But just out of curiosity, what is it?"

"That you come back and visit me again," he said, doing humble now. "You have no idea how *brutal* the monotony is—every day like every other, never changing, always predictable. I sit in this cell and see nothing and no one I haven't seen before, while the seconds march past in lockstep like they did yesterday and all the days before, and like they will tomorrow and all the days to come."

Without another word, she turned on her heel and rapped sharply on the door of his cell to let the guard know she was ready to leave. The Joker smiled after her as she left. Without a word. Because she didn't know what to say.

Gotcha.

◆

Harleen maintained her dignified bearing all the way back to her office, not letting herself relax even a little until she closed the door behind her. Slumped at her desk, she called the nurse on D ward to say she was running behind and she'd see Mr. O'Brien an hour later. Deuce O'Brien wouldn't mind, if he even noticed. Unlike the Joker, who was obviously starved for company.

It wasn't that Harleen wanted to give up on O'Brien, or any other patient; she simply wasn't sure she could do anything more for him. The world was full of people who were content to be mediocre. Why would the criminally insane be any different? Still, she'd have thought anyone who bothered to transgress wouldn't settle for being an underachiever.

The Joker, on the other hand, had actually challenged her to make a difference in his life. And if there was anything Harleen Quinzel really relished, it was a challenge.

No, no—what was she thinking?

Too late. She couldn't un-think it.

◆

Just being in the Joker's cell had given her all kinds of ideas and, despite her best efforts to turn them away, they chased her for days, refusing to leave her alone. The man was an exhibitionist, an extrovert turned up to eleven. The worst thing anyone could do to a man like that was bury him alive in a sub-sub-sub-sub-basement and restrict his social contact to near-zero. That wasn't therapy, it was torture. It would only serve to make him obsessed

106

with breaking out. The obsession would keep building up until the pressure became so great, he had to escape or his head would explode. And of course once he had, his compulsion to act out inappropriately would take over. Humor with a body count.

Eventually he would be recaptured—by Batman, according to his file—and returned to Arkham where the cycle would start over again. Stifling confinement, pressure build-up, break-out, high crimes and misdemeanors, re-apprehension, back to Arkham. Good God, why did no one see the man was trapped in a vicious cycle courtesy of the criminal justice system?

Or, to be more precise, the criminal justice system as personified by Batman. Who was *not*, in fact, legally part of the justice system. How unconscionable was that? So what if Batman was supposed to be on the side of the angels, one of the good guys—how was a masked vigilante a good guy?

There was no answer to that because it was the question nobody wanted to ask. It didn't fit the Batman-as-hero myth everyone in Gotham had embraced. Anyone who didn't toe that line was a bad guy and ended up in jail. Or in Arkham.

That was it in a nutshell: if you dissented, if you didn't buy into Batman, you were a criminal or crazy. Or both.

If resistance to Batman was a crime, then crime was a revolutionary act.

It was this insight that made Harleen certain she could help the Joker step off the terrible treadmill the justice system had condemned him to. She could help him find a better way to express himself, a way that wouldn't give Batman an opportunity to drop him back into the black hole of Arkham Asylum.

◆

Dr. Leland looked up from Harleen's new proposal, her expression troubled. "I'm really not comfortable with the suggestion that

Arkham Asylum is a blind alley with no exit."

"That wasn't what I said." Harleen tried not to be defensive. She had spent almost three weeks rewriting the proposal to make it sound more objective and less emotional. But when you were passionate about something, it was damned near impossible to come across as coolly reserved. After the group session fiasco, she knew Dr. Leland would look very carefully at anything else she proposed, so she had to make her boss see her as calm and professional, not enthusiastic and eager. "I simply pointed out that many patients at Arkham will never leave."

"And that's because they'll always pose a threat to everyone around them," Dr. Leland said. "Not because Arkham Asylum is a dead end."

"Yes, I know, I agree," Harleen said, hoping she didn't sound as impatient as she felt. "But that doesn't mean we shouldn't try just as hard to help them as we do patients who *can* someday be discharged. No, they won't get well, but we could try to help them be less ill, to find a way to express their feelings—"

"Most of them feel homicidal," Dr. Leland said, sitting back in her chair. "And expressing themselves is what put them in here."

"Really," said Harleen, unable to help herself. "A lot of the files say it was Batman."

Dr. Leland gave her a look. "Batman captured them, often *in flagrante delicto*. Their being diagnosed as criminally insane put them in here."

"But can we really be sure about that?" Harleen said. "Nobody knows who Batman really is. He could be the doctor who signs the commitment papers or a higher-up in the police department. For all anyone knows, he could even be the judge who sentenced them."

"Gotham City isn't like anywhere else," Dr. Leland said with a faint, sad smile. "People who come here from other, more conventional cities find it hard to understand our brand of normal."

"Someday I'd like to get Batman in for therapy," Harleen said.

Dr. Leland gave a single short laugh.

"Oh, I know no one ever will," Harleen added. "He can't risk being unmasked." She sat forward in her chair. "But just suppose you were in private practice in Gotham and you discovered one of your patients was a masked vigilante. What would you think— 'My, isn't he well-adjusted, I wonder if he's single?'"

Dr. Leland laughed. "Only if he were Batman."

"You're missing the point," Harleen said, exasperated.

"No more so than you, Dr. Quinzel," Dr. Leland said. "Because— as I'm sure you're tired of hearing—you're not from around here."

Harleen bristled. "So you're saying I don't get it because I don't get it. Fine, I don't get it. But that doesn't mean I'm wrong about there being room for improvement in how we do things here." She nodded at the folder on the desk. "That proposal is one idea on how to make a start."

Dr. Leland's smile was flat. "Your becoming the Joker's therapist will fix everything that's wrong with Arkham Asylum? Oh, relax, I know that's not what you mean," she added as Harleen started to protest. "But some of your proposal reads very close to that kind of oversimplification."

"It's just that I feel it's a tremendous waste to bury such an active intellect in a rock-bottom sub-basement. Someone so energetic will be better served by treatment that will address his issues by working with him as he is, instead of trying to make him into something he isn't. I know my last idea didn't work out very well— it was a mistake to take on a whole group. My real strength is in one-on-one. Just me and the J—the patient."

"We don't have enough doctors on staff to allow you to focus on only one patient," Dr. Leland said firmly.

"I wasn't planning to give up my other patients," Harleen lied, hoping her disappointment didn't show. "I propose to devote extra time to the Joker—"

"We have no budget for overtime," Dr. Leland reminded her.

"I'll do it on my own time."

Dr. Leland didn't say anything for a few seconds. "If I say no, you're just going to keep coming back with more arguments, until you either get me to say yes, or I snap and start taking hostages. Am I right?"

Harleen blinked. "I'm not sure how to answer that."

"Never mind." Dr. Leland hesitated. "I have a feeling I'll regret this and it will all end in tears before bedtime, but go ahead—under certain conditions. Namely, I want written daily reports documenting every moment you spend with that man. Be *extremely* careful—his cell is the one and only room that has no monitoring."

Harleen blinked at her. "That's... surprising. I'd have thought you'd have him under all kinds of surveillance."

Dr. Leland sighed. "First of all, we can't afford all kinds of surveillance. We make do with keeping an orderly, sometimes two, outside his door twenty-four/seven. And second, the sub-sub-sub-sub-basement is the one place in Arkham that no one, not even the Joker, has ever managed to break out of."

Harleen wasn't sure she believed the Joker's cell wasn't monitored beyond an orderly with his ear pressed to the door but she told herself to let it go and just take the win.

"Any change in medication has to be okayed by me well ahead of time," Dr. Leland was saying, "and if I tell you no, it's no. And if I decide to shut it down, you don't try to get around me. Or you'll find yourself on the wrong end of a disciplinary action. Are we clear?"

"Sure, boss, sure," Harleen said in her tough-Brooklyn-cookie voice. "Anything you say, I'm on the case."

Instead of laughing, Dr. Leland stared at her stonily. "This isn't a joke, Dr. Quinzel."

"No, of course not," Harleen said quickly. She had only wanted to dispel the tension. Batman probably never dispelled the tension with a joke, so nobody else should, either. Unless they wanted to end up in Arkham Asylum's deepest, darkest sub-basement.

Harleen marveled; Batman had made joking a crime.

13

Before Harleen embarked on her program of concentrated therapy with the Joker, Dr. Leland insisted she read or reread everything about him—not just his patient file, which was as thick as the latest edition of the DSM, but also his arrest reports, correspondence from various experts and authorities, and writing by the Joker himself, which Harleen was most interested in.

There was quite a lot of it, ranging from lively and chaotic to cold and focused; to surprisingly astute; to disturbing things she was certain he'd written specifically to bait his doctors. Any writing he'd done at Arkham was in crayon, which didn't always photocopy well. One more reason why Harleen intended to get her hands on the originals—she had to feel the texture of the actual paper and see how much pressure he had applied with whatever crayons he'd used. All of that, she was sure, would be of great importance if she were to understand him well enough to help him, not to mention write a book about him.

Harleen would gladly have talked anything over with Dr. Leland, but her boss was busier than usual, juggling her caseload with unannounced visits from board members. Harleen felt sorry for her. The board members had a knack for showing up at the most inconvenient times, often with experts in tow, expecting Dr. Leland to essentially make more hours in the day to meet with them.

At the same time, however, Harleen's feelings toward Dr. Leland had cooled somewhat since she had come to Arkham. Part of it was simply the end of the honeymoon period. Another part was that, like all authority figures, Dr. Leland sometimes felt the need to remind everyone she was the boss.

But it wasn't just that. The latest discussion about Batman bothered her. She tried to understand Joan Leland's point of view but it seemed so *off*. Batman might have the approval of the police department—even the police commissioner was pro-Batman—but it didn't change the fact of law. Batman was a criminal who wasn't locked up because he only picked on other criminals.

So good intentions made the difference. But that begged the question: How did anyone know Batman's intentions really *were* good? By that token, if the Joker promised he meant no harm to innocent bystanders, only other criminals, they should release him immediately.

Okay, not really—not yet, anyway. The Joker needed a lot of therapy before Dr. Leland would even consider moving him out of the sub-sub-sub-sub-basement.

But if the Joker actually *could* be released—which Harleen privately thought might not be impossible with the right program of concentrated therapy—he would be sent to a halfway house in a city where the police department openly colluded with a criminal. But the criminal was Batman and Batman was a good guy.

Which raised another important question: how good was he really? The fancy car and all those fancy high-tech gadgets wouldn't come cheap. Ergo, Batman had to be a rich guy—and not just rich, super-rich, a billionaire at least. No one had ever become a billionaire by being a great humanitarian.

Perhaps Batman was a group effort—a bunch of super-rich guys who shared the costs. But why would super-rich guys do that—for tax breaks? Money laundering? Or just to have their own private cop?

Or maybe Batman was blackmailing them into paying for everything. Was that the kind of thing a good guy did?

She was getting sidetracked. Harleen pulled her attention back to the report she was supposed to be writing about one of her other patients. Dr. Leland had sent her a memo reminding her not to neglect them, which Harleen found especially irritating. She had already promised she wouldn't. If Dr. Leland didn't know she was a conscientious therapist by now, she never would. Even with patients like Phil "the Phish" Phrobisher.

Phil "the Phish" had been an arsonist-for-hire. Anyone who wanted to burn down a property for the insurance contacted the Phish and their problems went up in smoke. He charged half the going rate and was so skilled, investigators seldom found any definitive signs of arson—no burn patterns that indicated the use of accelerants or improvised explosive triggers.

The man had a good streak but his luck finally ran out. He was caught in the act of inducing an electrical fire with his laptop by an IT expert consulting for Gotham PD. There were whispers that the expert had actually been a hacker hired by Phil's competition in cooperation with a group of insurance companies desperate to stop Phil before they all went broke. Only in Gotham, Harleen thought.

Phil the Phish was a genuine firebug—he really liked burning things and he didn't care whether the properties were empty or not. There had been a number of deaths, six of them occurring in the fire that had put him away.

Everyone had expected him to be troublesome. But as long as he could watch fires on his laptop—news, movies, or TV shows, Phil wasn't fussy—he was docile enough. In fact, he had never seen any of his own fires in person, only on a screen, which was atypical. Firebugs usually loved witnessing their handiwork as it happened.

He was difficult to communicate with because he didn't like looking away from his computer. Harleen had done her best but Phil showed no sign that he cared. As long as he was allowed to watch fires on his laptop, he was content.

One afternoon, at the end of another fruitless attempt to reach him, Harleen had said, in a fit of exasperation, "Don't you *want* to get better someday?"

The question had astonished him. "'Get better someday?'" he said, as if the words were a foreign language. "I'm the best right now."

Then he had put on *Gone with the Wind* and fast-forwarded to the burning of Atlanta. Apparently that one never got old.

But then, there was no percentage in getting well for him. According to the terms of his commitment, once he was declared legally sane, he would go on trial for arson and murder. A conviction might encourage investigators to reopen old cases, a prospect that didn't thrill anyone who had collected a big insurance payout.

It occurred to Harleen that if she took a look at Arkham Asylum's finances, in particular the record of donations received since Phil the Phish's commitment, she could probably figure out which commercial property owners in Gotham City had a vested interest in Phil's remaining mentally ill for the rest of his life.

But if she did, would Dr. Leland congratulate her on her crimefighting? Or would the loss of desperately needed funds give Dr. Leland a good reason to fire her?

Dr. Leland might feel differently if Batman dropped by to give her a pat on the back. *Kudos on your excellent detective work, Dr. Quinzel*, Batman might say. Her boss would swoon.

Abruptly Harleen felt ashamed of her thoughts. She was a doctor, not a cop—she was supposed to treat her patients, not investigate them.

What if she talked to a detective at GCPD?

Oh, sure, that was a *great* idea. Had she actually forgotten what had happened the last time she'd gone to the police to report a crime? They'd arrested her father for getting beaten up, thugs had planned to kill her mother, and she'd almost been handed over to a perv. (Delvecchio. Bruno Delvecchio. She was *still* going to get the s.o.b.)

God only knew what would happen if she went to Gotham City cops. If she got nervous and cracked a joke in her tough-Brooklyn-cookie voice, they'd call Batman to lock her up in Arkham. Probably in the cell next door to Poison Ivy, and Dr. Leland would go along with it because Harleen hadn't grown up around here.

Whew. Just thinking about it made Harleen feel as if she'd had a close call. Which was totally silly. Nonetheless, she was going to stay away from cops, and Batman, too. Better safe than sorry.

Harleen told herself to think more constructively, the way she had when she'd come up with the idea to get the women together. Even if it hadn't worked, the idea itself had been constructive, a positive action. Like writing a book, for instance—that was still a good idea, too, only now her subject would be the Joker.

It had to be more than just a lurid true-crime book, though. Sure, there needed to be a bit of tell-all exposé for the sake of selling it. But it had to come across clearly that Gotham City made criminals via its own special recipe—one part felony, one part cosplay—along with the double standard embraced by the police and endorsed by the courts, which followed one set of rules for Batman and a different set for everyone else. Under those conditions, it was a wonder that half of Gotham's population hadn't been declared criminally insane. And of those who were presently committed to Arkham, how many were people who had merely pissed Batman off?

Unbidden, the mental image of Dr. Leland reading her book bloomed in her mind's eye. She didn't look impressed at Harleen's insights; she looked sad and betrayed. *I shouldn't have trusted you—after all, you're not from around here.*

Maybe she could paint her boss as the unwitting victim of a corrupt system, someone trying to do good while fighting against a rising tide of chaos and corruption.

No, Dr. Leland probably wouldn't think much of that, either. "Clueless pawn" wasn't a compliment, and it didn't describe the Joan Leland she knew. Neither did "conniving calculating opportunist who didn't care where the money came from just as long as it came."

Dammit, she had become a psychiatrist to figure out why people were the way they were and sometimes she felt like she knew less now than when she'd started out.

Best to keep her book focused on the Joker, Harleen decided. She had to tell *his* story, how he'd been shaped and then bent and twisted by Gotham City's unique warped social order. Although now that she was thinking of it, was there any social order that *wasn't* warped in some way? Brooklyn was no Utopia. The cops there had arrested her daddy for being the victim of an assault without any help from Batman.

Harleen's gaze fell on the unfinished report. Damn, her mind was all over the place. She had to concentrate on her regular patient reports first. Then she could concentrate on the Joker.

14

"I've studied up on you," Harleen told the Joker.

"Have you indeed?" The Joker was lying on the bed in his cell in a way that made him look like he was lying on a psychiatrist's couch. Deliberately, of course. The man did nothing without reason or point. "I would expect nothing less from my psychiatrist."

Harleen felt her heart thump as she made a note on her tablet with her stylus. *My psychiatrist.* Somehow he had imbued those two words with a possessive quality. It put her on her guard, but it also gave her a warm feeling. Inappropriate; she had to be above such reactions. She wasn't socializing with this man and it was too soon for countertransference. (Wasn't it?)

Abruptly she realized the Joker was staring at her expectantly. "I guess you didn't hear me," he said as heat rushed into her face. "I said, did you learn anything significant that all my numerous other doctors missed?"

"I heard you," she lied, looking down at the tablet and pretending to read over extensive notes. "Give me a minute, I was just trying to decide where to begin. While I'm thinking, let me ask *you* a question: are you going to tell me anything you haven't told all your numerous other doctors?"

The Joker smiled, but despite his chalk-white clown face, the expression was oddly serious. She had never seen that look before.

"Give me a minute," he said. "I'm trying to decide where to begin."

"You must be *completely honest* with me," Harleen told him. "Otherwise—"

"—You won't know how to help me and this won't work," he finished for her. "Heard it before. That gag's so old, it's got whiskers."

"It may have whiskers, but it's not a gag." Harleen pushed her glasses up on her face and a strand of hair came loose just over her left ear. She would fix it later; grooming was inappropriate here, even something as slight as tucking a curl back into place. She had to maintain an air of strict formality to keep the doctor–patient boundary clear and well-defined.

"We'll see about that," the Joker said, chuckling.

"Excuse me?" Harleen stared at him, baffled.

"It's all in the name, my dear. You do remember my name, don't you? The Joker."

"I do," she told him smoothly. "You seem to have forgotten mine. It's 'Dr. Quinzel,' or 'Doctor' for short. Not 'my dear' or 'sweetheart' or 'doll-face' or any other little nicknames men use to undermine a woman's professional standing in her place of business."

The Joker stared at her. He was so used to dominating every room he was in, but she'd caught him off-guard with that one. It had wiped that smug smile right off his clown-face; Harleen felt pleased with herself although she kept her expression neutral.

"I hardly meant to offend, my d—my doctor," the Joker said after a few seconds. "Please forgive me. I'm a creature of habit and old habits die hard."

"I can see that," Harleen said. "In fact, I've been wondering how long it will take for you to stop playing all your little games so we can finally get down to business."

"And what business is that?" asked the Joker. "Delving into the mysteries of my mind? Finding out what makes me tick? Getting to the root of my problems?"

"Determining how you can get well," Harleen said, just to see how he would react to the idea.

The Joker made a scornful noise. "And you said you were serious."

"I *am*," Harleen replied, wincing inwardly at how defensive she sounded.

"Oh, sure." The Joker rolled his eyes. "Getting me well—that's a joke I haven't heard since Tut was still a prince. Wasn't funny then; isn't now."

"I'm not like other doctors," Harleen told him. "Your previous doctors may have decided you couldn't be helped but I don't give up so easily—"

"Who said anything about my *previous doctors?*" The Joker hooted laughter at the ceiling. "I don't know if they wanted to cure me or kill me or send me to Mars, and I couldn't care less." He sat up on the edge of the bed and leaned forward. "And I don't give a damn what *you* think, either. I *can't* be helped. I *can't* be adjusted or rehabilitated or salvaged or brainwashed or any other damned thing! I took a good, long look at myself and I saw the truth: There's *no hope* for me—*no* chance, *no* possibility, *no* cure! None, nada, zero, zilch, the big goose egg!"

The Joker got to his feet and Harleen immediately did the same; he was taller than she was but he couldn't loom over her quite as much when she was standing too. "You don't give up? Well, good for you. Congratulations! You don't have to—I've given up *for* you, Dr. Sweetheart, Dr. Doll- face. Get used to it—*I* have!"

Harleen drew herself up to her full height and looked into his grotesque, twisted-up features without flinching. "I see we're not going to make any progress today," she said in a quiet, unruffled tone, as if he hadn't just been yelling. "I'll be back when you're less—*this.*" She turned on her heel and left.

Yelling incoherently, the Joker tried to follow her but the two husky orderlies who had been standing by in case of trouble caught him at the door. The yells became screams as they subdued him, and Harleen had to force herself not to look back in concern.

To her surprise, Dr. Leland was waiting for her in the hall. "Are you all right?" she asked.

Harleen nodded. "That actually went better than I thought it would," she lied. "Now if you'll excuse me, I'm going back to my office so I can write this up while it's still fresh in my mind."

◆

Harleen expected that Dr. Leland would want to talk more about what had just happened, perhaps try to comfort her, even though she didn't need comforting. She was afraid Dr. Leland would tell her the Joker's reaction was too extreme and that she was withdrawing permission for Harleen to treat him.

But Dr. Leland didn't knock on her door. Harleen heard her lock up her own office and leave for the night. All the other doctors were already gone except for Dr. Wendell, who was on call overnight. Harleen could work uninterrupted on her report, then make some notes about how to approach the next session.

How many sessions would it take, she wondered, before he stopped putting on a show? He'd said he was a creature of habit, which meant, among other things, he had to do everything he could to drive her away. Even after it became obvious that she wasn't going to make it easy for him, he'd probably continue subjecting her to The Joker Show Starring The Joker simply because he no longer knew how to do anything else.

Harleen was still making notes when there was a polite *tap-tap-tap* at the door. She glanced at her watch as she got up to answer and saw she had stayed an hour later than she had intended.

It was one of the orderlies who had come into the Joker's cell when she had left. His name-tag said Adam. "Sorry to bother you, Dr. Quinzel," he said, his big face contrite, "but he insisted."

"'He?'" As if she really didn't know.

"The subterranean homesick clown," Adam said. "I mean, the Joker. He insisted I come and find you. He wants to apologize."

Harleen's eyebrows went up. "He's awake again already?"

"He's developed a high tolerance to sedatives," the orderly said.

It was on the tip of her tongue to ask how the Joker could have known she was still here. She decided not to. "I'm just about to leave," Harleen said pleasantly. "Tell the Joker I'll see him at our next scheduled session."

Adam grinned at her with approval. "Will do, Doc. You have a nice night."

That would teach him, Harleen thought, as she closed the door.

◆

She woke at four a.m. from a nightmare of finding the Joker had hanged himself in his cell with a rope made from his clothing.

Two orderlies, both of them Adam, cut him down. Dr. Leland stood beside Harleen, wringing her hands like a damsel in distress. *When this gets out, the patients'll riot. They'll burn Arkham to the ground.* She turned to Harleen. *I have to tell Batman how the Joker wanted to apologize but you went home instead. He'll be so mad. So mad.*

Harleen took a sip of water from the glass on her nightstand and lay down to go back to sleep. But as soon as she did, she was back in the Joker's cell, standing over his body with Dr. Leland moaning about Batman. She forced herself awake and padded into the kitchen to put on the coffee. Today was going to be a helluva long one.

◆

"If you're asking me whether you did the right thing," Dr. Leland said, frowning, "I can tell you yes, absolutely, without a doubt, and I don't know why you have to ask. The Joker has to understand that no, we do *not* come running every time he calls, not even when he wants to apologize for behaving badly."

Harleen nodded. "That was my thinking at the time."

"You think differently now?" Dr. Leland looked wary.

"As doctors, we are always in the power position," Harleen said. "There's a fine line between being appropriately assertive and bullying."

Dr. Leland laughed a little. "I heard the whole thing from the hall. Someone *did* get bullied but—spoiler—it was you."

"Not really," Harleen said. "I didn't *let* him bully me."

"You're splitting hairs," Dr. Leland said. "But okay, have it your way. The Joker *tried* to bully you. We can't allow that, either."

"Still, he knew he'd done wrong and wanted to apologize." Harleen sighed. "But I made him wait, and not just a few hours. I left him hanging all night." She winced.

"Something wrong?" Dr. Leland looked concerned.

"No, just a poor choice of words," Harleen said. "I was so annoyed. I wasn't thinking of what was best for my patient. I only wanted to teach him a lesson."

"Which happened to be the right thing anyway," said Dr. Leland. "Sometimes we do the right thing even when our motives are less than pure. We're only human."

"But we have to rise above selfish considerations," Harleen said.

"You can rise above next time," Dr. Leland said, chuckling a little.

"Leaving something unresolved overnight is one of the worst things you can do," Harleen said. "My parents never went to bed mad. Even during the times when my father was in—uh, was away, they never let anything fester between them. And never, *ever* overnight."

Dr. Leland grimaced. "You aren't your mother, the Joker's not your father, and the doctor–patient relationship is in no way a marriage."

"But it's every bit as intimate," Harleen replied. "Maybe more so. Patients tell therapists things they'd never tell their spouses. And the relationship is lopsided—we have all the power and personal information."

"And thank God for that!" Now Dr. Leland looked alarmed. "Otherwise we'd all be doomed! The patients here are crazy but they aren't stupid, and the Joker is positively diabolical. *Never* tell him *anything* about yourself, no matter how trivial you think it is. He might use it to ruin your life."

Harleen frowned. "Nobody's *that* good."

"Narcissism and the need for immediate gratification tripped him up, not a failure of intellect," Dr. Leland said. "I recommend you not see him for another six days—a week from yesterday's debacle."

"But that contravenes my whole program of concentrated therapy," Harleen protested. "We're supposed to have *daily* sessions. If I wait a whole week before seeing him, we'll have to start all over from the beginning."

"You're still *at* the beginning," said Dr. Leland. She put up one hand as Harleen started to say something else. "Never mind, I gave you the go-ahead and interfering before you've even started isn't fair. That said, I wish you'd give it at least two or three days before your next session."

"The point is that action, response, and reaction must be dealt with in the moment, as things happen," Harleen said. "That's why I shouldn't have let him stew overnight. But it's done now. I want to proceed with the program as outlined."

"Five years ago, I'd never have gone along with this," Dr. Leland said, her voice heavy with resignation. "I probably shouldn't now. But I did, and I am, and I will. Just don't see him until the end of the workday."

"I didn't plan to do otherwise," Harleen lied. She had intended to go straight from Dr. Leland's office to the Joker's cell. Now she'd have to wait nine hours. Already she couldn't stand it but she had to, and she couldn't stand that, either. She hadn't thought quickly enough to say she should see the Joker early in the day, while she was fresh. She'd have to rise above that next time, too, she supposed.

"I did promise I'd see the Joker on my own time, after all," she added as she stood up. "I've got three patients to see before lunch and I don't want to run late all day. So if you don't mind—"

Dr. Leland made a shooing motion at her. "Go, go. Once more into the breach, walk tall, heal. You know the drill."

"I know the drill," Harleen said and left, stopping at her office to get her tablet and lock the door. She considered going down to the Joker's cell anyway, but Dr. Leland would find out and hassle her about it. She sighed; no day was ever so hard that it couldn't get harder.

Harleen made short, efficient work of her morning sessions. Not that she shortened them, exactly. But she had to face reality. Jake Maxwell, the paranoid schizophrenic, was decompensating again—the meds weren't working and he was sure the government was conspiring with aliens to replace all non-human life on the planet, including fish, with robots. When Harleen asked why only non-humans, Maxwell had said, "Because it's cheaper—no uniforms to buy." It was probably the most sense Maxwell would make for a while.

Maxwell wasn't usually violent but he had a way of inciting violence in others. One of the consulting psychiatrists had suggested Maxwell be tested for pheromones, but nothing in his file indicated any follow-up. Harleen made a note to write up an isolation order for him in advance. By the time isolation became necessary, Maxwell wouldn't know where he was.

Her mass murderer, Gordy Sovay, claimed to hear voices just like Jane of Arc ("Most people think it's Joan, but they're wrong.") They had told him how to get hold of an automatic weapon, and the Archangel Clansy ("He spelled it for me.") had ordered him to take it into a crowded shopping mall.

To Harleen, he was one more sad case of mediocrity, and she was stuck listening to him tell her about the voices, which sounded like Twitter for unimaginative psycho killers.

Harleen broke for lunch after a session with the charitable serial killer. Stanley Stockwell preferred to be called a "serpent of mercy." He had volunteered at care facilities for the elderly where he had gently dispatched those diagnosed with dementia. He might have gotten away with this indefinitely if he hadn't decided to expand his victim pool to include any older person who had moments of confusion or forgetfulness.

A disorganized resident at one of the care homes who had almost drunk a cup of poisoned coffee had been his undoing. Stanley's total lack of remorse had sent him to Arkham. In a just universe, Harleen thought, the man would develop Alzheimer's himself. So far, however, he was just stultifyingly bland; it made Harleen want to slap him. When she had gone into psychiatry, she'd had no idea just how many psychotics were just plain *boring*. Hannah Arendt sure had been right about the banality of evil.

Harleen ate lunch alone in her office so she could think about her evening session with the Joker. He was so unpredictable; she never really knew what was going to happen or what he'd do. It could be scary but it was also challenging. Not to mention exciting.

Unlike her afternoon appointments, who were as predictable as wind-up toys. Her other serial killer, Durwood LeBlanc, became so rude and confrontational that she had to have the orderlies take him to a quiet room. No surprise—he'd been building up to it. Durwood always said the same old things—same old profanities, same old insults, same old accusations and threats. *She* might as well have been a wind-up toy, Harleen thought, for all the difference she made to him.

Her last two patients barely kept her awake, even with extra cups of strong coffee. Well, yes, she had gotten up obscenely early but Harleen had dealt with sleep deprivation as an intern and she knew the difference between physical fatigue and excruciating boredom. Boredom was tougher. But she did her job, listened to them tell her things they had told her numberless times before, made the right I'm-listening noises, and got away from them as fast as she could without breaking into a run.

Since it was one of those days when all the doctors were in, Dr. Leland had called a staff meeting for that afternoon. It wasn't quite as boring as her patients but it seemed to last forever, and she could barely hide her impatience. As always, she took notes, if for no other reason than to keep her mind from wandering too much. But when she got back to her office afterward she discovered all her notes had been about the Joker:

Get to real cause of anger. More than frustration with confinement — how much more? Origin of persona — Card games? — Parent with gambling problem? Or sideshow/freak fixation? And what IS his real name?

That was the truly astonishing thing about him—of every wild-and-crazy, larger-than-life, multicolor criminal that had ever made a splash in Gotham City, only the Joker had managed to conceal his identity completely, including his given name. It was as if he had just sprung up out of nowhere, coming into existence simply because he'd felt like it. No one had ever known him as anything but the Joker.

Everyone came from somewhere. But Harleen thought if anyone *could* have magicked himself into existence by sheer force of will, it was this clown.

There was one more hour left in the workday after the staff meeting. Harleen used it to write reports, make corrections, reread patient files. Then she finally gave up and reorganized her Joker materials in the special ring-binder devoted exclusively to her most challenging patient. There wasn't much in it yet besides photocopies of newspaper articles and her private preliminary notes.

Dr. Leland asked the staff to digitize their notes for easy access from the Arkham cloud. But Harleen always kept hardcopy backups. Any cloud could be hacked, and if a hacker altered or erased data, the original was gone for good—unless it existed as something other than bits or bytes. There were off-line archives but Harleen had been through enough computer meltdowns to know there was no such thing as too many backups.

Harleen also felt it was wise not to put *everything* in the cloud. Her private notes on her patients were just that—*private*—and they couldn't be archived because they were dynamic, changing as she learned more. She had a feeling her private notes on the Joker would be extremely dynamic.

Harleen's desire to go down to the Joker's cell was so strong now she thought it must have been radiating from her like heat. She half-expected Dr. Leland to suddenly barge in and say she had decided to cancel the proposed treatment plan because she thought Harleen was too personally invested and who did she think she was anyway, Sigmund Freud or Carl Jung? Arkham Asylum wasn't a place for breakthroughs; it was a storage facility for people too toxic for a standard human warehouse. People like the Joker had to be handled like the hazardous materials they were.

She heard Dr. Leland lock up for the night, then walk past without stopping. Still, Harleen made herself sit at her desk until she heard Dr. Leland's car leave the parking lot. Then she picked up her tablet and her ring-binder and walked sedately through Arkham down to the Joker's cell in the sub-sub-sub-sub-basement, taking the stairs instead of the elevator.

15

Well, *of course* she would come back, he'd never doubted it, the Joker thought when Angus told him the lovely Dr. Quinzel was on her way. First thing that morning, he'd asked the orderlies—politely, even—to tell him if or when the good doctor was headed in his direction. Now he was sorry he'd said *if*; it made him sound like he wasn't sure of himself. Fortunately, Angus was a moron who lived in a nuance-free world—anything subtler than a pie in the face was wasted on him.

But never mind; Harleen Quinzel was coming back because she was well and truly hooked. She was treating him now, and what a treat she would be. Such a relief not to have to tolerate those other sorry schlubs that passed for psychiatrists at Arkham, Dr. Leland excluded. She most definitely wasn't a schlub—he had to watch his step around Joanie La-La Leland. In fact, he'd probably see her a little more often now—she'd be checking up on Dr. Quinzel, monitoring her work, making sure this wasn't a mistake like the Looney Ladies club. He'd have to be careful.

Did she know how gorgeous she was? Or was she one of those women who couldn't see her real reflection in the mirror? So many beautiful women couldn't. According to the information he'd wheedled from the orderlies, Dr. Quinzel had been a gymnast; gymnastics was full of knockouts with body issues, reinforced by the very nature of the sport.

Why had Dr. Quinzel never competed in the Olympics, he wondered. Had she tried out and not been good enough? Did the failure eat at her? Or had she never had the chance because Mommy and Daddy couldn't afford the right coaches?

Maybe her parents hadn't even cared—how classic. Heartless mothers, absent fathers, abusive brothers, twisted sisters—thanks to screwed-up families, there would always be an endless supply of potential hench-wenches to choose from.

At the same time, however, neurotic women were *so much trouble.* They always wanted to talk about their feelings and your feelings and their feelings about your feelings and your feelings about their feelings about your feelings, ad nauseam. It wasted time better spent devising and executing crimes outrageous enough to keep the twenty-four-hour news cycle abuzz for weeks, and have all the nobodies speaking your name in an awed whisper.

But this was in the outside world, where he wasn't. He was buried alive in the loneliest cell on the lowest level of Arkham Asylum, courtesy of that caped buffoon, Batman.

Well, Batman didn't know it yet but he was going to learn that even the sub-sub-sub-sub-basement of Arkham Asylum wasn't deep enough. Not when there was a neurotic beauty on the premises who wanted only to help him.

And here she was now, with good old Angus the orderly bringing a chair in so the good doctor wouldn't have to sully her behind by sitting on the bed where every night he lay in his criminally insane repose and dreamed his criminally insane dreams.

Angus offered to stay but the very professional Dr. Quinzel shooed him out in the name of doctor–patient confidentiality. She sat down, crossed her long, graceful legs, and finally deigned to look directly at him.

"Are you up to a civilized exchange this evening or are you still not using your indoor voice?"

The question almost brought tears of joyful laughter to his eyes. Bless her beautiful, professional, clueless little heart.

◆

"Are you up to a civilized exchange this evening or are you still not using your indoor voice?"

The Joker didn't answer right away. Harleen blinked; were those *tears* in his eyes? Or was that just a trick of the light?

"I was really afraid you might not come back after I treated you so shamefully," he said after a few seconds. "As much as I hoped you'd let me apologize, I wouldn't have blamed you for wanting nothing more to do with me. When you didn't come back last night, I tried to tell myself it was simply that you'd already gone home. I didn't sleep very well."

It must have been a trick of the light, Harleen thought; the Joker's voice was serious but steady, no cracking or breaking. Not that he'd have fooled her with crocodile tears. His face was so utterly forlorn, though, she found it hard to look at him; she gazed down at her tablet instead and pretended to take notes. The man had so much presence and vitality—the humiliation must have been unbearable, as bad as physical pain.

Harleen cleared her throat. "How well do you sleep normally?"

"I don't know what that means," the Joker said in the same low, serious voice. He sat up on the edge of his bed and rested his elbows on his knees. "'Normally,' that is. I don't think I've ever done anything 'normally.'"

"I meant, what's normal for you," Harleen said, suppressing a smile. Contrite, humble, but still trying to take control of the conversation; it was probably a habit. Getting the upper hand was how prisoners survived. And crucial to her understanding of him was knowing he saw Arkham as a prison in hospital scrubs. (That was good, she thought, writing it down; she had to use it in the book.) "Do you usually sleep well?"

The Joker tilted his head, gazing at her in a speculative way. Trying to gauge something about her—the word that appeared most often in his files was "manipulative." What might he be trying to discern?

"That's a good question," he said after a few seconds. "Do I wake up refreshed, singing with the birds every morning? Hardly. I doubt anyone's life is that good. But here in Arkham, I don't have very much to occupy my mind so I'm prone to things weighing on me."

"What kinds of things?" Harleen asked, using the stylus on her tablet screen.

"The usual suspects," said the Joker. "Things I've done. Or not done. Things done to me. Or not."

Did he think she was an amateur, Harleen wondered? She frowned down at her tablet. Someday, someone would make a stylus that didn't make her handwriting look as if she were recovering from a stroke. Until then, she'd stick with low tech. She swapped the tablet for the binder.

"Go on," she said, pencil poised over a blank page. "Do any particular things weigh on you more than others?"

"Other than the fact that my misdeeds are without number?" the Joker said brightly. "Nah, not really."

"What about things that have happened to you?" Harleen asked. "Any of those repeating on you like bad chilli?"

The Joker looked at her disapprovingly. "Isn't that a bit racist?"

Harleen smiled with half her mouth. Some patients would pounce on the most ridiculous things in an effort to throw their doctor off-balance. "Any cuisine can suffer from failure of execution. Bad curry. Bad pizza. Bad apple pie."

The Joker put his head in his hands and stayed that way for so long, Harleen worried she had somehow hit a nerve. She was about to ask him what was wrong when he suddenly sat up straight and said, "Damn, I miss that *so much*."

Harleen blinked at him. "Bad apple pie?"

"Intelligent conversation. Banter." He moved to lean back against the wall. "I swear sometimes I feel my own brain atrophying, my mind shrinking. It takes a lot more than crossword puzzles and killer sudoku to keep an intellect alive and kicking. My other doctors hardly ever said anything to me about—well, *anything*. We never *talked*, never *conversed*. They'd just look at me, check the box next to 'still crazy,' and they were done for the day.

"And before they put me down here in isolation," he went on before Harleen could respond, "it wasn't much better. I mean, who among the other nut jobs in this joint could I have even a halfway intelligent conversation with—a serial killer? An arsonist? Half the loonies in Arkham hear voices so it's impossible to get a word in edgeways. And it probably wouldn't be worth the effort anyway."

Harleen opened her mouth to say something but he was too fast for her again.

"And don't get me started about the so-called *fairer* sex," he went on. "The choice of female companionship is strictly limited in here. Now, I'm not one of those men who has problems with women being who they are or asserting themselves. But I'd rather talk to a woman who has more to say than 'I did-unt *mean* to!' Or 'Shiny! *Shiny!*' And a woman who calls herself Poison Ivy and grows *plants* in her freakin' *hair* probably hasn't read any good books lately!"

Harleen tried pressing her lips tightly together but it didn't work. She burst out laughing. The Joker laughed a little himself as he watched her; she could practically feel his gaze as a physical pressure.

"Well, thank God," the Joker said as she wound down. "I was afraid you had no sense of humor."

"Now what would make you think a thing like that?" Harleen asked, still a little breathless.

"I dunno," he said, shrugging. "Maybe because you hardly ever smile. Or because the only way you ever react to what I tell you is to make notes." He smiled in a way that was actually gentle, not much like his standard Joker grin. Harleen's heart went *thump!* "It's nice to know I can make you laugh."

"I'm not here so you can make me laugh," she said, sobering quickly.

"I meant, as opposed to driving you away to avoid therapy." The Joker leaned forward as he looked into her face with an unguarded earnestness that made her heart go *thump!* again. "To be brutally honest, I'd still rather avoid therapy. But seeing you react to me so positively—I can't remember the last time that happened. It makes me want to believe that maybe what I've needed all along is the right person to help me look myself in the eye and see what's really there. I don't need a lot of yak-yak-yak about pathologies and disorders. I need the right person to connect with, who gets me so well that I can make her laugh, not run away."

Abruptly, there was a knock on the door and Angus poked his head in. "Everything okay, Dr. Quinzel? I thought I heard something."

It was all Harleen could do not to scream at him and whack him in the face with her binder. "You heard no good reason to interrupt a scheduled session of therapy," she told him, her voice tight with indignation. "Unless you hear me explicitly call for help, *don't* barge in here again. Got that?"

Angus nodded solemnly and withdrew.

"Oh, my," the Joker said, wide-eyed. "I think you scared him."

"He's lucky that's all I did," Harleen said darkly.

"I've *never* seen Angus scared of anyone." The Joker paused. "Well, except Mary Louise Dahl, but she creeps everyone out."

"Very funny," Harleen said. "We've already established that you can make me laugh so it isn't necessary to keep doing it. If you can connect with me, then connect with me instead of deflecting with humor. Ya get me, Mistah J?"

The Joker burst out laughing.

Oh, God, why did I do that? Harleen thought, appalled at herself. What had possessed her to do exactly what Dr. Leland had told her not to? She hadn't intended—

*I did-*unt* mean *to*!*

If she'd caught Mary Louise Dahl's crazy, Harleen thought, she would kill herself.

"Dr. Quinzel, you are full of surprises!" the Joker said, wiping his eyes. "Where did *that* come from?"

"Brooklyn." Harleen cleared her throat again and spoke in her normal voice. "Now, where were we?"

◆

Despite her misstep with the tough-Brooklyn-cookie voice, the session was brilliantly fruitful, so much so that Harleen let it run thirty minutes longer than she had originally planned—and then discovered that she had actually let it go on an hour longer. That was Angus's fault, Harleen decided. His interruption had thrown her timing off.

"I've enjoyed this more than I thought I would," the Joker said as she got to her feet and gathered her things together.

"I'm glad you feel that way," Harleen told him. "We'll be doing it again tomorrow."

"I suppose I'll have to wait all day for you," he said, a bit sadly.

"That's the arrangement," Harleen said. "If you show improvement, however, the schedule might also change for the better. You never know."

"I'll do my best, Dr. Quinzel," said the Joker. "I pro—"

"*Don't.*" Harleen put up a hand. "Don't promise anything. It's too early for promises. Change takes time, even when you're ready and willing."

"I look forward to our next meeting," the Joker said. "No matter how hard it is to wait."

Harleen headed for the door, then stopped and turned back to him. "By the way—what you said when you made me laugh?"

"My rant *du jour*?" He smiled, obviously pleased with himself.

"I think if we recorded that and played it for juvenile first-offenders, it might be more effective at scaring them straight than any other program the social workers have tried."

"*Well!*" The Joker folded his arms, pretending to be deeply offended. "I'll thank you not to repeat that slander where anyone can hear it. You'll ruin my reputation as a bad influence."

"Good night, Mr. J.," she said, resisting the urge to use her tough-Brooklyn-cookie voice.

"Until tomorrow, my dear Dr. Quinzel," said the Joker.

My dear Dr. Quinzel crept all the way up to the edge of her rule as to what he could call her, but, Harleen decided, it stopped short of going over. She'd allow it.

She also liked the way it sounded.

16

The Joker collapsed on the bed, wrung out but satisfied. This was going to be beyond good. It would be a major event, a genuine extravaganza—

"Excuse me, Joker, I'm just coming in to get the chair," Angus said. "Since she's gone, I'm not interrupting."

"Make it quick, you're interrupting my therapeutic train of thought," the Joker informed him loftily.

"You missed your calling," Angus said. "That performance deserves an Oscar."

"As if *I* care what *you* think," the Joker said, waving one hand dismissively.

"How long can you keep it up?" Angus asked. "A week? Three weeks? A month?" Pause. "You'll break that poor girl's heart."

The Joker made a disdainful noise. "Everyone's a critic."

◆

Joan Leland wanted to be reassured by Harleen Quinzel's daily reports. From the beginning, they were enthusiastic accounts rich with detail about the banter she and the Joker engaged in, all their conversations heavily annotated. She could imagine Harleen at home with her laptop, typing up her notes, adding insights as they occurred to her. There seemed to be a lot of those. The reports arrived promptly; every morning when she got to work, one was waiting in her inbox.

The length of some reports made Dr. Leland wonder if Harleen was getting enough sleep. But she didn't look sleep deprived—she showed up every day looking fresh and energetic, as if she were sure that something good was going to happen before the day was out. Seeing her like that was worrisome.

Dr. Leland talked with the nurses as well as the orderlies who were on duty during Dr. Quinzel's sessions. The orderlies were all certain the Joker was having a ball playing Dr. Quinzel, because that was what he did. He had nothing else to do, and nothing to lose.

Maybe she shouldn't let it continue, Dr. Leland thought. Dr. Quinzel didn't deserve to be toyed with by a psychopath. No one did.

Except according to the nurses, the Joker actually showed improvement. Not all the nurses, of course, some of the long-timers had seen too much. But none of them were especially credulous. The nurse who took his vitals every day reported he was polite. When he came down with a bacterial infection that put him in isolation in the medical ward for a few days, there had been no practical jokes, no booby traps, no physical assaults, and no verbal abuse, just *please, thank you,* and even *excuse me.*

Dr. Leland wanted to be skeptical, to agree with Angus that the Joker was Arkham's own Meryl Streep. Sociopaths could be skilled actors, good at simulating someone with a conscience and a working moral compass.

They also had an extremely low boredom threshold, however, so they had trouble maintaining the act. Unless there was a quick payoff, they'd drop it and look for a new thrill. Arkham was pretty short on thrills these days. Dr. Quinzel's arrival was the most thrilling thing to happen to Arkham since Hugo Strange's downfall.

If the Joker had been anyone else, Dr. Leland would have had no doubt his interest in Dr. Quinzel was prurient. But the Joker was about as sexual as a Bugs Bunny cartoon. His interest in Harleen Quinzel was something else entirely. It may have been merely that she hadn't already heard all his jokes. Or she may have been the star of a paranoid fantasy he was making up as he went along.

The Joker had been in a number of institutions, prisons, hospitals, facilities that didn't even have names, and had never been discharged from any of them—he got out only by escaping. He had even managed to escape from Arkham more than once. But his ridiculously over-the-top criminal activities inevitably resulted in his recapture.

A normal person—a normal criminal—might have left town to do something less destructive, like go straight. But not the Joker. He did what he did simply because it was what he did.

And then Dr. Harleen Quinzel had come along with all her new ideas about treatment and rehabilitating people even if they were never going to rejoin the outside world. She worked hard, believed in everything she was doing, even coming in on her days off for sessions with the Joker and, somehow, her desire to make a difference actually seemed to be doing just that—making a difference.

Joan Leland wanted more than anything for that to be true. She was well aware that hope could make even the most dispassionate professionals lie to themselves. But as time went on, she couldn't deny something good was happening. Not fast or ostentatiously, which was all the more reason to believe it was true: the Joker was changing from a caricature of a human being into a person.

Not that anything was resolved—it would be some time before the Joker was fit for polite company. And there was still the possibility that it was some kind of trick, although the possibility seemed to be getting progressively smaller.

Time would tell.

♦

Harleen was worried.

Not biting-her-nails, thin-edge-of-hysteria worried but a constant hum of anxiety at the back of her mind, like an almost-headache. And not because everything wasn't going well, but because it was.

After a month and a half, the Joker had gone from the Mad Clown Prince of Crime with a death wish for Batman to a man tentatively finding his way out of a psychotic fog.

Dr. Leland was so impressed with what Harleen had accomplished just with talking therapy that she had done what she said she wasn't going to do—she had transferred all Harleen's other patients to other staff members, bringing in part-time help as needed. There was enough room in the budget for anyone who didn't require vacation time, sick time, health insurance, or any of the other benefits of full-time employment.

But Dr. Leland also made Harleen promise to speak up if the Joker's therapy became overwhelming.

"While I can't deny you're accomplishing something that no one else has," Dr. Leland said at a lunchtime meeting in her office, "I still have some reservations. Just because the Joker is benefiting from this concentrated therapy of yours—"

"Concentrated, full-immersion therapy," Harleen corrected her between bites of the corned beef, pastrami, and capocollo hero sandwich she'd brought from home. The cafeteria food was, like all cafeteria food, uninspiring, except for the pudding cups, which she'd heard were a form of currency among the inmates.

Dr. Leland nodded. "Just because the Joker benefits from your concentrated, full-immersion therapy doesn't mean it's doing *you* any good. I don't think you've considered how this is affecting you."

"I'm *fine*," Harleen assured her. "Better than fine—I'm super. Knowing a therapy program I developed is having a real effect on a hard-core criminal everyone else believed was hopeless—Dr.

Leland, if there's a better feeling than knowing you're helping someone by doing the very thing you love to do, I don't know what it is. You know what they say—if you can find what you're most passionate about, you'll never work a day in your life."

Dr. Leland gave a short laugh. "They say a lot of things, don't they? Sometimes they're even right. But sometimes they oversimplify things just to be pithy. Loving your work doesn't mean it *isn't* work. You loved gymnastics, didn't you?"

"I still do," Harleen said. "I get to the gym whenever I can. At least three times a week." Which wasn't actually true; the Joker's therapy had cut into her workout time. But her boss didn't need to know that.

"Well, good for you," Dr. Leland was saying. "But it's still a physical effort, isn't it? And if you overdid it, you'd hurt yourself. You can even hurt yourself when you don't overdo it. And certainly you must get bored with it sometimes—you're not always in the mood for tumbling or cartwheels?"

Harleen's nod was reluctant. "The Joker's treatment doesn't require that kind of physical effort from either of us. And I have yet to pull a muscle just from sitting and listening to my patient."

Dr. Leland laughed again. "Wait till you get a bit older—you can pull a muscle just crossing your legs. But never mind. This isn't a debate; having an answer for everything doesn't mean you win."

Heat rushed into Harleen's face. She was doing good work, better than anyone else had done at Arkham for a very long time, and Dr. Leland had just rapped her on the knuckles for it. Cheaper than a pay-raise, Harleen supposed. If she ever made a real breakthrough, Dr. Leland would probably line up the entire board of directors to punch her in the face. Because Dr. Leland was *the boss.*

The boss seemed to catch something of what she was thinking. "I'm sorry. I don't want to sound like I'm reprimanding you," she told Harleen. "But I have to look out for the well-being of everyone here—'everyone' being the staff as well as the patients.

I'm responsible for what happens to everyone at Arkham. Which means I have to make certain that, in your eagerness to help a patient, you don't hurt yourself."

Harleen still felt as if she were being disciplined but she made herself smile and nod.

"There's also the matter of feasibility," Dr. Leland went on. "The effectiveness of this treatment plan comes at a cost to other patients. I've transferred yours to your colleagues just to be sure they get the proper amount of attention."

"But *you* made that decision," Harleen said, not caring if she sounded defensive. "I didn't ask you to, and you'd said you weren't going to. But then you did it anyway, even though I kept my promise not to neglect any of them."

Dr. Leland didn't answer for a few seconds. Harleen could practically see her mind working as she chose her words. "That's true. But I felt I had to lighten your load before problems developed because you were neglecting *yourself*. And to be honest, some of the reports on your other patients seemed a bit—" she hesitated. "Perfunctory."

"I'm pretty sure I know which ones you're referring to," Harleen said, forcing herself to sound pleasantly professional rather than argumentative. "I'll admit that a couple of my patients seem to be stuck in a rut. The problem is, they *like* the rut. They know they're never getting out; Arkham Asylum has become their comfort zone. They wouldn't leave now if they found all the doors wide open and unguarded. You'd have to call Batman to drag them out."

Dr. Leland smiled fleetingly. "Which brings us to the question of why you feel the Joker is worth so much effort when we all know he'll never be discharged." She looked at Harleen expectantly. "I think that's a fair question."

"The Joker's *not* complacent," Harleen said. "He's *not* in his comfort zone. He's *not* resigned to being an inmate for the rest of his life. He wants more for himself."

"He's not going to get more," Dr. Leland said, with an edge of warning in her voice.

"That's not entirely true," Harleen said. "No, he'll never be set free but if we can heal his mind even a little, he could learn to redirect his energy into more constructive things—reading or appreciating art and music, maybe even educating himself. He'd get a lot more out of life in here, maybe even a college degree. Wouldn't it make all our lives better if he were studying instead of sitting down in the sub-sub-sub-sub-basement thinking up new ways to torment everyone just for spite?"

"You think you can get him to a point where he could reconcile himself to the fact that he's never getting out?" Dr. Leland asked.

Harleen hesitated. At least Dr. Leland had said *reconcile* rather than *resign*, although she was pretty sure the Joker wouldn't see the difference. "That would be part of being rehabilitated," she said slowly as she tried to think of how to sound like she was answering the question while changing the subject. "Look, he's got a big, bold personality—Gotham City's most flamboyant criminal. Rehabilitating him would show him that there's no point in using all his brilliant energy to be the biggest problem child in Arkham and that trying to escape isn't worth the effort because he'll only end up back here again. Wouldn't it be great if he *weren't* the most troublesome inmate we have?"

Dr. Leland sighed. "You make some good points. I'd like to believe you're onto something—"

"Then just believe it," Harleen said, her face growing warm again. "Don't give in to cynicism or so-called 'compassion fatigue.'" *And don't blame me for decisions you've made,* she added silently. *I never asked you to lighten my case-load, and I refuse to feel guilty because I'm glad you did.*

"All right," Dr. Leland said with another sigh. "But with reservations. It's part of my job to have reservations. I'm the boss. I have to play devil's advocate not because I want to stomp all over good ideas but because everything has to be questioned from as many different angles as possible."

"Point taken," Harleen said, meaning it, even though she had lost count of the number of times the other woman had reminded her she was the boss just in this one conversation. Was Dr. Leland feeling threatened?

"Did you have anything else you wanted to talk over?" Dr. Leland asked.

"Well, while we're on the subject of good ideas," Harleen said cheerfully, "has anyone ever talked about the possibility of putting in a swimming pool?"

17

Harleen had thought Dr. Leland might actually faint when she dropped the swimming-pool bomb on her. Dr. Leland must have pictured an Olympic-sized swimming pool full of bodies floating face down; Harleen had had the same mental image herself.

She hadn't been a bit serious about the idea. She simply hadn't been able to help herself. A swimming pool was such an outlandish suggestion, a perfect way to distract her from any misgivings or second thoughts she might have.

But now that Harleen had given it a little more thought, a swimming pool didn't seem *that* far-fetched. Swimming was the ideal exercise for people who didn't move around much—it was low impact and high intensity, good for people of all ages and levels of fitness. Swimming laps would let patients blow off steam in a non-destructive way. Maybe they could even hire someone to give water aerobics classes. There was plenty of room for a pool on the sub-sub-sub-sub-basement level.

Harleen wrote a note to herself to explore the possibilities further, at some future time, then headed down to the Joker's cell. Normally they'd have had lunch together, except Dr. Leland had pre-empted the time with her need to be *the boss*.

To make up for the time lost, Harleen had given the Joker a sort of homework assignment—he was to come up with three to six activities he'd enjoyed early in his life and think about when he had stopped doing them and why. Harleen had been very careful to avoid the word "childhood," as the Joker shied away from discussions having anything to do with the word. But no therapy was complete unless it covered a person's childhood. Rather than acting like an interrogator and bullying him into talking about it, Harleen decided to try sneaking up on the subject in a roundabout way. She had to get him there soon—the longer the Joker put the discussion off, the harder it would be on him. So much of his life had been hard on him already—enough was enough.

The Joker looked as if he hadn't moved since she'd left; he was still sitting on the edge of his bed, elbows digging into his knees and his chin in his hands. The sheet of paper and felt-tip pen sat apparently untouched beside him. She slipped the pen into her blazer pocket immediately; he was forbidden to have anything with a sharp point, but making him write with a crayon seemed so insulting that Harleen couldn't bring herself to do it. The Joker hadn't betrayed that little bit of trust; he hadn't stolen a pencil or pen to use as a weapon. In fact he'd always reminded her to take all her writing instruments when she left. If Harleen were caught treating him with that much respect and dignity, she might lose her job.

Fortunately, whoever had brought his lunch tray hadn't noticed this blatant violation. It was Taco Tuesday, Harleen remembered; the Joker loved Taco Tuesday. He'd eaten well, leaving the pudding cup for later. All the inmates loved pudding, the Joker included.

"I'm sorry I couldn't stay for lunch," Harleen said gently. "But, as I told you, *the boss* summoned me and *the boss* must be obeyed. You know how that is."

Or maybe he didn't, Harleen thought. The Joker was used to being in charge. If there had been a time when he'd been a henchman or sidekick, she couldn't picture it, any more than she could picture what he had looked like before the incident that had given him his distinctive appearance.

As she sat down in her chair, the Joker scooted back from the edge of the bed and put a pillow between his back and the wall.

"So if you weren't able to come up with things you enjoyed doing in the past," she went on as she picked up her notebook and took out her pen, "perhaps you'd like to tell me what you *did* think about."

Instead of giving her his usual equivocations, he said, "You know, my father used to beat me up pretty bad."

The words hit Harleen with a force that was almost physical. For a fraction of a second, the world seemed to tilt sideways. Harleen sat up straighter in her chair. Her own emotional reaction had to wait for later; right now, her patient needed her. He was staring past her at something only he could see.

"Go on," she said calmly.

"Every time I got outta line—" the Joker took a swing at the air. *"Bam!"*

Outta line, bam! Harleen wrote, her hand shaking a little.

"Or sometimes I'd just be sitting there doing nothing and—" the Joker took another swing. *"Pow!"*

Nothing—pow! Harleen wrote.

"Pops tended to favor the grape, ya see," he continued. "And people who tend to favor the grape *don't* tend to be *upbeat.*"

Grape people, not upbeat, Harleen scribbled, nodding at him. "I see."

The Joker fell silent. Harleen waited, not wanting to interrupt his thoughts or break the spell that had put him in the mood to disclose. But as the silence stretched, she worried that he might suddenly scurry away from the subject and hide. Was there anything she could say to encourage him without being too overbearing?

"There was only *one* time I ever saw Dad really happy," he said finally. "He took me to the circus when I was seven."

Dad happy, circus, seven, Harleen wrote, keeping her gaze on the Joker so he would know she was paying close attention.

"And there was this one clown—crazy-looking geek with checkered pants." He laughed a little as he stared into the distance.

Harleen could see him seeing the crazy-looking geek all over again as she wrote *crazy-looking checkered geek*. "He was running around the ring with this tiny dog snapping at his heels."

Ring dog snapping heels, Harleen scribbled, still looking at the Joker and not the paper.

Abruptly, the Joker jumped to his feet. "And every time the clown stopped to kick the pup—*zwoop!*—he dropped his pants and fell on his butt!"

ZWOOP! Pants, butt, Harleen scribbled, nodding.

The Joker doubled over with laughter for a moment, then straightened up, wiping his streaming eyes.

Tears—of laughter? Harleen wrote.

"Jeez, I thought my old man would bust a gut laughing," the Joker said, a little breathless himself. "I saw how happy he was, so I decided I'd make him laugh, too!"

Old man happy laugh too. Harleen underlined the words.

"So the next night, when Dad staggered home from the bar," said the Joker, still laughing a little, "there I stood at the front door wearing his best Sunday slacks around my ankles!"

Harleen tried to write *bar, staggered, door, slacks ankles* but she was laughing too hard now. The Joker had dropped his own trousers, revealing boxer shorts covered with a pattern of hearts, flowers, and Cupids. She couldn't decide what was funnier—the boxer shorts or the way the Joker was acting out the story. His laughter was so contagious, she couldn't have stopped laughing if Dr. Leland had marched in wanting to know what was so funny.

"'Hi, Dad!' I squeaked. 'Look at me!'" the Joker said in a high, squeaky kid's voice.

Squeaked! Harleen wrote, laughing even harder.

"And *zwoop!*" said the Joker, making a swooping motion with one hand. "I took a big pratfall and tore the crotch right out of his pants!"

Harleen gave up trying to write anything and laughed along with her patient. Her stomach muscles were starting to ache now. How much longer would this go on, she wondered? She was also weeping with laughter, so much so that her whole face was wet. She was dabbing at her cheeks with a tissue when the Joker suddenly stopped laughing and looked directly at her, his face cold and expressionless.

"And then he broke my nose," he said.

Harleen's laughter cut off sharply, as if he had slapped her. *No,* she thought, trying to catch her breath. *Please, no—*

"I still like to think he was aiming for my behind and missed," the Joker added, his voice calm and matter-of-fact, as if he hadn't just been laughing his head off with her for minutes on end. He'd pulled his pants up and he was back on the bed with the pillow between himself and the wall. "At least that's what I told myself when I woke up in the hospital three days later."

"*Three* days later?" Harleen managed, her voice faint and horrified.

"But hey, that's the downside of comedy!" The Joker jumped to his feet again and spread his hands, grinning broadly. "You're always taking shots from folks who don't get the joke—like my old man." His grin disappeared, replaced by an expression of pure loathing. "Or Batman."

The way he said *Batman* made it sound like a profanity, Harleen thought as he plumped down on the edge of the bed with his elbows on his knees. "Wow," he said, shaking his head a little. "That was—" he thought for a few seconds. "Exhausting. I guess I've been holding that in for so long, I didn't realize it would be so draining to let it go." He turned to her with the expression of a man who had been struggling with something for years only to have it vanish, leaving him discombobulated and uncertain. "I know it's time for our afternoon discussion but suddenly I'm just so tired. Would it be okay if I took a nap?"

"Of course," Harleen said. She was tempted to ask if she could stay with him in case he had a bad dream and then thought better of it. He was in a vulnerable state; she could give him a bad dream via the power of suggestion. Besides, he really needed to be alone for a while. She could go back to her office and write this up while it was still fresh in her mind.

She needed some time to digest this herself. It wasn't just that he had opened up to her for the first time—he had told her something he had never told anyone else. She knew it because after reading his file over and over and over, she had never come across an account of a trip to the circus or any mention of his father being either abusive or an alcoholic.

This wasn't just big—this was colossal. This was a game-changer.

♦

Harleen went back through his files anyway, just to make sure. Then she asked Dr. Leland—*the boss*—if she had ever gotten wind of any abuse in the Joker's background.

"Not even a hint, although it's likely it's a no-brainer, as the kids used to say." Dr. Leland had several file folders spread out on her desk; all of them seemed to be financial records. She made a pained face. "Dr. Quinzel—Harleen—I'm sorry, you've caught me at the worst possible time. Ordinarily, I'd drop everything to sit down with you and we could hash this out until we were both satisfied. There's a problem with Arkham's financials—I'm sorry but it would take too long to explain—"

"It's okay, boss, you don't have to," Harleen said. She had a vague memory of something in the news about a possible corruption scandal; a couple of the names mentioned were on the Arkham board. Had Dr. Leland been caught up in it? She couldn't imagine such a thing, but this was Arkham; anything was possible.

"Is there something in particular you need?" Dr. Leland asked her, sounding harried.

"Just information on the Joker's first eighteen years," she said.

"We've already talked about that," Dr. Leland replied, sounding even more harried. "Everything we've ever found connected to his childhood or adolescence has been falsified in some way, a forgery or whatever. We don't even know exactly how old he is—we only have estimates based on medical and dental examinations. Close enough for government work but not much else."

"But we're *doing* government work," Harleen said.

Dr. Leland was too busy looking for something among all the papers on her desk to comment.

Abruptly, Harleen had another idea. "What if it's something like witness protection?"

The other woman straightened up, looking at her with an incredulous expression. "Now that's one I've *never* heard."

"Not the *real* witness protection program," Harleen added quickly. "But something *like* that. Maybe there was something the Joker was so afraid of that it wasn't enough for him to assume a new identity—he had to completely obliterate his old one and become the Joker."

"There's only one problem with your theory: anyone that scared would stay in hiding. The Joker has never hidden from anything or anyone."

"Because he knows whoever he's afraid of isn't interested in the Joker—they're after the person he used to be. It's possible. Highly unlikely, but not impossible."

"Too improbable," Dr. Leland said. "I doubt *anything* scares that man. I doubt anything *could*."

"Isn't that rather dehumanizing?" Harleen said.

"Many sociopaths are thrill-seekers because they don't feel fear, at least not in the sensible way the rest of us do," Dr. Leland said. "They're also talented liars. The Joker has lied so much, he may not even know the truth about himself anymore. It's a bit hard to keep track when you keep losing touch with reality."

"But don't you think that after so many years—a lifetime really—

even the most accomplished liar would want to tell the truth to someone?"

"Sure," said Dr. Leland. "Just don't make the mistake of thinking that liar is the Joker and that someone is you. I'm sorry, I've really got my hands full, so if there's nothing else…?" Her expression said she hoped not.

Harleen shook her head. "Just that I don't think I'd want your job if they paid me a million dollars."

"Right now, I don't want it, either," said Dr. Leland, looking unhappy. "And if I can't prove they don't pay me even half that much, the Joker's pathology will be the least of my problems."

◆

All the staff psychiatrists had treated the Joker at one time or another, some more than once. It had been standard practice to rotate his doctors simply because he was so difficult and stressful. A chat with Dr. Davis confirmed that he had, in fact, removed some of his notes from the Joker's files.

"Can I see them?" Harleen asked.

"No," Dr. Davis said flatly. "They're gone. Destroyed."

Harleen was shocked. "Altering files—"

"I didn't *alter* anything," Dr. Davis said, almost snapping. "I *un*-altered them. The Joker fed me a pack of lies. I removed the lies and repaired the record, to prevent problems in the future. You'd have done the same if it had been you."

"I'm not so sure about that," Harleen said, offended.

"Easy for you to say, because it *wasn't* you," he said grumpily. "This is Arkham Asylum. You don't know how different it is because you've never worked anywhere else—you have no basis for comparison. We *have* to do things differently here. Otherwise the gargoyles would already have had us for lunch, in hideous and terrible ways. Now if you'll excuse me, I have to meet with a patient. A former patient of yours, as it happens. Dr. Leland has decided the best way for you to do your job is to make more work for *me*. I guess that's why you have so much time to pore over old records and wonder what's missing."

There goes a man with no sense of humor, Harleen thought, staring after him as he stumped away.

18

As the weeks passed, Harleen became convinced the man the world called a homicidal madman was in fact a tortured soul crying out for the same thing everyone else wanted—love and acceptance.

She was aware of how melodramatic that sounded. But people *were* melodramatic. People were messy, desperate, full of urgent emotions. Like in the half-remembered poem from one of her college lit classes, they fell upon the thorns of life, they bled. In the next moment, they were jumping for joy, and the moment after that, they would die for love.

That was the human condition.

Leaving that aside, she decided the Joker was *not* a homicidal maniac. She knew a homicidal maniac when she saw one. She had come face to face with three of them in the middle of the night on Coney Island when she was seven years old and barely escaped with her life.

When it came to homicidal maniacs, Harleen Quinzel was an authority.

◆

Harleen had trouble organizing her jottings. Not because she couldn't remember what they meant—just looking at them, she could remember what the Joker had said word for word. It was that it was becoming more difficult to write them up as reports for Dr. Leland, to strip out the raw thoughts and emotions that gave them meaning and make them into something cold and antiseptic.

```
The subject admits to suffering childhood abuse—
alcoholic father; father/son trip to circus
(potential bonding experience)—subject beaten
when prank went wrong—3 days in hospital!!


Father <——> Batman?
```

Harleen didn't like referring to the Joker as "the subject." She didn't like calling any her patients "the subject," even though it was standard terminology. It was supposed to help you maintain professional objectivity and avoid becoming personally involved with a patient. But Harleen thought it dehumanized the patients, objectifying them so they became their symptoms and case histories instead of human beings, something the Hippocratic Oath explicitly warned against.

Maintaining professional distance made sense; doctors couldn't make every patient personally important or it would tear them apart. Still, every patient deserved to be treated like a person, and not written off just because they'd been diagnosed as incurable or dangerous. For one thing, a person wasn't a diagnosis. And for another, what if the diagnosis were *wrong*?

Diagnostic errors happened in every area of medicine—tests gave false positives or negatives, people read X-rays or scans wrong or got them mixed up, and even the best doctors weren't infallible, especially in psychiatry. A well-intentioned doctor could interpret symptomatic behavior in a particular way because of an unconscious bias, and no one would think to challenge it, because of the doctor's reputation or position. And once in a while, someone like Hugo Strange came along and did all kinds of damage before anyone could stop him.

In light of all these things, Harleen wasn't surprised the Joker had been misdiagnosed. She had discovered the mistake only because her own unique life experiences had given her a special understanding most doctors didn't have. She could see that labels like "homicidal" and "maniac" had been too easily applied to someone who was really just a lost, injured child trying to make the world laugh so it would love him—or at least not hit him so hard that he was unconscious for three days.

Harleen understood that. She'd done the same thing on the worst night of her life. The Joker was a more extreme case; the very people who were supposed to take care of him and protect him had terrorized him so much in his childhood, he must have devised his own version of witness protection, disguising his true identity without having to hide from the world.

Why not? The justice system had failed to protect him so he'd had to protect himself. And the system was *still* failing him. Instead of understanding him as the abused, terrified child he had been, it locked him up for being a victim.

But he hadn't let abuse and fear turn him into a tearful, quivering wreck. He had stood up to the world and fought back by making fun of it, and the system didn't like that at all. They called that "having a bad attitude." He'd refused to give up his self-worth. So the system had called in a specialist to teach him the error of his ways—viz., that state-approved terrorist and self-righteous bully, Batman.

After that, the Joker hadn't stood a chance. Once you got on Batman's radar, there was apparently no way to get off it. You became his twisted idea of a hobby or project; he'd never stop making you miserable.

Harleen pulled the file folders from her previous, less successful project with the female patients and reread her notes. Batman had loomed large in their anger. All the women had stories about being frightened, trapped, and overpowered as he'd taken them into custody. He'd never asked for their side of the story, never stopped to think that they might have been victims, not criminals.

Sometimes Harleen wondered if Batman had ever been with the Brooklyn police department. He would have fit right in.

19

When Dr. Patel applied for permission to take three of his patients swimming at the County Pool, all of Joan Leland's alarm bells went off.

Dr. Patel proposed to hire an unmarked prisoner transport van so no one would know these were Arkham inmates. The pool could be reserved for a private swim so they wouldn't have to worry about members of the general public. The van would have two expert drivers, and Dr. Patel had lined up staff members willing to volunteer for extra duty. Should any problems occur, the patients could be quickly subdued and returned to Arkham.

The safety and security arrangements weren't what Dr. Leland was worried about. What had set off her alarm bells was the fact that the proposal was completely unlike Chetan Patel. He was a man of cool reserve who normally believed in keeping psychotic patients calm and avoiding excessive stimulation. In Dr. Patel's view, their minds were already prone to chaos; many of them had visual and auditory hallucinations even when they weren't agitated. Keeping them peaceful prevented undesirable behavior, which, in many cases, was the best anyone could hope for. Dr. Leland thought swimming sounded like the antithesis of what Dr. Patel was trying to accomplish.

"On the contrary," Dr. Patel told her when they met in her office to discuss it, "I'm not talking about a free-swim situation where they all splash around and jump off the diving board. I'm talking about attaching water wings or belts to my three most well-behaved patients so they can float quietly, perhaps with soft, New Age music in the background. There'd be enough room in an Olympic-sized pool for them to drift about calmly, each with a nurse to look after them so they wouldn't bump into each other. Buoyed up, relieved of even the minimal struggle against gravity, they might even achieve a meditative state."

"I'm not so sure about the New Age music," Dr. Leland said.

The joke went past Dr. Patel unnoticed. "Then we'll play recordings of whale songs," he said. "I hear that's even more calming. Very spiritual. These people are in dire need of something to feed their spirits, but without any dogma, of course."

"I don't know about the patients but I'd like to try that myself," Dr. Leland said.

"So would I," said Dr. Patel with a chuckle. "I've been familiarizing myself with various forms of hydrotherapy. There are flotation tanks where you float in very salty water with no sensory input—"

"Forget it," Dr. Leland told him firmly.

"I know," said Dr. Patel. "That kind of therapy might be appropriate for only a very few patients. It occurred to me while I was researching that we have to avoid becoming too set in our ways. There's a fine line between calm and monotony. In our desire to avoid trouble, that line can become blurred to the detriment of patient care."

"Good point," Dr. Leland said, meaning it even as she wondered about him. Patel was conscientious and kept current but he wasn't an innovator. "I'd like to read this research of yours before I make a decision."

"I knew you would so I've prepared a folder I can email you as soon as I get back to my office." Dr. Patel's smile was actually eager, like he hadn't spent a dozen years trying to erase the line between calm and monotony. "There are also a few videos but they aren't too long—forty-five minutes at most. When would you like to meet again to discuss it?"

"I'll let you know," she said.

Dr. Patel's smile faded. "Well, we're all busy," he said with a disappointed sigh. "But I wanted to move on this as soon as possible—"

"I'm sorry I can't tell you we'll get together at the end of the week or first thing Monday," Dr. Leland replied, irritated. "I've been subpoenaed to testify before the grand jury in the corruption case and I have to prepare. There may be a preliminary hearing."

Now Dr. Patel looked utterly baffled. "What for?"

Dr. Leland wondered if *he* were kidding now. "There have been financial irregularities connected to some Arkham board members. It's been all over the news."

The man shook his head. "I never watch the news. Too agitating." He started to get up.

"One question before you go," she said suddenly. "This swimming idea of yours—did you get it from Dr. Quinzel?"

Dr. Patel's dark brown eyes were astonished. "Good heavens, no. She's the *last* person I'd get an idea from."

"Oh?" Dr. Leland's eyebrows strained toward her hairline. "Do you have a problem with her? Or do you feel that I'm wrong to let her concentrate on one patient?"

Dr. Patel hesitated, then sat down again, moved his chair a little closer to her desk and lowered his voice. "That was your decision to make," he said. "And I know you've taken more of her patients so the rest of us wouldn't be too overburdened. It's not how I would have done things but I'm not in charge."

Dr. Leland nodded. "And your feelings about Dr. Quinzel?"

"She's young," Dr. Patel said. "If it had been up to me, I don't think I would have hired someone so inexperienced and, for lack of a better word, *eager*. She's quite brilliant; I don't dispute that. But she's—well, *young* and brilliant. Compared to everyone else here, she's practically an innocent. I don't mean to disrespect her. I can see she's intelligent and, personally, I like her. But I wouldn't ask her to consult on one of my cases."

"You might feel differently if you'd seen her handle a fire extinguisher," Dr. Leland said, more to herself. "Never mind. I'd just like to know where you got the idea."

Dr. Patel shrugged. "I read some articles and they stuck with me. It seems to be very current in the field right now. I'm not one for being trendy but I won't dismiss a good idea just because it's the topic *du jour*."

The hell he wouldn't, Dr. Leland thought, hiding her amusement. "So nobody mentioned putting in a swimming pool here?"

"At *Arkham*?" Dr. Patel looked appalled. "That's a *horrible* idea! The first day, it'd be full of bodies floating face down by lunchtime."

◆

A few days later, a nurse named Jack Abraham sought her out as she was on her way back to her office after a session with Phil the Phish Phrobisher. Harleen Quinzel had not used the term "boring" in Phrobisher's file but Dr. Leland wouldn't have blamed her. He seemed determined to follow the path of least resistance to entropy. Dr. Quinzel's concentrated, full-immersion therapy would roll off him with no effect. Dr. Patel, on the other hand, would have regarded his treatment as successful in that he didn't engage in any undesirable behavior.

Phrobisher definitely deserved to be confined for life but, in Dr. Leland's opinion, in prison, not Arkham Asylum. Unfortunately, his lawyer had made an iron-clad deal. When she had queried it, the board sent her a terse note saying they were sure the head of Arkham Asylum had more important things to think about, like possible budget cuts. Whoever was looking out for Phrobisher had probably been well insured, especially against fire, Dr.

Leland thought, and turned her attention to next year's budget.

"You got a minute, Dr. L?" Jack Abraham asked, falling into step beside her. He was an ex-Marine with combat experience, husky though not linebacker-sized like most of the orderlies.

"Give or take ten seconds," she said cheerfully. Jack Abraham seldom asked for anything or made complaints. "What's on your mind?"

"I was wondering what your thoughts are on Dr. Patel's proposal for swimming therapy," the nurse said chattily. "I told him I'd volunteer as support."

"I see," Dr. Leland said, slightly unsettled. "Let's discuss this in my office. But I really don't have more than a minute." She unlocked the door, gesturing for him to take the chair in front of her desk. "Why the sudden interest in swimming?" she asked as she sat down, opening one of the file folders she'd been carrying to remind him she was busy.

"It's not really sudden," Jack said, looking ever so slightly defensive. "I've always believed exercise is great therapy—been a gym rat all my life, even before I joined the Corps. I still hit the Gotham Health Center three or four times a week. Arkham doesn't have a gym and, considering who our patients are, it's just as well. But they all need exercise, and swimming is good for all ages and every level of fitness."

Dr. Leland nodded, glancing down at the contents of the folder without really seeing them. "So I've been told by Dr. Patel, at length and in detail." She paused, frowning thoughtfully. "He didn't put you up to this, did he?"

"Oh, no, not at all," Jack said, looking worried now. "He doesn't even know I'm talking to you, I swear."

"Your support and willingness to volunteer is noted, and I'll take it into consideration," Dr. Leland told him. "But now I really can't give you any more time."

"No problem," Jack said, getting to his feet. "I appreciate your letting me give you my input on it."

"I promise I'll think it over carefully," she said, pretending to be absorbed in the file. "Anything else?"

"No, just thanks again for listening." He was cheerful but there was a hint of disappointment in his voice.

◆

"So have *you* joined the swimming campaign?" Dr. Leland asked the Joker. It was just the two of them in his cell, while Dr. Quinzel waited in the hall. Dr. Leland swore she could feel the woman's apprehension coming through the wall like heat.

The Joker blinked at her in what seemed to be genuine bewilderment. "What swimming campaign?"

"Don't you want to go to the County Pool?" she asked. "Enjoy the numerous benefits of hydrotherapy and no-impact aerobic exercise?"

"Is this some nefarious plot hatched by the Looney Ladi—excuse me—by the female patients to get me into a Speedo? Don't answer, that's a joke." Pause. "I hope."

"So you *don't* want to try out for the Arkham Asylum swim team," Dr. Leland said, amused.

"Not to be flippant or disrespectful, doctor," the Joker said slowly, "but do I look like a man who *wants* to be seen in swimming trunks?" He studied her for a moment. "Does Dr. Quinzel know we're having this conversation?"

"Of course," said Dr. Leland. "She agreed to let me interview you at any time, on a moment's notice if need be, without her being present."

"With all due respect, this feels more like an interrogation than an interview," the Joker said. "And I have enough experience with each to know the difference."

Dr. Leland was sure he did. "Has Dr. Quinzel said anything to you about swimming therapy or exercise?"

"She's mentioned maybe getting me a stationary bike or a treadmill," he said. "But walking or riding a bike to nowhere seems more like an exercise in futility." He sighed. "No, Dr. Leland, we've never discussed swimming. Although a Jacuzzi would be nice."

♦

Harleen didn't pace or hop from one foot to the other—Nathan the orderly sitting outside the Joker's cell would have reported that to Dr. Leland, and there was no telling what she'd make of it. At the moment, Dr. Leland was very much in favor of her therapy program for its salutary effect on the Joker. Even some of the orderlies were saying he'd changed for the better. But Harleen wasn't taking any chances, especially now.

After the women's group fiasco, her current success made her want to do cartwheels through the halls for joy, and yet she had to be more guarded than ever. Because professional achievement wasn't the only reason she loved coming to work every day. It wasn't even the biggest.

At first, she'd tried to deny her feelings, telling herself it was only countertransference—very intense and powerful, but nothing more. It was perfectly normal. People became psychiatrists in the first place because they wanted to help people and doing that stirred up a lot of emotions. But the therapist couldn't let them interfere with the treatment. The patient's best interests were the most important consideration; the doctor had to put the patient first.

Yes, but suppose acting in the patient's best interests stirs up even more, uh, positive feelings for them? Harleen had asked one of the instructors during her psychiatric rotation.

You do what's best for your patient because it's the right thing to do, the woman had replied, *not because it makes you feel all warm and fuzzy. Those things might overlap but your feelings can't be your* motive.

The instructor's words had helped Harleen clarify her thoughts and feelings, especially during her first clinic experiences. For a while she had seriously considered writing a book to explore the contradictory dynamic between therapist and patient: an intimate, personal relationship that could not be intimate or personal. It was a fascinating topic in its own way, but she hadn't become a psychiatrist to study other psychiatrists.

Arkham Asylum was her dream job—sometimes nightmarish, but that came with the territory. Her patients were many things besides psychotic—passive-aggressive, obsessive-compulsive, depressed, borderline, narcissistic, psychopathic, self-destructive, and most of all exhausting. Next to these things, countertransference was a non-issue.

In the back of her mind, however, she had wondered if, in some instances, it wasn't that simple. Could it be that, in certain circumstances, two people who had initially come together as doctor and patient had actually been meant to find their way to each other? Wouldn't they then realize their lives had been incomplete, lacking something to make them work right? For example, one of them might have turned to crime, even gone crazy—or maybe just seemed crazy to everyone around him.

Wasn't it possible that Fate could bring that person's soulmate to him in the form of a doctor? In which case, would the doctor have the wisdom and courage to accept the truth—that they were meant to be together? Or would she knuckle under to convention, hiding behind jargon like "countertransference" because the prospect of professional censure and disapproval made it too hard to do the right thing? If she chose the latter, she wouldn't just be giving up her chance at happiness—she'd be one more sorry excuse for a human being following that ever-popular path of least resistance to mediocrity.

God, the world was so irrational! Things that were perfectly natural—love, for example—were fraught with complications and obstacles. If you didn't get arrested for being a victim, some so-called authority was telling you what emotions you weren't allowed to have—or even that your feelings weren't real.

As crazy as the patients in Arkham Asylum were, they had nothing on the outside world, where The Golden Rule was *Love thy neighbor*, and you'd be punished if you did.

20

Despite her insight, Harleen struggled with her feelings. For the couple of weeks she'd tried to deny them, she had been extra careful to do everything by the book, to cross no lines, break no rules. In the time she had been at Arkham, she hadn't put a foot wrong. She never even took more office supplies than she needed, unlike Dr. Davis. What was he *doing* with all those paperclips? *Eating* them?

She felt she had to hold herself to a higher standard, just because of how her co-workers saw her. Except for Dr. Leland, the other doctors often treated her like a little girl—clever but still wet behind the ears.

It wasn't really that anyone disrespected her; the progress she'd made with the Joker impressed them and the nursing staff as well, although a lot of the orderlies were sure she was being played. But there were always cynics everywhere, people who had been eroded by life rather than enriched, who, like the old adage said, knew the price of everything and the value of nothing.

Harleen was so lost in her thoughts that the sound of the Joker's door opening made her jump. Nathan jumped, too, probably because he'd been dozing. Not that she faulted him for that— guard duty was pretty boring. Besides, she liked Nathan. He was one of the orderlies who had gathered up Killer Croc; later, she'd overheard him telling some of his co-workers not to sell the new shrink short just because she was a pretty blonde.

She watched Dr. Leland typing with one hand on her tablet.

When she finally looked up, Harleen said, "Everything okay?"

Dr. Leland's smile was perfunctory. "Seems to be." She headed down the hall toward the elevator, beckoning for Harleen to follow. "Tell me the truth," she said, pressing the call button. "Are *you* behind the swimming trend?"

"'Swimming trend?'" Harleen did her best to look innocent.

"Not too long ago, you asked about the possibility of putting in a swimming pool here. The next thing I know, even Dr. Patel is extolling the benefits of swimming. He wants to take some of his patients to the County Pool." She paused, looking intently into Harleen's face. "I'm not accusing you of anything, I'd just like to know if you gave him the idea."

"Dr. Patel wouldn't take my word for it if I told him the sun rose in the east," Harleen said, laughing a little. "I don't mean anything bad—I like Dr. Patel; he's really smart and he works hard to stay current. But he sees me as his junior. *He'd* give *me* suggestions, not vice versa."

"Did you talk to anyone else about swimming? Maybe the nurses? Or your patient?"

"Is that what my patient said?" Harleen asked, hoping she didn't look as apprehensive as she felt.

"No." Dr. Leland laughed a little. "When I mentioned it to him, he thought it was a female conspiracy to get his clothes off." She laughed some more and Harleen laughed, too, despite a sudden flash of irrational jealousy.

"Was it?" Harleen asked after a bit. "A conspiracy?"

Dr. Leland laughed harder, putting a hand over her mouth to stifle it. "Oh my goodness," she said finally. "I really don't think he's Pamela Isley's type and he's *definitely* not Harriet's. He's not shiny enough for Magpie, and he's too tall for Mary Louise."

"It certainly wasn't *me*," Harleen said, forcing herself to grin hugely so her boss would know what a joke that was.

"I didn't think so," Dr. Leland said, still laughing a little. "More like wishful thinking on the Joker's part—he *is* an exhibitionist, after all. He claims he doesn't want to be seen in swimming trunks but methinks he doth protest too much."

"*I* don't," Harleen said. "Not after what happened to him, with all those chemicals."

Dr. Leland was still laughing when the elevator doors opened. "Normally I don't make pronouncements about someone else's patient but I've known that man longer than you have," she said, stepping into the elevator. "He's an inveterate show-off. Crime gets him a lot of attention but he'd take off his clothes in a pinch." Dr. Leland's phone rang just as the elevator door slid shut.

Harleen hurried back to the Joker's cell. Nathan let her in and locked the door behind her without budging from his chair.

The Joker was stretched out on his side on the bed, his head propped up on one hand. "She wanted to know if you talked about swimming with me," he said. "I posited a female conspiracy to put me in a Speedo."

Harleen didn't say anything. They stared at each other in silence for a few seconds before they both burst out laughing.

"She thinks I've instigated a campaign for swimming therapy," Harleen said, when she could speak. "As if!"

"Where do people *get* such *silly* ideas?" the Joker said, laughing. "You would never do anything like that; you're too professional, too much of a straight arrow." He paused and sat up. "But with hidden depths that only someone who knows you well enough can see."

Harleen sat down in her chair, opened her notebook, and jotted the date and time at the top of a blank page. "Are you saying you know me that well?"

"I'd say I'm the only one who does, my dear doctor," he said. "Because hidden in those depths are things that only *I* would think of."

"Is that so?" Harleen's laughter died away as she felt her heart go *thump*. Her heart was doing that a lot lately. She pushed her glasses up on her nose. "Can you give me an example?"

"Well, there's the secret of your name," the Joker said, learning forward and lowering his voice a bit. "Camouflaged within Dr. Harleen Quinzel is Harley Quinn—harlequin, the classic clown character who originated in a form of Italian theatre called *commedia dell'arte*. Harlequin is the spirit of fun and frivolity. When I heard your name, I felt drawn to you immediately."

What's in a name? Harleen thought. "So it was only my *name* that made you want me for your therapist?" she asked uncertainly.

"Like everyone else, I heard about your heroic takedown of Killer Croc. I wanted to meet this beauty who could repurpose a fire extinguisher at a moment's notice and your name only made you that much more intriguing." The Joker looked into her face, openly earnest. "Then you showed me you didn't need a fire extinguisher to put an unruly patient in his place." He gave her a brief apologetic smile. "I knew then I wanted you—*needed* you."

Harleen's heart went *thump!* again, so hard she thought he must have heard it.

"I knew you were the only one for me—that I could put myself completely in your hands because even as you slapped me down, I saw a twinkle in your eye. Not because you didn't mean what you said, I knew you did," he added quickly. "But as a sign there was a fire inside you. I was afraid it was just a trick of the lousy fluorescent lighting. Then you laid out your plan for this concentrated, full-immersion therapy program and I saw it was no trick. You're the one I've been waiting for—the only person I can ever open up to, the one person in the world who can understand me. And the harlequin who would get all my jokes."

His successful therapy was all down to *her name?* Harleen felt uncertain, as if someone had yanked the ground out from under her and she was a cartoon character standing in midair, about to fall a long way into a ravine.

No, I'm not, Harleen told herself firmly. The injured child in him had responded to the twinkle in her eye. It had reassured him that she would accept him, not hurt him, and never hit him so hard he woke up three days later. An injured and neglected child had a profound understanding of "validation," "inclusion" and "kindred spirit" as things they yearned for, even if they didn't know the words.

Besides, deep, life-changing relationships of all kinds had to start somewhere, usually with things like a smile, a word of greeting, small talk.

Harleen's gaze fell on what she'd been writing.

My one true love in all the world. One soul in two people.

$$HQ + J = \heartsuit$$

◆

In general, Dr. Leland was good about not micromanaging the staff and she didn't intrude on their lives outside Arkham. But one thing she did insist on was that all the staff psychiatrists saw a psychiatrist on a regular basis.

Harleen had no problem with that. Like anything else, crazy could rub off on other people, and not always in ways that were as easily recognizable as mass hysteria or *folie à deux*. The problem for Harleen was finding a shrink she felt comfortable with in Gotham City, aka Batmanville. Speaking of crazy being contagious.

Most of the psychiatrists she tried refrained from the open displays of hero worship endemic to the locale, but none of them found Batman as questionable as she did. When she expressed her feelings about the so-called Caped Crusader, they all immediately chalked it up to the fact that she wasn't from the Gotham City area.

A couple were willing to admit that, under federal, state, and local laws, Batman was problematic. But, they added, there had always been something odd about the area, even before Batman.

Something in the soil, the water, the air, or all three affected people in a way that caused the sleep of reason to produce monsters, of a kind that persisted even after reason was awake.

In Harleen's view, this was rationalization with a side of self-aggrandizing—*We're not like the rest of the world, we're different, we're special*—which they used to justify violations of the social compact and normalize Batman's aberrant behavior.

Eventually she found Dr. Fay Silver, an older woman who sometimes consulted for Dr. Leland. Harleen chose her simply because she displayed a sense of humor about most things, even Batman. Harleen dutifully checked in with her once a month and never told her anything important. Dr. Silver probably knew as much, but so what? The rule said she had to see a therapist; it didn't say anything about actually having therapy.

Harleen could just imagine the look on Dr. Silver's face if, during one of their monthly appointments, she suddenly said, *Oh, by the way, my father spent most of my childhood and all my adolescence in the Coxsackie Correctional Facility. That's a maximum security prison in New York. He got out just in time to see me graduate from high school.*

The good doctor would probably look at her the same way her first college roommate had when Harleen had foolishly been honest when Olivia had asked what her father did for a living. Harleen had finally moved to a dorm across campus just to get away from the stares. Nice people's parents didn't go to prison. Well, not unless it was Club Fed, where all the inmates had been framed for banking irregularities and taken a plea to spare their families the expense of a trial they'd probably have lost. White-collar crime wasn't like real crime.

Harleen had known better than to tell anyone about the scariest night of her life, and she certainly wasn't going to tell Dr. Silver about it, either. If anyone found out she had seen *two* murderous psychos die violently in the same night when she was seven years old, she wouldn't be working at Arkham Asylum. She'd be locked up in it, just on general principle. Then they'd go after her mother for saving her life. The police beat up victims of crimes—Harleen didn't want to know what they would do to someone who dared to fight back.

Especially here in Batmanville.

Only one person in the whole world would understand how hard she'd had to work to put her background behind her, and how that had meant putting her goals ahead of everything else. Only one person in the whole world could comprehend how frustrating it was to have done all that hard work only to find herself surrounded by people who settled for less because it was easier than striving for more.

Only one person in the whole world knew how much it pained her that, on a planet full of adventure, so many people were just sleepwalking through their lives. Only one person in the whole world could see how natural it was for her be drawn to someone larger than life, wide-awake, fearless, and energetic, with the power to make her laugh and cry within seconds.

There was only one person in the whole world she could bare her soul to, who would listen to her admit that, despite her best efforts to conform to the standards and expectations of her profession, she had fallen in love with her patient. Only one person in the whole world would not immediately condemn her.

And the only person in the whole world who really understood her didn't let her down. "You're a true rarity, a woman of daring who welcomes the challenges of a world full of bold, bright colors and is brave enough to enjoy it rather than hiding from it, by running on a human-sized hamster wheel and calling that life."

"Somehow you know exactly what's in my heart," Harleen sighed. "You get me like no one else ever has."

"Of course I do, my dear Dr. Harley Quinn," said the Joker.

It was like the sun was shining inside her, Harleen thought with another happy sigh. She'd never known how good it could be to have someone who knew *exactly* who she was—who she *really* was. And who she *really* was, was Harley Quinn.

172

21

Harleen had been truthful when she'd told Dr. Leland she hadn't given Dr. Patel the idea for swimming therapy. Harleen Quinzel was a consummate professional who'd never even think of doing anything untoward. The mischievous Harley Quinn, however, wasn't so inhibited and thought nothing of screwing with the status quo for a good laugh—you could tell by the twinkle in her eye.

It was Harley Quinn who had written a piece about the virtues of swimming therapy; then formatted it to look like it was a transcript of a talk given at the International Congress held by the Royal College of Psychiatrists in London last year. Harley Quinn left a copy in the staff lounge where Dr. Patel was sure to find it. Pretty soon he was pontificating on the benefits of swimming to anyone who held still long enough. Harley let one of the nurses tell her all about Dr. Patel's new obsession over lunch one day.

Song Guo, R.N. had a PhD in psychiatric nursing; if any of the doctors pissed her off, she made them address her as Dr. Guo. Harleen admired her intelligence and enjoyed her company. Harley knew that Guo was most likely to see through the "transcript" as a fake and was having lunch with her just to find out if she was suspicious. She wasn't, so Harley salted the staff lounge with a few more "articles" tricked up to look like reprints from professional journals and then had the good luck to find an issue of the *North American Journal of Psychiatric Professionals* with a real piece on the benefits of swimming for hospitalized psychiatric patients.

Harleen Quinzel might have been a bit surprised when Dr. Patel began talking about taking a few of his low-risk patients to the County Pool for a private swimming session, but Harley Quinn wasn't. Harley knew that, on Dr. Patel's planet, anything good enough for the Royal College of Psychiatrists in London was a bandwagon worth jumping on. What surprised both Harleen and Harley was how many of the staff were taking him seriously.

Not everyone thought it was a good idea. A number of orderlies thought Dr. Patel was losing his mind. At Arkham, patients could be well behaved on the premises but still too dangerous to go outside. Yet Dr. Patel had enough support that Dr. Leland had to give it serious consideration.

Harley tried not to hope. It was still all talk, and at Arkham, things could get talked to death. If swimming didn't make it, Harley thought, she'd just have to think of another way to get her puddin' out into the daylight and fresh air.

As impressed as Dr. Leland was with the Joker's improvement, she wasn't even ready to consider moving him out of his cell. There was a much longer way to go before Dr. Leland was willing to risk letting him take a short walk on the grounds even with armed guards standing by and snipers stationed in the windows. In the meantime, the air in the sub-sub-sub-sub-basement was so filtered, it was cleaner than outside air. He was given supplements to prevent vitamin D deficiency and the fluorescents in his cell were supposed to be the kind that mimicked daylight. Harley was pretty sure they weren't, but contradicting her boss wouldn't help.

And then, a minor miracle came to pass.

♦

When Harley heard Dr. Leland had okayed a trip to the County Pool for Dr. Patel and his three most well-behaved patients, she thought it was a joke. But Dr. Patel assured her it was true.

"Dr. Leland will be going with us," Dr. Patel told Harley when she asked, "along with two nurses and three orderlies, in a prisoner transport van with two drivers experienced at transporting high-risk prisoners." He gave a short laugh. "None of my patients are high risk at this point, and I doubt that Dudley Garan ever was. They didn't call him the Dud ironically."

"Maybe at one time they did," Harley said.

Dr. Patel gave another short laugh. "As if criminals even know what irony is," he said, and walked off before she could ask him when the trip was scheduled for.

Harley stared after him, thinking the way he underestimated his patients' intelligence was abusive and unfair. She would have pointed it out to him but he'd never have listened because he underestimated her, too.

A little later, Harley learned from Nurse Guo that the trip to the County Pool was two weeks away. Dr. Leland had reserved the pool for the entire day, so the patients would have the whole place to themselves without anyone staring at them. Plus, if anything did happen, there'd be no risk to innocent bystanders—or by-swimmers. Dr. Leland herself would not be going in; she would remain fully clothed and observe.

Two weeks was a nice, long grace period, too, Harley thought; it gave Dr. Leland plenty of time to change her mind. It would also let her gauge how the other patients at Arkham would react. If the upcoming trip created too much unrest, she could call it off. Dr. Leland was nothing if not shrewd.

Shrewdness, however, was no match for a perfect storm of circumstance.

◆

The day before Dr. Patel's trip to the County Pool, Joan Leland found herself on the phone with Assistant District Attorney Dale Morrissey saying, "No, this is impossible. I was told the grand jury would be convened next week. I *can't* testify tomorrow. Does the DA think other people are just hanging around waiting for him to say 'Jump'? We're *busy*."

"The DA has stage four lung cancer," the other woman replied bluntly.

"*What?*" Dr. Leland almost dropped the phone. "That's impossible! Darius Hunt never smoked a cigarette in his life!"

"Believe it or not, Dr. Leland, an awful lot of lung cancer patients *aren't* smokers. As I understand it, Darius has a rare form related to extreme stress."

Dr. Leland put her elbow on her desk and rested her forehead on her free hand. "How in God's name did he let it go on for so long?"

"He's *busy*," Dale Morrissey said flatly, and Dr. Leland felt stung. "He's arranged for the grand jury to hear testimony in the corruption case tomorrow. At the end of the day, he goes straight into the hospital for surgery the next morning. After that, we'll handle everything, but he feels it's crucial that he's on hand if they indict. Do you want to tell him you have something more important to do?"

"No, of course not." Dr. Leland sighed. "Only in Gotham City."

"I hear you, sister." For the first time, Dale Morrissey sounded sympathetic. "See you tomorrow."

A moment after Dr. Leland put the phone down, there was a tap at her office door.

"Come in," she said wearily.

"Pardon my nose, but I could hear you," Dr. Quinzel said. "You sounded upset. Is everything all right?"

♦

Harley was amazed at how eager everyone on the staff was to go ahead with the trip to the County Pool rather than postpone it. Even staff members who hadn't originally been in favor of it wanted it to go ahead as scheduled.

The doctors and half of the nursing staff gathered in the staff lounge to talk it over.

"These patients *already* have outdoor privileges, they're well behaved," Dr. Patel said. "The worst thing I can imagine is Dudley the Dud falling on his face and breaking his nose. If he does, we'll pick him up and put a Band-Aid on it—problem solved."

"What do *you* think, Dr. Quinzel?" Dr. Leland asked suddenly.

"Me?" Harley asked as everyone turned to look at her. It was startling to be the center of attention but she had to admit it felt good, too; no wonder the Joker was so flamboyant. "Well, I'm not as experienced as my colleagues," she began, her voice small and humble.

"Oh, just spit it out already," said Dr. Davis impatiently.

Harley gave him a wounded look. "It's not just Dr. Patel's patients we'll be disappointing if we cancel. All the patients are waiting to see if we'll really go through with it. If we cancel, they'll never trust us. Not for a long time, anyway."

"So what's *your* solution?" Dr. Leland asked Harleen.

Harley took a breath. Everyone was still looking at her, as if she were important and what she had to say mattered. "I would send Dr. Davis in your place with Dr. Patel and his group because he's in charge when you're not here." She paused; no one argued so she continued. "Dr. Percival is the next most senior so he could be in charge here and work from your office for the day." She flashed a smile at him. "I promise we'll be good, Dr. P—we'll save all our problems for Dr. Leland when she comes back." She actually got a few polite laughs on that one.

Dr. Leland stared down at her hands folded in her lap for a few moments. Then she looked around the room. "All those in favor of Dr. Quinzel's suggestion?"

Everyone said *Aye*. Harley hoped she didn't look as boggled as she felt.

"The ayes have it," Dr. Leland said. "I'll have my phone with me except when I'm testifying, so I'd like updates via text and email throughout the day, even if it's just to say everything's great or boring or whatever. I'll leave other contact numbers with everyone in case there's an emergency and my phone battery dies. And I want extra staff on duty here tomorrow. I'll authorize a full day of overtime for everyone who comes in."

"You can depend on us," Dr. Davis assured her solemnly. Everyone made noises of agreement.

"I still don't like letting this go ahead without me," Dr. Leland said, talking over them. "But I agree with Dr. Quinzel—cancelling at the last minute will hurt patient relations."

As the meeting broke up, Dr. Leland asked Harley to come back to her office for a few minutes. Harley was still feeling a bit bowled over. Perhaps the other doctors would have said exactly the same thing she had, but Dr. Leland hadn't asked them. She'd made it Harley's suggestion, then followed it.

"Does your star patient have any feelings about this excursion?" she asked, motioning for Harley to take the chair in front of her desk.

"I think he's just waiting to see what happens, like all the other patients," Harley said. "I should get back to him. He's probably getting anxious."

"Oh?" Dr. Leland's expression turned wary. "Does he have a problem with your absences?"

Harley shook her head. "Not with my scheduled absences. But unscheduled absences are different. He's so dependent on me right now. If I'm away for too long, he starts feeling a bit lost."

"Please tell me you go home to sleep," Dr. Leland said.

"That's a *scheduled* absence," Harley said. She didn't mention she'd given the Joker a smart-phone for those times when he woke up in the middle of the night feeling frightened and alone. Patients weren't allowed to have phones. But who else was he going to call? His old gang was scattered, in jail or on the run. He had no one else in the world, only her.

"Did he say in so many words he feels lost without you?" Dr. Leland asked.

"Not in so many words exactly. But almost. He's—" Harley caught herself before she said he was an injured, abandoned child. She knew Dr. Leland wasn't ready to think of the Joker in that way—the woman had only begun to see there was more to him than the label *homicidal maniac.* Dr. Leland didn't know him the way Harley did and probably never would, which was just as well. Harley wasn't comfortable with the idea of her boss getting that close to her puddin'.

"Dr. Quinzel?" Dr. Leland was looking at her with concern. "Are you all right?"

"I'm sorry." Harley felt herself flush with embarrassment. "I've got so much on my mind."

"You were saying the Joker is somewhat dependent." Dr. Leland's concerned expression intensified.

"Rather dependent, yes. Transference—you know how it is," Harley replied. It was the first thing she could think of.

"Still? I would have thought that would already have peaked," the other woman replied, studying Harley's face. "You're not struggling with countertransference, are you?"

"Oh, heavens, no!" Harley laughed a little, hoping she wasn't protesting too much. "I've always understood how vital it is not to become emotionally entangled with a patient, especially one so damaged."

Dr. Leland scribbled something on a small notepad. It could have been anything, Harley told herself—a just-remembered dental appointment or a reminder to buy milk on her way home, nothing to do with her or the Joker.

"You know, since you've been making such good progress with him," Dr. Leland said, tearing the note from the pad and sticking it in her pocket, "I was wondering if you'd given any thought to when you might resume treating other patients again."

"Uh," Harley said, momentarily lost for words. "Well… no."

"Don't worry about it right this minute," Dr. Leland replied. "We can talk about it after I get back, the day after tomorrow."

"Sure," Harley said as she stood up. "I really should, uh, go. Back to work." She headed for the door.

"Not so fast," Dr. Leland said. Harley froze with her hand on the knob. "You've fallen behind with your daily reports."

"I have?" Harley said, hoping her tone of innocent surprise sounded genuine.

"I've seen nothing from you for the last four days."

"Really?" Harley turned around. "I know I sent them. I remember."

"Well, re-send them, if you don't mind," Dr. Leland said.

"Of course," Harley said. She didn't think Dr. Leland sounded suspicious but she wasn't smiling. "Suppose I wait till after you get back so it won't be one more thing piling up—"

"No, send them before you go home tonight." Dr. Leland's tone was matter-of-fact but she still wasn't smiling. "I'll have my tablet with me tomorrow so I can download them and read them while I'm waiting to be called. The legal system is *made* of hurry-up-and-wait."

"Sure thing," Harley said and hurried out before Dr. Leland thought of something else.

Dammit! She'd never be able to magic up four detailed, objective reports on the Joker by the end of the day. Maybe she could tell Dr. Leland her computer had eaten them and offer her a four-day summary. In her opinion, weekly summaries should have been enough by now anyway. Harley hadn't broached the idea for fear of rocking the boat. The less Dr. Leland thought about her and the Joker, the better.

Of course, not turning in her daily reports was no way to keep her boss from getting too curious, Harley thought ruefully. She needed all the approval she could get from Dr. Leland if she was going to move the Joker out of the sub-sub-sub-sub-basement. It would be a major victory just to get him transferred to an aboveground cell, one with windows for natural light. From there, she would maneuver him to a part of the building where the windows actually opened. There would be bars on them but at least he could breathe fresh air.

Eventually, she thought she could persuade Dr. Leland to give him yard privileges—very brief at first. But when she saw how well behaved he was, she'd let him stay outside longer, and with fewer armed guards. Maybe even *no* snipers.

And then someday, it would be the Joker's turn to go to the County Pool. How proud she would be! It was all a matter of helping him take one step at a time. They would take those steps together and then one day, those steps would lead the two of them out the front door of Arkham Asylum, through the gates, and back into the real world. He would be a free man and she would be right by his side.

Harley had the whole thing mapped out in her mind by the time she got back to the Joker's cell. Except when she laid it all out for him, his reaction wasn't what she'd hoped for.

"And how long will this brilliant scheme of yours take?" the Joker asked her. "How many decades?"

"Not more than one," she told him, maintaining a cheerful, encouraging attitude. "Or not *much* more. But you can't look at it that way, not all at once. You have to take one step at a time, and I'll be right there with you—"

"Easy for *you* to say." The Joker gave a hard, humorless laugh. "One step at a time, you're with me all the way. But you're not.

When it's quitting time, you get to knock off, go home and leave me here, buried alive. And what are the big rewards I get if I'm a good boy—an extra minute of hot water in the shower? A dinner only *half* the orderlies have spat in rather than all of them? If that's it for the next ten years, I gotta tell you, I'm just not feeling the love."

Harley was shocked. "Who spat in your dinner?"

"How should I know? I can't tell one of gob of saliva from another," the Joker said bitterly. "What time is it? How long before you leave me again like you always do? How am I supposed to sleep tonight knowing that tomorrow three schlubs are getting out of this godforsaken snake-pit to go *swimming*. And all they had to do was sit and nod like bobble-heads at whatever that quack Davis babbled at them."

The Joker dug his fingers into his hair and, for a moment, Harley was afraid he was actually going to rip it out of his head by the roots. Then he looked up again, his face agonized.

"I'm trying, Doc, I really am. But I don't think I can stand having to sit down here and think about those three *nothings* paddling around in water-wings." Tears began to well up in his eyes; Harley felt her jaw drop. "Like I said, I'm trying. But when I look ahead, all I can see is a long straight empty road through a place more barren than a desert. And at the end of it is an open, unmarked grave in Potter's Field."

"Don't!" Harley sat down beside him. "You mustn't think like that." She touched his arm lightly.

The Joker shrugged her off. "When you leave tonight—when you walk out that front door into the cool night air—I want you to imagine how you'd feel if you knew that the only way you'd ever leave this building was on a stretcher with a sheet over your face."

"Don't *talk* like that!" Harley had meant it to sound like a command but it came out as a desperate plea. "I would never let that happen to you!"

The Joker looked at her, and she had never seen his eyes so sad. "I want to believe that, my dear Dr. Harley Quinn, I really do."

"It just takes… a little time," she said lamely.

The Joker dropped his head. "Of course it does," he said in a low, mournful voice. "But maybe not much more than a decade, so I guess I should be glad about that." He took a long shuddering breath. "I thought you were different. I thought you understood that you have to be bold—*daring*! You have to grab the world and shake it up, not creep through it like a mouse."

Harley knelt in front of him and took his face in her hands. "Have faith in me," she begged him. "I won't let you down. You'll see."

He took a deep shaky breath and looked up. His eyes were shiny but not quite tearful.

"You'll see," Harley said again in a whisper.

The Joker leaned forward and, for a moment, she hoped this was the moment she had dreamed about, hoped for, yearned for.

It wasn't.

When his lips were bare inches from hers, he drew back and lay down on the bed with his back to her. "Good night, dear doctor," he said, speaking through a yawn. "Sleep well. Maybe tomorrow will be better."

Oh, puddin', you have no *idea*, she told him silently.

22

Everyone in the van, including the patients, stared at Harley with the same dumbstruck expression.

"Is this some kind of *joke?*" Dr. Patel demanded.

"No," the Joker chuckled, "it's some kind of Joker."

Harley stepped on his foot, giving him a warning glance. "It's part of his therapy," she said. "The decision was last-minute but it's completely authorized." Before Dr. Patel could argue, she stepped back from the van's open side-door and urged the Joker to get in. She was about to climb in after him when she saw that every seat was taken.

"Looks like you just got *de*-authorized." Dr. Patel twisted around to look at the Joker in the seat behind him. "You. Out."

"Stay right where you are," Harley ordered the Joker, who hadn't moved. "I'll follow in my own car. My patient can ride with me."

"No, he can't," said the man in the passenger seat up front. "It's against the rules to transport a prisoner in a private vehicle."

"He's a *patient*," Harley corrected him.

"I don't care if he's a kumquat," the man replied. "No Arkham inmate is allowed to travel unsecured in a passenger car."

"He shouldn't really be here, either," said Dr. Patel, glaring at Harley. "We're set for three patients, not three patients and *him*." He turned to the Joker again. "*Out.* Better luck next lifetime."

"He can ride if there's a seat for him," Harley insisted. "Which there is, right?" She looked at the guys in front. It crossed her mind that there shouldn't have been *any* extra seats, but she couldn't think why and there wasn't time to wonder. She was too busy taking bold action, grabbing the world and shaking it up, which was the only way you could make any real progress.

"Dr. Quinzel could sit on my lap," the Joker said helpfully. Harley glared at him and mouthed *Don't.*

"Nice try, but it's one seat to a customer," said the man in the front seat. He looked at Dr. Patel and shrugged. "Relax, Doc. We still outnumber the, uh, patients."

"Then it's settled," Harley said quickly, before Dr. Patel could argue. "I just have to run up to my office and get my car keys."

When she came out again, the van was gone.

◆

Harley told herself she was only irritated the van hadn't waited, not flooded with an overwhelming sense of impending doom. Maybe the driver had fully intended to wait for her but Dr. Patel ordered him to go, just out of spite.

Well, he'd get his, Harley fumed as she got behind the wheel of her Smart Car. When Dr. Leland came back tomorrow, she would find Harley's detailed report on how the Joker had been on his best behavior throughout the trip to the County Pool, with no thanks to Dr. Patel, who had been obstructive and uncooperative.

Of course, Dr. Leland would be shocked at her daring to take such bold action. In fact, she would probably yell a little—or, okay, a lot. But once she got past that and Harley explained about bold action and grabbing the world and shaking things up as the key to making progress, Dr. Leland would be impressed. In fact, she might actually be awestruck. She'd try not to show it because a boss wasn't supposed to be awed by their employee. But Harley would know she was.

Then maybe Dr. Leland would see she shouldn't have been surprised. After all, she had taken Harley's advice letting the trip go ahead. Surely she'd see Harley's taking the Joker to the County Pool really had been the best way—the only way—to demonstrate how successful her program of therapy had been. She'd probably have to remind Dr. Leland how it was always easier to get forgiveness than permission.

Harley just hoped her boss wouldn't praise her so much that it alienated the other doctors. Dr. Patel's head might explode.

◆

Two miles from the County Pool, Harley spotted the van on its side in a ditch. All three of Dr. Patel's patients were sitting on the shoulder looking traumatized. One of the nurses was shouting into a cell phone and gesticulating with his free hand. Dr. Patel was nowhere to be seen; worse, neither was her puddin'. Harley's heart was pounding so hard it was painful as she pulled into the breakdown lane, and she had trouble getting her door open because she was shaking with terror.

"What happened?" she asked, running up to the nurse with the phone. "Where's my patient?"

Nathan the orderly pulled her away from the nurse, who turned his back to her. "We had an accident," Nathan said.

"Thanks for that, Captain Obvious," she snapped. "Now *where's my patient?*"

"Dr. Patel is in the van," Nathan went on, holding her by her shoulders and talking into her face earnestly, as if he thought she might not understand him. "We can't move him. The driver was knocked unconscious by the airbag—"

"*My patient!*" she yelled. "How badly was he hurt?"

"I don't know." Nathan looked annoyed now. "I'd say not at all, since he was the first one out of the van. Another car came along—"

"*Oh my God*. Did it hit him?" Harley tried to pull away but Nathan was too strong.

"No, it didn't hit him," Nathan said impatiently. "The driver stopped, picked him up, and drove away. Like they knew each other."

Harley felt a dropping sensation in her stomach. "I didn't pass anyone—"

"They went the other way, toward Gotham." Nathan gave her a little shake. "Dr. Quinzel, please—*listen to me!*"

Harley stared at him. "I *am* listening." God, what was *wrong* with him? Maybe he was in shock.

"Emergency services are on the way but I need you to take a look at Dr. Patel and check everyone else for signs of concussion or Traumatic Brain Injury," Nathan said, trying to speak quickly while over-enunciating. "Can you do that for me, Dr. Quinzel? Someone could be hurt bad. We need you."

The words snapped Harley into focus. "Of course," she said. "Where's the first-aid kit?"

◆

The ten minutes it took for the paramedics to arrive seemed like hours. By then, Harley had determined that everyone, including Nathan, had at least a mild concussion but no one had sustained a TBI, not even the driver. Harley sniffed his breath surreptitiously and checked him for a flask or pills but found nothing. If he'd been DUI, he'd hidden it well. But she'd tell the paramedics to test his blood for everything. If he was drunk or on drugs, she would kill him with her bare hands.

Dr. Patel was in very bad shape. He had dislocated his left hip and broken his tibia and possibly his fibula on the same side. Why he wasn't screaming was beyond her. His three patients had come through with contusions that would be multicolored by tomorrow, but they were all right. She'd thought Dudley the Dud's nose was broken but his eyes weren't black; apparently he just had a crooked profile.

When the paramedics finally showed, the police were right behind them. Harley let Nathan deal with the paramedics while she told the cops her patient had been forced into a car and taken away from the scene right after the accident. They listened intently, taking lots of notes, all the way up until the moment she told them who her patient was.

Immediately, they started pushing her toward their squad car, even though she told them she hadn't been in the accident and she had her own car. They assured her she would get her car back undamaged. Why had they felt they had to specify it would be undamaged, Harley wondered. Why wouldn't it be?

Then they opened the back door of the cruiser expecting her to climb in, and she flashed back to the last time she'd been in the back seat of a cop car. She knew damned well what would happen next.

Harley pulled free and sprinted down the middle of the road, screaming for help.

23

"I *wasn't* hysterical," Harley told Dr. Leland, barely managing not to shout. "But I'd just discovered my patient had been kidnapped—"

Sitting in the chair beside her bed in the Gotham City Hospital ER, Dr. Leland squeezed her eyes shut for a moment; when she opened them again, she looked weary. "That's not how Nathan tells it."

"What does *he* know? He's concussed; he probably didn't even know where he was," Harley snapped. "My patient was in shock when he clambered out of the van after it had rolled over who knows *how* many times—"

"It tipped over on its side after it went into the ditch. It never rolled, not even once." Dr. Leland sounded like she was having trouble keeping her patience. What did *she* have to be upset about? *Her* patient hadn't been kidnapped.

"Did they give that driver a blood test?" she asked, lowering her voice. "How does a so-called experienced driver end up in a ditch in good weather with almost no traffic on the road?"

"Dr. Quinzel, what is *wrong* with you?" Dr. Leland demanded, her face red with exasperation and anger. "What possessed you to put the Joker in a van without restraints or armed guards? Please tell me he overpowered you and threatened your life. Tell me you acted in fear of your own safety."

Harley shook her head, bewildered. "I don't understand."

"*What* don't you understand?" Dr. Leland said, looking more exasperated.

"I wanted to show you how far he had come," Harley told her. "So when you came back, you'd see how much he's recovered. There wasn't a seat for me so I had to take my own car." She went on to explain how the driver had left when she had gone inside to get her car keys and how the van was already in the ditch when she caught up with them. Her Smart Car had a top speed of eighty mph. The van driver must have been on something and driving like a maniac.

"Experienced prisoner transport driver, my eye!" Harley said, getting worked up again. "I *demand* he be tested for every drug there is. Where are you going?"

Dr. Leland didn't answer as she left the treatment bay, pulling the curtain shut behind her. Then she poked her head back in. "*Don't move,*" she ordered.

"I won't," Harley said in a small voice.

◆

It didn't take long for Joan Leland to put together what had happened. A couple of miles from the County Pool, the Joker had removed his seatbelt, attacked the other passengers, especially Dr. Patel, and then gone after the driver, forcing the van off the road and into a ditch. After giving Dr. Patel a few extra kicks, the Joker had climbed out of the van and made a cell-phone call. A minute or two later, a car appeared and picked him up. No one got a look at the driver, and the best description anyone gave of the car was that it had been a light color, beige or cream.

The cell phone interested Dr. Leland more than the car. Nathan said the Joker had it with him, and on hearing this, her heart sank. Harleen Quinzel knew patients were forbidden to have cell phones and staff members could be fired just for letting a patient borrow one. If she confronted her, the silly little girl probably wouldn't even deny it.

She should just fire Dr. Quinzel and be done with it, Joan Leland thought, except that would leave them shorthanded. And now they also had to do without Dr. Patel.

Everything might have been different if Dr. Davis hadn't been late for work.

Dr. Davis was almost never late but this morning he had gone out to his car and found three flat tires. Because it was rush hour, he'd had to wait ages for a tow truck and then even longer at the garage for someone to change the tires.

While he'd been waiting, he had called Dr. Patel to say he'd had some car trouble and he'd meet the group at the County Pool. Dr. Patel had wanted to wait for him but Dr. Davis insisted they go ahead—if they weren't going to cancel it because Dr. Leland couldn't be there, they shouldn't delay it just because he was running late.

Dr. Leland asked the nurses and the orderlies why they had gone along with Dr. Quinzel's putting the Joker in the van. They all said the same thing: *Dr Quinzel told us it was authorized. We assumed that meant you okayed it. You okay everything she does.*

So there it was, the awful truth: it wasn't Dr. Davis's fault or Dr. Patel's or even the Joker's. Joan Leland had only herself to blame for this breathtaking instance of FUBAR. By allowing herself to be dazzled by Harleen Quinzel's fancy psychiatric footwork, she had somehow given her too much credibility.

This is the way the world ends, Joan Leland thought miserably; *not with a bang or a whimper but by assumption. Better luck next universe.*

Only the world *wasn't* going to end, of course—that would be too easy. The world would go on and she'd have to answer for every misstep and wrong that had resulted in the Joker's escape.

When the board asked her what she had to say for herself, would she have the nerve to tell them she had allowed Harleen to treat the Joker exclusively because it had been the easiest thing to do? Yes, it had made extra work for her and the other staff psychiatrists, but it had kept the Joker too busy to stir up trouble. He hadn't been bribing her orderlies to smuggle things in or out for him, or instigating disturbances among the other patients, or dreaming up how to prank the staff in new and dangerous ways whenever he got bored.

Dr. Leland had thought—hoped—he'd be so infatuated with his pretty young therapist, he might cooperate with treatment and improve in spite of himself. And it had kept the new doctor too busy to come up with another fiasco like the women's group. It also kept her too busy to ask more questions about board members who came and went at all hours, and the odd characters and even odder equipment they brought with them.

Dr. Leland sighed. If this were any other hospital, she would already have been fired. It was still a possibility—if the board of directors ever found anyone stupid enough to take her job.

Only in Gotham.

♦

The GCPD said the Joker would likely have all the employees' home addresses. Until he could be recaptured, their families would be taken to safe houses while staff were to remain under guard at the asylum, which was the one place the Joker would avoid.

Harley was the only one who argued. She pleaded with them to let her go back to her apartment. If the Joker knew she was there, he would come straight to her and she could bring him back to Arkham without anyone getting hurt. Or rather, without the cops giving the Joker a beatdown for being kidnapped by some lunatic. But she didn't say that out loud.

She tried to talk to Dr. Leland, but her boss wasn't having any of it.

"Harleen, the only reason I haven't fired you is it would take ages to find a replacement who isn't just as bad or worse." Dr. Leland wasn't yelling as much as before but Harley thought she was still too emotional, which made her feel disappointed and a little heartbroken. Her boss was letting her personal feelings interfere with her job. The woman was losing her edge.

On the other hand, maybe she shouldn't have been surprised, Harley thought. Like everyone else in the vicinity, Dr. Leland was Team Batman.

And now that she was thinking of it, had Joan Leland ever really had an edge?

Harley thought back to her first day on the job—only a few months back but it seemed like a lifetime ago now. When Killer Croc had come charging up the hallway, who had laid him out with one blow—the Chief of Psychiatry? Hardly—Dr. Leland had frozen like a rabbit in the high-beams of a Humvee. The orderlies chasing him were twenty feet behind. If she hadn't started work that day, Dr. Joan Leland would have been Killer Croc's brunch.

Management made people soft. Their reflexes went first. Then they started missing things because they spent so much time reading or writing reports; it ruined their eyesight. Then they lost their nerve—they got too scared to do anything that hadn't been pre-approved by a bunch of bureaucrats. They didn't do anything too difficult or complicated, either. They traded the road less travelled for the path of least resistance and, having also lost their stamina, went home exhausted every night.

Harley couldn't feel all that sorry for Dr. Leland, not when she was so worried about the Joker. He was out there all alone, without her to comfort or guide him, possibly still in the clutches of a kidnapper crazier than anyone in Arkham.

What if some of his old gang had been in the car, the few that weren't in prison? What if they'd been plotting to free him—but then after taking him away, they discovered he wasn't a criminal anymore? Harley couldn't even imagine what they might do to him; they were such bad people.

◆

JOKER STILL AT LARGE…BODY COUNT RISES…GC MAYOR DEMANDS SWIFT ACTION…

"This is Yolanda MacKenzie, outside City Hall. It's day three of the Joker's crime rampage and the police seem to be no closer to taking the Clown Prince of Crime back into custody. Commissioner James Gordon has ordered all police leave, vacations, and days off cancelled as the manhunt continues. When asked if this means he's lost faith in Batman, the commissioner said—quote—'The GCPD does not sit around eating doughnuts and waiting for the Caped Crusader to do their job for them.' Unquote. The mayor met with the city council this morning…"

Harley put her head down on her desk and let the sound from the flat-screen TV on the wall wash over her like so much meaningless noise. Dr. Leland had insisted the board install TV monitors in all the doctors' offices as well as the nurses' lounge. The staff needed to keep up with the latest developments.

When Harley had thanked Dr. Leland, her boss had looked at her coldly and said, "It's for your office. Not you." Apparently her boss was still pretty mad at her.

Harley kept waiting for Dr. Leland to have her arrested or report her to the medical board for disciplinary action. But then she'd overheard the nurses talking about how the Arkham Board of Directors were adamant that Harleen's involvement in the Joker's escape must never come out. The scandal could close the asylum, everyone would lose their jobs, and the patients would be sent to facilities or prisons not equipped to deal with their brand of crazy.

Didn't that just figure, Harley thought. In wanting to be honest and straightforward, she had become a scandal to be covered up. It was the bureaucrats' version of beating someone up for being a crime victim.

She couldn't win for losing.

◆

Early in the morning of the seventh day after the accident, Harley had just gotten dressed in her office after a shower in the nurses' facilities when Nathan pounded on her door.

"Dr. Quinzel, he's back! The Joker's back!"

Harley ran to open the door. "Is he all right?"

"He's fine," Nathan said and went to pound on all the other office doors.

Dr. Leland came out into the hall, tucking her blouse into her skirt. "Where is he?" she asked.

"Downstairs at the main reception desk," Nathan said.

"How did he get here?" Harley called after him as he headed off with Dr. Leland.

The orderly looked over his shoulder, grinning. "Batman caught him!"

Harley felt a surge of panic and ran after Nathan and Dr. Leland without bothering to lock her office. "Is he all right?" she asked.

Dr. Leland gave her an annoyed glance as Nathan said, "He's okay. Batman had to tune him up a little but he'll get over it."

Her panic doubled. Harley rushed past them and tore down the large, curved staircase to the main reception desk near the front door.

There he was, the hero of Gotham City and guardian of the public morals, the mighty, mighty Batman. This was the first time Harley had seen him in person and he was somewhat the worse for wear—the right sleeve of his silly costume had been torn off, a large portion of his cape was shredded, and his fancy tights were torn. But his mask was intact, because God forbid Batman should ever show his face to the world, Harley thought bitterly.

He was holding up what appeared to be a cluster of bloodstained rags. Then the rags groaned.

"Puddin'!" Harley shrieked and lunged for the Joker just as Batman let go of him. She wasn't strong enough to hold his dead weight up by herself but she managed to lower him gently to the floor, and cradled him in her arms while everyone else stood around gawking at what the bat had dragged in.

(A *bat*, for crying out loud. Harley knew if any of these people ever saw a *real* bat, they'd have tried to kill it with a broom. How could they idolize someone dressed like a flying rat?)

The Joker groaned again, resting his head on her shoulder. One eye had swollen shut, his nose was broken, and both his lips were split. He looked up at her with his one good eye. Harley wasn't sure he recognized her. But then he smiled painfully with his poor, split lips. "My dear Dr. Quinzel," he said, his voice weak. "I missed you so much. I yearned for you—*tragically.* So *very* tragically."

Harley looked from his battered face to the costumed vigilante looming over her. She wanted to scream her hatred at him. She wanted to rip off his head and spit down his neck, but she had to hold onto her puddin'. Infuriated, she heard herself growl, low in her throat; it was a surprisingly vicious noise.

It should have been hard to read someone wearing a mask but Batman's reaction couldn't have been plainer. He was completely nonplussed, obviously not used to being confronted by someone who wasn't an adoring fan, who didn't think his brutality deserved a gold star and a parade. Harley might have enjoyed it but the Joker was in such bad shape, she worried about permanent damage. Now she noticed that besides the ruined costume, the Bat-stard had a fat lip and blood trickling from the corner of his mouth. Her puddin' had gotten in a few licks. Whoever he was when he wasn't Batman, he'd have to stay out of sight for a few days.

Right now, he was still gaping at her in disbelief. Harley glared right back defiantly.

Believe it, you thug, she thought at him. *Not everyone loves you.*

Then the nurses and orderlies lifted the Joker away from her, detaching him from her with efficient movements to put him on a gurney. Harley gave Batman one last, furious glare and tried to follow the Joker to the medical ward. But Dr. Leland took hold of her arm.

"We need to have a little talk." Dr. Leland blocked her from getting into the elevator and hustled her up the stairs to her office.

♦

"We've already had a little talk," Harley said. "My patient needs me—"

Dr. Leland pushed her down on the sofa. "No, he doesn't," she said in the bossy voice Harley found so rankling.

"You don't understand—" Harley began.

"No, *you* don't understand," Dr. Leland said. "From now on, things are going to be very different around here."

"I know," Harley said. "Thank God we can all finally go home."

"Harleen—*focus!*" Dr. Leland snapped her fingers in Harley's face, making her jump. "I'm going to contact the medical board about disciplinary action. In my opinion, you should lose your license to practice any kind of medicine. And you should be barred from any work involving counselling or therapy. Certain members of the Arkham board want to give you another chance—I don't. But all they'll allow me to do right now is suspend you for two weeks."

"But you can't," Harley said, on the verge of tears now. "My patient *needs* me—"

"You're the *last* thing he needs," Dr. Leland said angrily. "In fact, I'm going to file a restraining order to keep you away from him."

"But you can't!" Harley said again as tears spilled down her cheeks.

"Oh, just *shut* the *hell* up!" Dr. Leland yelled. "That homicidal maniac got loose because of *you*! He forced the van into a ditch. Dr. Patel was seriously injured—he could have been killed, along with everyone else in the vehicle. I share the blame, for making the biggest, stupidest, most egregious mistake of my career— of my *life*! I believed you were a *grown-up* when in fact you're an adolescent with more hormones than sense! You're a disgrace to this profession and *I'm* a disgrace for putting my faith in you, something I have to live with for the rest of my life!"

"That's not all you'll have to live with, is it?" Harley asked darkly, no longer crying. "Or do payoffs from the board of directors give you selective amnesia?"

Dr. Leland looked as if Harley had slapped her.

"You're a pretty big disappointment to me, too, *Joan.*" Harley practically spat the name. "I thought I wanted to be like you. I told myself, yeah, you're corrupt, but only a tiny bit, and only to get things Arkham needs. But you're no better than that leotard-wearing bully you call a hero."

Dr. Leland looked down at her as if from a great height. "I should have realized your antipathy to Batman was a sign of a deeper disturbance, a pathological resistance to authority that—"

"Can it, lady," Harley said. Her tough-Brooklyn-cookie voice came out unbidden and it wasn't kidding around. "Save yer misplaced hero worship for when you talk to your shrink about how ya always go for unavailable guys, especially ones dressed like vermin. Don't bother firing me, I'll fire *myself,* effective immediately. And then I'll file my own court order, to take custody of my patient on the grounds that your so-called therapy is actually the legalized abuse of people with no legal recourse so they *haveta* escape!"

Dr. Leland's complexion had gone a bit ashy and for a moment Harley thought she was going to faint. *Good,* she thought with a hot rush of spiteful glee. It was about time she found out the world didn't actually belong to antiseptic, buttoned-down people like her no matter how bossy they were. Harley stood up and felt even more gratified when the other woman took a couple of quick steps back.

"You can't do that," Dr. Leland said. She was trying to be stern but her voice shook and there was fear in her eyes.

"Just watch me, sistah," Harley said. "Some o' dose *specialists* yer precious board membahs bring in here look an awful lot like known associates of Hugo Strange. Ya think Channel Seven Investigative News might be innarested? I'd bet your pension they would." She turned to leave.

"Where do you think *you're* going?" Dr. Leland demanded, then backed up a few more steps when Harley whirled on her.

"Whadda you care?" Harley said, sticking one fist on her hip. "I don't work here."

"Well, you'd better be back here at nine a.m. tomorrow morning for a meeting with the board," Dr. Leland said, still trying to reassert her authority. "You're still answerable to Arkham Asylum and the board of directors for what you've done. They may decide to file criminal charges."

"Izzat so?" Harley laughed in her face. "You can try an' make me but my money ain't on *you*, Joanie."

"If you don't show up, the consequences will be serious," Dr. Leland replied, her voice shaking even more. "*Extremely* serious."

Harley laughed again. "Yeah? Watcha gonna do, fire me? Tattle to Batman?"

"You just be here!" Dr. Leland called after her as she walked out and slammed the door behind her.

Harley stopped only to grab her purse and raincoat from her office—her ex-office. On her way out, she ran into Nathan.

"Hey, bud," she said and slipped a twenty-dollar bill into his shirt pocket. "I need a favor. You up for it?"

Nathan gaped at her. She couldn't tell what he was more astonished by, her Brooklyn accent or the money or both. But he nodded. "Okay."

"I want ya to tell my puddin' the situation's temporary and I'm workin' on a solution," she said. "Can you remember that?"

He looked even more flabbergasted. "You want me to talk to your *dessert*?" He blinked. "Uh, what flavor?"

Harley forced herself to smile at him instead of grabbing him by his hair and ramming his head into the wall. "Not my *pudding*," she said, over-enunciating. "My *puddin'*. *The Joker*." She paused, watching his face as he took this in. "Will ya do that for me, hon? I'll know if ya don't and the consequences will be serious. *Extremely serious.*"

"Tell the Joker the situation's temporary, you're working on a solution," he said dutifully.

"You got it, sweetie." Harley pinched his cheek hard enough to make him wince and swept out the front door with a flamboyant swish of her raincoat.

24

"Don't get many folks looking for these," the car salesman said, nodding at Harley's Smart Car. "Everybody wants hybrids or something they can plug their iPods into, along with GPS and a camera in the rear—"

"Not me, toots," Harley said. The tough-Brooklyn-cookie voice seemed to have settled in for good. She looked out over the sea of cars in the lot. "I know where I'm goin' so I don't need GPS. If I wanna see what's behind me, I look in the rear-view mirror. Ya got any cars that, you know, ya just get in and drive?"

He laughed. "Not afraid of car thieves?"

"Nah. Everybody wants hybrids they can plug into their iPods or something," she said. "That's what a good-lookin' used-car salesman told me, anyway." She tapped the end of his nose with her index finger. "Boop!"

The man laughed again, blushing, and Harley realized he was a nice guy. How could a used-car salesman be a nice guy? What was the world coming to? It was probably Batman's fault.

"We do have a few vehicles that don't come equipped with all the latest bells and whistles." Taking her elbow, he walked her through the dealership building and out the back door to where several older cars were parked.

"I gotta tell you, they're all high mileage and one or two have rebuilt engines," he said. "But they run just fine. Used to be parents got one of these for their kid—Junior's first car, you know? But nowadays, Mom and Dad want GPS and lo-jacks."

Harley shook her head. "No respect for their kids' privacy." She ambled over to look at a dark blue four-door hatchback.

"You don't have kids, do you?" asked the man.

"No. But if I did, I'd respect their *boundaries*," Harley said. "So tell me about dis one."

The man was still blushing a little. "Well, it actually *was* someone's first car…"

◆

After almost an hour and two brief test drives, Harley decided on the hatchback. Four doors meant no struggling to get into or out of the backseat and the hatch was handy for groceries and things. Her puddin' needed good food to make him well. No proper trunk, but cops always looked there first anyway.

She was a little sorry to let the Smart Car go—it had been cheap to run and easy to handle. But there was no way her puddin' could ride comfortably in it; his knees would be up around his ears. Besides, it was too noticeable, whereas the hatchback was so nondescript that as soon as you looked away, you'd even forget what color it was—the perfect getaway vehicle.

Since she'd left Arkham, Dr. Leland had been calling her two or three times an hour and texting her even more frequently, demanding that she call back. So her next stop was a convenience store where she picked up half a dozen burner phones and a few extra prepaid SIM cards, along with sandwiches, grape soda, and a picnic cooler. Then she stocked up on medical supplies at a drugstore—only over-the-counter stuff, nothing she had to show her medical license for, just in case Leland had already put out the word on her.

Her last stop before home was Just For Laughs, which claimed to be Gotham City's one-stop shop for costumes, novelties, tricks, and party goods.

♦

"You don't want that," the clerk said matter-of-factly as Harley held a red-and-black costume in front of herself and looked at her reflection in a mirror. He was colorless and doughy; probably lived in his parents' basement and wasn't planning to move.

"Why not?" she asked.

"Because you're a *girl*. Harlequin's a *guy*." The clerk pointed at a fluffy dress with a corset-style bodice. "*Columbine's* the girl."

Harley wrinkled her nose. "No, thanks. *This* is me."

"But Harlequin's *supposed* to be a *guy*," he insisted. "It's a character from a form of theatre called *commedia dell'arte* from Italy—"

"I don't care if it's a la carte from Kalamazoo," Harley said. "*I* call the shots an' *I* say it's *me*."

"Yes, ma'am," he said. "No offense."

"Okay. Now back off, I'm tryin' ta shop here."

"Whatever you say," he told her, backing off. "I'll be at the counter when you're done."

Harley had already known what she wanted when she'd gone in, but now that she was here, her mind was filling up with even more ideas. By the time she checked out, she was practically euphoric, but a lot of that feeling was just from quitting her job. It was like she'd escaped from a prison she hadn't even known she was in, a prison made of dos and don'ts. Mostly don'ts. Why hadn't she realized how stifled she'd been at Arkham? She should have done this weeks ago.

Except that would have meant abandoning her patient, and she never would have done that. Good thing the Joker was in the medical ward. It would be easier to break him out from there than his regular cell.

She paid cash and turned down the clerk's offer of help to carry her purchases to her car. Men always treated women like little babies who couldn't do anything without help.

Harley smiled. Tonight, a bunch of men were going to need a whole lot of help when she finished with them.

◆

All practical jokes had an underlying nastiness to them; the funniest ones were usually the meanest. Those unfortunate enough to be the butt of a practical joke were expected to laugh along with everyone else, be a good sport who could appreciate the comedic value of their humiliation. If they didn't think looking stupid in public was hilarious, they were party-poopers with no sense of humor.

Well, tonight's festivities would divide the good sports from the party-poopers, Harley thought as she filled some rubber chickens with ball bearings and sealed them with superglue. Replacing the light, aluminium springs in the fake snakes that jumped out of the can labelled PEANUTS with more heavy-duty coils wasn't too hard, but cramming them back into the cans was really difficult. The rocks she attached to the top of each new snake actually helped.

When she was done with the props, she tried on the costume and was delighted at how well it fit. That stupid clerk had been full of it—no guy would have looked half as good in this Harlequin suit. But then, it *was* her name—Harley Quinn—just like the Joker said.

Harley took it off, made herself a light supper, and then settled down to wait. In comedy, timing was everything. It wasn't time yet.

◆

Every place has its own kind of time zone, and nowhere is this truer than in a mental hospital, especially an asylum for the criminally insane. Late at night, time bifurcates. The staff live in one temporal reality and the patients inhabit an entirely different one.

Two a.m. PT—Patient Time—sits at the border between staying up late and insomniacs' purgatory. Anyone still awake after two a.m. is on a direct, sleepless course to Suicide O'Clock at three a.m. Patients who hear voices won't hear anything comforting; if they have visual hallucinations, they won't be pretty.

Four a.m. is officially Dead of Night. Insomniacs aren't asleep but they aren't as awake as they think they are. Four a.m. is the nadir before morning begins its approach. Breathing and respiration become sluggish, not just for patients but for the staff on the graveyard shift. This is when the two worlds of patients and staff are at perigee and the boundary between them becomes porous. Rational and irrational are not as easily distinguished from each other as in the daylight hours.

In the Dead of Night, anything can happen.

♦

The guard at Arkham's main reception desk tonight was a forty-four-year-old man named Gavin McDaniels. After a brief career as a minor-league football player and a longer sojourn as a bouncer for several of Gotham City's more notorious clubs, he had fetched up as a security guard and part-time orderly at Arkham. He was calm, not easily riled, and not so corrupt as to exacerbate Arkham's existing problems.

The remarkable thing about him, however, was that he slept with his eyes open. More remarkably, he didn't know it. He was happily single and childless. If any of the ladies he had occasional, brief relationships with ever noticed this quirk, they failed to mention it.

Paul Mendez, the head of security of Arkham, was among the few who did know, and it was why he always assigned McDaniels to the main reception desk on the graveyard shift. Anyone wanting to break in probably wasn't going to use the front door. But any potential intruders casing the joint would likely go elsewhere if they saw an apparently wide-awake guard on the front desk.

Harley had found out about McDaniels' eyes-wide-shut condition on her way out after a marathon therapy session with her puddin' and filed the knowledge away for possible future usefulness.

◆

McDaniels had been asleep for almost two hours when the distant sound of a car engine worked its way into his vague, random dreams without waking him. The front door opening woke him, but when he saw the red-and-black harlequin with tiny bells on the floppy points of her hat, he thought he *was* dreaming and started to doze off again.

"Hey, Gavin-baby!" said a comical female voice with a heavy Brooklyn accent. "How's it goin'?"

McDaniels blinked at the clown-white face grinning hugely at him with red-and-black lips, and he jumped, startled. He forgot the alarm button and his radio. All he remembered was that any time you saw something like this in Arkham, you were in deep shit. He also recognized the voice, as silly and high-pitched as it was.

"Dr. Quinzel?" he said, blinking.

"Smell my poi-fyume! It's from Paree!" The harlequin produced an oversized atomizer with a squeeze bulb. The cool mist she sprayed into his face did smell good. It was the last thing that crossed his mind before he hit the floor.

The harlequin leaned over the counter to look at him. "It's called 'Essence De La Lights Out,'" she added.

Gavin McDaniels didn't answer. He was out cold and, for once, his eyes were closed.

◆

The bells on Harley's jester-style hat jingled cheerfully as she moved behind the reception desk and woke the computer terminal. Disabling the alarms and the surveillance cameras was absurdly easy. Hacking in from outside was damned near impossible, but if you were on the premises, you could go nuts. Just like everyone else, Harley thought, giggling. She erased herself from the surveillance record, then programmed every camera to replay video from one a.m. to three a.m. on a loop. Much better than knocking the cameras out completely; by the time anybody noticed, she'd be long gone. *If* anybody noticed.

♦

Rosalind Bellefontaine, RN, didn't make a big deal about being Arkham Asylum's first transwoman on the nursing staff. She was innately modest—she had chosen a service profession because the focus was on other people, not herself. But she had also learned to be circumspect; being trans meant having to be ready to deal with situations that could, without warning, turn hostile or even dangerous, not just in Arkham but anywhere.

While Gotham City wasn't the Deep South in 1956, it still had hazards for her that cis-gender people never had to think about; e.g., a neighbor who nodded hello every morning might, on learning you were trans, start slipping death threats under your door; or a belligerent drunk might follow you down the street, calling you "It."

By contrast, Arkham Asylum could actually be more straightforward. You knew the patients were all potentially dangerous; you knew anything could galvanize the demons in their brains—or nothing in particular. However, the signals that presaged trouble could be surprisingly similar in both the supposedly rational and the diagnosed psychotic. Nurse Bellefontaine had become adept at sensing a change in the weather and either heading it off or taking cover, depending.

There were also times when, suddenly and without warning, all bets were off. When Nurse Bellefontaine looked up from her desk outside the medical ward where she was filling in for someone on vacation and saw the figure of a harlequin in the hallway, her first thought was that some rough beast slouching toward Bethlehem had got off at the exit for Arkham again.

Though the Joker was the only patient in medical, Bellefontaine had insisted on having two orderlies on the ward with him. He was too feeble to create even a minor disturbance, but she wanted extra help in case the Joker's gang tried to break him out. They were certainly crazy enough and a harlequin costume was pretty much their dress code.

In the bottom right-hand drawer of Bellefontaine's desk was an electrified baton—essentially a cattle prod. Bellefontaine wouldn't touch it, didn't even like the idea of having something so barbaric in easy reach. But the head of security had insisted, saying it was better to have it and not need it than to need it and not have it. Bellefontaine settled for locking the drawer and leaving the key in a bowl of paper clips on the desk. Now she grabbed the key out of the bowl and stuck it into the lock—and then, ashamed of herself, left it there.

The harlequin laughed loudly in a high, silly voice that made all the small hairs on the back of Bellefontaine's neck stand straight up. Patients laughed, screamed, cried, wailed, or ranted at all hours of the day and night. This was not a patient, and the sound she made was far worse; Bellefontaine recognized the voice.

"Dr. Quinzel?" she asked. For a second, she held onto the desperate hope that the doctor had been at a costume party and someone on the staff had called her, even though she'd walked off the job that day.

"Good night *noice!*" the doctor said in a heavy Brooklyn accent. "Ya got it in one!" She dipped and made a sweeping motion like a bowler; something slid along the polished floor all the way to the desk. Bellefontaine stood up to look; it was a large sack with a rubber chicken stuck to it. The chicken was very lumpy, like it was stuffed full of marbles or ball bearings and Bellefontaine knew she was in deep shit at an unprecedented level.

Dr. Quinzel cartwheeled up the hallway, doing a double airborne somersault before bounding to a stop next to the sack. She bowed, grabbing up the rubber chicken with a flourish as Bellefontaine lunged for the panic button on her desk, pounding it over and over.

Nothing happened.

"Security breach! Help! *Help!*" she hollered. She heard the distant sound of feet running up the stairs and, behind her, the two orderlies in the medical ward rushing to unlock the doors. She stepped back and her gaze fell on the still-locked bottom drawer of the desk.

Dr. Quinzel giggled merrily, as if this were all just a harmless prank.

No, she couldn't. She just couldn't. But maybe someone else might have to. Bellefontaine crouched down and opened the drawer just as Tony and Marcus came out of medical.

"Stay clear, Roz," said Tony, "we've got this." He lunged at the harlequin and she swatted him with the rubber chicken. There was a sharp rap as it struck the orderly's head and he went down with a soft, slightly surprised grunt. Bellefontaine crawled under the desk just as Dr. Quinzel swung the chicken at Marcus; there was another sharp crack and Marcus hit the floor. Nurse Bellefontaine hugged her knees, trying to will herself invisible.

"Hi!" Dr. Quinzel peered at her upside down over the edge of the desk with a zany smile. "Bettah cover yer ears, Roz!"

The doors to the medical ward exploded in a blinding flash of light.

◆

Harley strode into the ward with her pop-gun in one hand and her chicken in the other.

"Knock-knock, puddin'!" she said joyfully. "Say hello to your new, improved Harley Quinn!"

The lights were low but Harley spotted him right away. They had him in the bed farthest from the now non-existent doors. She did a couple of flying cartwheels as she rushed to him, then threw back the covers and made a quick assessment. He didn't look any better than the last time she'd seen him—if anything, he looked a little worse. His poor nose! His poor lips! She ran her hands over him in a fast once-over-lightly. Underneath the hospital gown, everything from the neck down was in bandages or plaster but there was nothing to indicate he couldn't be moved. Under other circumstances, of course, she'd never have considered such a thing, but these were the desperate times that tried a doctor's soul and called for desperate measures. Fortunately, he was well medicated; the morphine bag was almost full and she found another in the cabinet next to the bed.

She hauled him up out of bed, wedging her shoulder under his arm. "We'll just take this with us," she said, rolling the IV tree with them as they went. "Can ya walk if I help ya, puddin'?"

The Joker laughed as his bare feet stumbled. "Name the dessert, I can walk on it."

"That's the spirit!" Harley dragged him out of the ward and paused at the ruined entrance. The nurse was gone but there were several mean-looking orderlies coming up the hall. She waited until they were only a few feet away so they could get the full benefit of the flash-bang she tossed at them. Judging by the smell, she'd singed their eyebrows. Harley stopped only long enough to hang her bag of tricks on the Joker's IV tree.

"Ooh, did you mug Santa?" the Joker giggled.

"That lard-ass had it comin'," Harley said. They reached the end of the hall and started down the stairs. More security thugs came at them as they hit the landing on the next floor but Harley was ready for them. She tore open the chicken, spilling the ball bearings all over the floor. The security thugs skidded wildly and went down on top of each other.

"Now *that's* what I call *funny!*" the Joker laughed and Harley felt her heart soar.

Yet more thugs were running up the stairs from the ground floor but Harley already had a tin labelled PEANUTS in her free hand.

"How 'bout a snack, fellas?" she said and flipped off the lid. The snakes sprang out and hit them hard, the rocks on the business ends drawing blood. Instead of tumbling down the stairs, they collapsed where they were, blocking her path. "Shortcut!" Harley yelled. With one arm around the Joker and the IV tree in her other hand, she leaped onto the banister and slid the rest of the way down to the ground floor.

"I always wanted to do that," she told the Joker when they landed in the lobby.

"Don't let's do it again soon," he said weakly. "Or ever."

More security thugs poured out of an entryway on the other side of the reception desk. She opened another tin of PEANUTS on them. While they were all rolling around on the floor groaning, she found one more item in the bag and threw it into their midst.

There was a burst of light followed by an immense cloud of very thick, dark, and extremely foul-smelling smoke. Harley managed to get herself and the Joker out the front door before it reached them.

"I love the classics," the Joker sighed as Harley shoved him into the car.

"I love *you*, puddin'," she said, chuckling.

"Oh, my dear Doctor Harley Quinn," he said and tapped one of the bells on her hat, "I love you, too."

Harley thought her heart would burst with happiness as they drove off into the sunrise, laughing all the way.

25

They were still on the road when the early morning sunlight poured over the countryside. It occurred to Harley rather belatedly that she hadn't actually planned past the big moment they ran out of Arkham Asylum and drove away. The fairytale version of the story would have ended there, with them living happily ever after. Obviously this was definitely no fairytale—fairytales didn't involve running from the cops. Or Batman.

But that didn't mean she was out of ideas. They needed a place to hide out, and it so happened there was a defunct amusement park somewhere in the vicinity of where they were right now. And as if on cue, she spotted a very faded, weather-beaten sign.

HAPPY-HAPPY JOYTOWN AMUSEMENT PARK
exit 47, 25 miles east on Rte 51

Harley pulled over to see if the sign was as easy to knock over as it looked.

It was. So were the three on 51 East.

◆

Happy-Happy Joytown probably hadn't been much to write home about even in its prime. But all amusement parks had a certain *je ne sais quoi* that made them the same country, no matter how far-flung they were from each other.

Coney Island was where Harley's spirit had been tested, the place that had made Harley who she was. In a way, she had been born in Coney Island, not Mt. Sinai Hospital, and that drew her to Happy-Happy Joytown, ruin though it was. She felt at home as soon as she drove onto the grounds and she found the Tunnel of Love almost immediately, like it had been sending out a signal only she could follow.

"Are we there yet?" mumbled the Joker, stirring fitfully in his partly reclined seat. "It hurts."

"We sure are." She parked in front of the tunnel's dilapidated entrance. As ruined as it was, the word LOVE hadn't faded too much. The O was a heart.

Harley had turned down the drip rate on the bag dangling from the rear-view mirror, both to conserve it and to make sure her puddin' didn't get more than he needed. Now she could turn it up again. "Gotcha covered, Mistah J. You'll feel bettah in a second."

The Joker took a deep breath and let it out in a contented sigh. "My Harley Quinn always makes me feel better."

Harley allowed herself a moment of love-euphoria. Then she reclined his seat all the way, kissed his forehead, and told him she'd be right back, remembering to take the keys with her. She didn't want him waking up disoriented and driving off to look for her.

◆

There was no water in the Tunnel of Love but a few of the boats were still attached to the rail and pulley system. It took only a minute for Harley to walk through the canal to the largest chamber.

Without any direct daylight, the glittery, multicolor paint on the rough, faux-stone walls was still fairly bright. Two fake mermaids sat on fake rocks, frozen in the act of combing their fake hair with fake clamshells. The large open space behind them must have depicted some kind of undersea fantasy. There were still a few fake pink and purple starfish lying around.

At the very back of the area, behind a waist-high wall of fake rock, she found a real treasure: a stack of old quilted blankets, the kind movers used to protect furniture.

"Bonanza!" Harley squealed; her voice reverberated, as if she were in an empty swimming pool. She shook the dust out of the blankets and spread them on the wooden floor. This was some genuinely good luck—she and her puddin' could sleep on them until she could find something better.

But then, she always had good luck in an amusement park. Even when she'd had bad luck, there'd been enough good luck to tip things in her favor. Not to mention that she was, after all, the one and only Harley Quinn.

◆

When she looked back on their time in the Tunnel of Love, when her puddin' had been so weak she'd had to do everything for him, it seemed like the closest she'd ever come to heaven on earth.

She took the Joker off morphine before he got addicted. By then the worst pain was over and extra-strength ibuprofen was enough to manage his discomfort. Reducing his pain medication was also a good way to remind him he had to take it easy and give himself time to heal. Still, Harley knew he'd be restive before long; it was hard to keep a big personality quiet.

He did need some gentle exercise to avoid blood clots, so Harley walked him around the park. Twice a day to start with; when she saw he was moving more easily, she increased it to three. The Joker complained mightily—he was stiff, everything hurt, why couldn't they go somewhere else besides this godforsaken ruin, it made him feel like they were the last two people on Earth.

Harley always had an answer for that last. "Aw, Mistah J, ya say that like it's a bad thing."

Usually he would just give her a pained smile. After a week, the smile began to shrink. By the end of week two, he stopped smiling altogether and barely spoke as he limped along the midway beside her, leaning on a walking stick she had found in one of the ticket booths. It was a rather amazing find—polished wood topped with a brass lion's head—but he was too cranky to appreciate it.

Harley tried telling him stories about Coney Island—not *that* story, he'd already heard it—but happy memories, heavily embellished. On the first day of the third week, in the idle of the last walk of the day, they had just passed the wreckage of the Ferris Wheel while she was talking about Nathan's hot dogs, when he suddenly stopped.

"Whatsamatta, puddin'?" Harley asked. "Ya gotta pain?"

"Have *I* got a pain?" The Joker drew himself up. "Have I got a *pain*? Oh, I've got *lots* of pains, all over, but worst of all, I've got this one great, big, *enormous* pain. Shall I describe it for you?"

Harley nodded, wide-eyed, as he advanced on her, leaning on the walking stick.

"It's a little over five feet tall, dressed like a harlequin, and when it isn't prattling on about its wretchedly happy childhood, it's asking stupid questions like have I got a pain! If I weren't crazy before, I am now *because my pain is driving me out of my mind!*"

Harley suddenly found herself backed up against a derelict game booth.

"And would you like to know *why* that is?" the Joker asked, suddenly quiet and matter-of-fact, as if they'd just been chatting about the weather. "Well? Would you?" An edge had crept into his voice. "*Would you?*" he bellowed, his face suddenly hideous with fury.

"S-s-sure." Harley nodded, making the bells on her hat jingle. The Joker yanked it off her head and tossed it over his shoulder.

"P-p-p—" she stuttered.

"If the next word out of your mouth is 'puddin','" the Joker said, "I will stab you in the eye *with my finger.*"

"Gotcha, Mr. J," Harley said shakily.

"That's better. Now where was I?" The Joker frowned as if he were concentrating. "Oh, yes—why my biggest pain is driving me out of my mind." He leaned closer. Harley looked to her left and he slammed his hand against the booth next to her head, blocking her so she couldn't sidle away from him. Then he did the same with his other arm.

"My pain is driving me crazy," he began in a dry, lecturing tone, "because it's keeping me in solitary confinement. I have no contact with *anyone* but *it.* It's almost like being back in my cell in Arkham—

"*Only this is worse!*" he screamed into her face. "The food's not as good—when there *is* any food! The bed's a lot harder—because there *is* no bed, *just furniture pads on the floor*! There's no hot shower, just a trickle of cold water from a stand-pipe. *And I don't even want to talk about the toilet facilities but—spoiler alert!—I'm probably going to die of disgustipation!*"

Harley shrank down under his rage until she was sitting on the ground hugging her knees.

"And the punchline to this very unfunny joke is, my pain keeps telling me *how much she loves me! She! Loves! Me!* And I tell myself, *thank God, because I can't imagine what she'd do if she hated me!*"

For a long moment, he loomed over her, panting from the effort of shouting. Harley had covered her head with both arms, waiting to feel a slap or punch. When it didn't come, she finally dared to lower her arms and look up.

The Joker was back on the paved walkway, leaning on his walking stick and gazing at her calmly as if he hadn't just been incandescent with rage.

"Well, my dear Doctor Harley Quinn," he said. "I do believe it's time for more pain medication, as the previous dose seems to have worn off. Shall we?" He jerked his head at her.

She should have known, Harley thought as she scrambled to her feet. Patients always got cranky when they needed pain meds. She hurried over to him but stayed a few inches out of reach as they started home. Just in case his pain got the better of him again.

"Dear, *dear* Doctor Harley Quinn," he said after a few moments, "would you mind terribly letting me lean on you? I'm feeling a bit weak."

Harley hesitated, then moved to his side. He put his arm over her shoulders. Struggling under his weight, she put an arm around his waist for balance.

"Don't do that," he said. "It hurts."

Harley removed her arm. He gave her shoulder an affectionate, possessive squeeze and it was like the last few minutes had never happened. She wouldn't think about that. She would just concentrate on being happy that he was himself again; he was her puddin'. She was so busy concentrating she forgot all about her hat until they got home. No big deal. She'd get it later. Everything was so nice right now; she didn't want to spoil it.

◆

Setting up the internet connection was the beginning of the end.

The Joker was pleased with her for getting them online and very appreciative of the tablet she gave him, although his thanks weren't as effusive as she'd expected. Or hoped. Or thought she deserved, which she tried not to dwell on because she had a much bigger worry—namely, he hadn't wanted an internet connection just so they could watch movies together. She managed to look happy when he gave her the good news that some of his old gang were coming to take them back to a great new hideout in the heart of Gotham City.

"No more camping out in this rehearsal for the end of the world as we know it," the Joker said gleefully. "We'll be able to get decent takeout—and it will still be hot when it arrives!"

"That'll be wonderful," she said, forcing herself to smile and nod.

"It's a new beginning," the Joker said, hugging her absently, exerting pressure he'd claimed was too painful, and then began limping toward the exit.

"Where are you going?" Harley asked in a high, anxious voice.

"To wait for them out front," the Joker replied.

"Bad idea!" Harley caught up to him and blocked his way. "The cops are still looking for us. Someone driving by could see you and call the tip line."

The Joker shrugged her off and kept limping. "The tip line gets thousands of calls. It'll take them a week before they get to that one."

"I don't think so, Mistah J," Harley said. "It's been a month. They won't be getting as many calls now. The cops might show up fast."

The Joker considered this. "You're right," he said finally and shoved his cell phone at her. "Text them and tell them to call for directions when they get to the entrance."

◆

When the gang arrived, there was another vehicle following their rather dirty gray van, an expensive-looking black car with dark tinted windows. The Joker eyed it nervously.

"You didn't bring the FBI along, did you?" he asked one of the henchmen who had spilled out of the van. He was short and squat, wearing a faded dark-green hoodie over a stained T-shirt and jeans he kept having to hitch up every couple of minutes. Harley thought he looked like a fireplug dressed in dirty laundry.

In fact, Harley thought uneasily, *all* the henchmen looked like fire hydrants in clothes, except for a couple of slightly taller ones. They could have been garbage cans. Very full garbage cans.

"Hell, no, boss, we don't roll with G-men!" the guy said. "Just a couple special surprise guests. They wanted to come say hello in person."

The car doors opened and Harley almost fell over with shock.

"Ducky!" March Harriet rushed at Harley with open arms. Poison Ivy approached more sedately, as beautiful and sophisticated as ever if not quite as bored, with even more vines in her hair. Her entire outfit seemed to be made of plants, like a wearable garden. Harriet was still in her Arkham pajamas; she grabbed Harley up in a bear hug, squeezing the breath out of her. Poison Ivy kept her distance and waved one gracefully blasé hand.

"So 'ow's me old china?" Harriet burbled.

"'Me old china'?" Harley said, baffled.

"China plate—mate," Poison Ivy said, exquisitely world-weary again. "Which is British for friend, not spouse. Two countries still divided by a common language."

"*Friend?*" Harley looked from Harriet to Poison Ivy and back again.

"Don't tell me you're holding a grudge, luv," said Harriet.

"Not against me, certainly," Poison Ivy said. "After all I've done for you."

"Oh, that's the God's honest, ducks," Harriet said. "I was quite cross with our Ivy, I was, not lettin' us 'ave our fun with you at the tea party after we'd been waitin' so long. But she said you was actually one of us and everybody knows you don't hurt a mate. I told her she was stuffed full of wild blueberry muffins, didn't I? I did. And then the next thing I hear, you tell Joanie Leland where she can stick the job. And *then*, cor blimey! The very same day, you go bustin' His Nibs out! And look at us now—three peas in a pod, we are!" Harriet bussed her loudly on one cheek and then the other. Poison Ivy rolled her eyes.

"How did you get out?" Harley asked.

"Ah, thereby hangs a tale!" Harriet laughed. "One for another time, I think. Looks like your bloke's gettin' ready to leave. Would you like to ride with us, ducky?"

Harriet was nattering on about three girls going out on the town together as Harley turned to see the Joker climbing into the van. She pulled free of Harriet and rushed over just as a henchman started to slide the door shut.

"Stop! Wait for me! I'm his doctor!" Harley yelled. "I've got his pain pills!"

The Joker's arm shot out and blocked the door. "Didn't you hear her?" he said to the henchman, annoyed. "She's my personal physician. She has my pain pills. Or do you think I *should* be in pain?" The Joker took her hand and pulled her up into the van. Harley had to force her way into a spot close to him, much to the irritation of the surrounding fireplugs.

Tough stuff, boys, she thought. *I outrank you—I'm his soulmate as well as his personal physician. Be nice to me or next time you get shot, I won't even give you a Band-Aid.*

"Uh, can I ask you something?" one of them said to her suddenly.

Harley nodded, making the bells on her hat jingle.

"Don't them bells drive you nuts with the jingle-jingle-jingle all the time?"

"You have *no* idea," the Joker said loudly before Harley could answer. "Do take that off, my dear doctor, before I snap and grab a machine gun."

Harley took off her hat and rolled it up tightly with the bells on the inside.

◆

The famous hideout was a cellar under an abandoned warehouse in one of Gotham's more rundown areas. It wasn't the comfy nest the henchmen had made it out to be, but she had to admit it *was* better than the Tunnel of Love, if only because it had a real bed—a queen-sized mattress in their own private bedroom. Harley felt bad—she had been so wrapped up in nursing the Joker back to health and making sure he knew he was loved, she hadn't registered the discomforts as keenly as he had.

Nonetheless, she was homesick for Happy-Happy Joytown from the moment they left. It was like her natural habitat; she'd felt more solid there, more real, more *Harley*. She knew who she was in an amusement park, even an abandoned one, which was a damned sight more than she could say for a warehouse cellar.

A big part of the problem was no longer having the Joker all to herself. Sometimes he acted as if she *wasn't* the most important person in the world to him. She knew better—he'd said he would be lost without her, and that they'd been destined for each other, just like she did. He'd even said he loved her, and more than once, although not often.

Also not recently, but only because his henchmen were always around. There were more of them now and they weren't all silly-looking fireplugs. The new guys wore suits and ties and always looked annoyed by the fireplugs. They gave her the same look when they thought she couldn't see, which was why she couldn't stand it when the Joker teased her in front of them.

Lately, all her puddin' seemed to do was tease her. She knew he was kidding around—he *was* the Joker, after all. But it was mean, hurtful teasing. Some things he said were so cruel she had to hide in their bedroom so no one would see the tears in her eyes. Maybe she wouldn't have felt so bad if she'd had other women to talk to but Poison Ivy and March Harriet had gone off somewhere else. They'd probably intended to do that all along, which made her glad she hadn't taken Harriet up on her offer of a ride—who knew where she'd have ended up? Certainly far from her puddin', with no idea where he was. But sometimes when his teasing was especially mean, that didn't sound so bad.

The Joker had explained why he had to do that. If the gang saw him showing any softness, even just to her, they'd think it was a sign of weakness, and if they thought he was weak, they'd think they could get away with being disrespectful. Then he'd have to kill them, and finding new henchmen was *such* a *bore.*

"The key to successful gang leadership," he said as she sat on his lap in his office, "is to make sure everybody maintains a profound fear of you. Which is to say, me."

"But *I'm* not afraid of you," Harley said, trying to sound confident rather than uncertain.

"I know you aren't," the Joker purred. "And that's the problem. I can't have you bouncing around here like you can do or say anything you want. I can't have them getting the idea I think of you as an equal."

Harley's jaw dropped. "Is that a joke?"

"Are we laughing?" the Joker asked.

"Well… no."

"Then it's not a joke," he said as his hand tightened on the back of her neck. "If it were, you'd be laughing your head off. Wouldn't you?" He made her nod her head. "Because I'm just that hilarious. Aren't I?" He made her nod again. *"Aren't I?"*

"Yeah, you are." Harley tried to smile but his grip on her neck hurt.

"Good. So let's review, shall we?" He sat back, took his arms from around her, and started ticking points off on his fingers. "No kissy-face, no hugging, no making out except behind closed, *locked* doors. Gang members must fear me, and you'd better start looking a little spooked yourself, as if you never know what I'm going to do from one moment to the next. Because *you don't.* Because we're *not* equals; I'm *always* your superior, and you do as you're told. Am I forgetting anything?"

Harley started to say something but he talked over her.

"Oh, yes. This is my *office.* I do *business* here. You and I *don't* do business—" He shook his legs and she almost fell as she got off his lap. *"So stop pestering me with your stupid girly issues! Get the hell out and don't come back unless I send for you!"*

Harley scrambled for the door.

"Out! Out! Out!" he bellowed as she fumbled with the doorknob.

A mix of suits and fireplugs were hanging around in the next room. Obviously they'd heard everything; they snickered at her as she came out. Harley straightened up, smoothed her clothing, and looked around at them, making her lower lip quiver, as if she were on the verge of tears. It wasn't hard.

"Don't rile him, guys," she said. "He's in a real mood today." She fled to the bedroom as they burst into loud guffaws that sounded nothing like a profound fear of their leader.

On the other hand, she thought as she slammed the bedroom door behind her and locked it, maybe they were covering the fact that they were terrified. She remembered how she'd reacted on the scariest night of her life—she'd burst out laughing. Harley threw herself down on the bed.

Yeah, yuk it up, fellas, she thought. *But he really is in a mood.*

She hoped her puddin' appreciated how supportive she was, although she had the sneaking suspicion he didn't.

♦

When Harley found herself taking a tray of chocolate chip cookies out of the oven, she knew she was dreaming. For one thing, she had never baked cookies, and for another, the hideout didn't have a lovely white stove with a ginormous oven. It didn't even have a kitchen, and certainly not one with sunlight streaming in through windows with a view of an idyllic street somewhere deep in the suburbs.

Harley looked down at herself. She was wearing an immaculate white ruffled apron over a red-and-black house dress and soft red slippers with fuzzy black pom-poms. As she straightened up, she heard bells jingle; the sound made her smile. June Cleaver had done the vacuuming in pearls; Harley Quinn baked cookies with bells on. Maybe if she listened closely, she'd hear a laugh-track.

No, what she heard was children. A little girl was yelling, complaining about her brother who was chasing her around the living room. Harley turned to look. The girl was wearing a smaller version of her harlequin hat, bells and all, and the boy was squirting something at her from a big fake flower on his shirt.

Daddy, daddy! JJ's poisoning me! the girl cried.

And there was her puddin', reading a newspaper in a recliner in the middle of the living room, which was cluttered with partially assembled bombs and a couple of junior-sized chainsaws.

Well, you just poison him right back, cupcake! the Joker said cheerfully. He had a little gray at the temples now and he needed reading glasses, but he was as handsome as ever. He rattled the newspaper; the headline on the front page said

THOUSANDS DIE IN MYSTERIOUS SANITATION EXPLOSION

Her dream-memory told her she and the Joker had done that together, blown up a toilet factory on the day the Quality Control Department were testing a new model.

The gray at the Joker's temples made him look aristocratic, royal even. He was the Clown Prince of Crime, and she was his consort.

Harley's eyes filled with tears of joy. Then she was staring up at the dark ceiling while they ran down her face. She had never been so happy. So what if it was just a dream—the feeling was real. She was so lucky. Most people went their whole lives and never felt half as good, not even in their dreams.

Harley rolled over to put her arm around her puddin', but he wasn't there. She sighed wistfully. He'd be in his office, coming up with a brilliant plan to teach Batman who was boss. She had a strong urge to get up and go to him, bring him a cup of cocoa. Instant cocoa was one of the few things they had in the cupboard, which was actually a cabinet with three shelves and a curtain instead of a door.

No, she couldn't. Mustn't. He'd already told her he couldn't look weak in front of his henchmen. He loved her so much, it wasn't fair to force him to be mean to her for the sake of maintaining his leadership. She didn't want him to be sad, ever.

She found a scrap of paper and a pen, and left a note on his pillow that said WAKE ME.

But he didn't.

Life went on.

And on.

26

Moses parting the Red Sea had nothing on Batman in midtown Gotham City on a busy afternoon. But then, Moses had had to make do with a staff and a little divine help; Batman had the Batmobile.

The Batmobile's engine had a particular sound—not loud, but distinctive, a pitch that cut through traffic noise. People described it variously as "solid," "forceful," "means business." Gotham City mechanics sometimes got customers wanting them to "make my hybrid sound like that." The mechanics suggested playing a recording of the Batmobile while commuting to and from work. (Rumor had it the Batmobile at high speed was the most popular sound-effect recording on Amazon and iTunes.)

Gothamites seldom saw the Batmobile except on the news or YouTube. Most of the videos from the latter were very, very dark— bats and Batman were both nocturnal. So when the Batmobile appeared in broad daylight in midtown Gotham City, traffic on both the street and the sidewalk came to a halt as people pulled out their phones. What they recorded was, for the average innocent bystander, a once-in-a-lifetime event.

Batman ejected from the Batmobile and, at the same time, shot a grappling hook up to the roof of the nearest building. He swung out over the heads of the awestruck pedestrians in front of Katz's Finest Deli (Come In, Have A Nosh), one of whom said she felt the breeze from his cape ruffle her hair. Then he was zipping upward and, when he got to the roof, he disappeared from the view of everyone except the Channel Seven Traffic Copter. For the next two days, they showed the video of Batman racing across rooftops, leaping from one to another until he rappelled down the side of the Cooley Building.

Due to flight restrictions over the city, the Channel Seven helicopter wasn't allowed to circle around for a better look, but it was a thrill for everyone lucky enough to see as much as they did. Other people on the street only got to see the Batmobile drive itself into a private underground garage a block away from Wayne Enterprises, but they were thrilled, too. One person was quoted as saying, "I never realized I had a bucket list until right then. But now I don't know what else to put on it."

◆

Commissioner James Gordon was not thrilled. He was sitting in his dentist's waiting room on the eighth floor of the Cooley Building. As usual, the dentist was running late. Also as usual, the magazines lying around left a lot to be desired. Gordon was starting to wonder if there was some kind of subscription service specifically for dentists' offices that supplied only the dullest, most boring periodicals, and all of them at least five years out of date. Even the *Highlights for Children* magazines were several years old; Gordon knew because he had read them all on his last visit.

Commissioner Goofus complains he's bored waiting for his dental appointment and hates his check-ups. Commissioner Gallant flosses and watches those between-meals snacks, and still has all his own teeth.

Gordon sighed. Damn, he *hated* these check-ups. He didn't like a single thing about them, not even the pretty dental assistant gushing about what great teeth he had, mainly because she kept adding "for a man your age." Well, she didn't look a day over twelve, so what did she know?

Dental Assistant Goofus lets the patient know she thinks he's older than dirt. She should read Highlights for Children Who Are Dental Assistants.

As if on cue, the receptionist looked up and said, "Commissioner Gordon? You're next. It's room fourteen today, last door on the left."

"Swell, thanks," Gordon mumbled as he got up and went through the door marked *Patients—Come In!* Every time he came here, he was struck again by what a big practice it was. He ambled along the hall in no hurry. Last door on the left, the receptionist had said. That didn't bode well. Nothing good ever happened at the last anything on the left. He should turn around right now and leave, pleading a sudden police emergency or a just-remembered prior obligation. An attack of beriberi.

Overwhelming existential dread. Labor pains. Terminator says I must come with him if I want to live.

But they'd charge him for the last-minute cancellation and he'd still have to come back for the check-up. Might as well get it over with, he thought grumpily, and then he'd be done with it for another six months.

Dammit.

He finally reached the end of the hall and door fourteen. He glared at it; unlike the many felons, miscreants, and all-purpose bad guys he had faced over the years at GCPD, door fourteen wasn't the least bit intimidated by him.

Jim Gordon pressed the handle and went in.

◆

"Have a seat. I'll be right with you," the dentist said. He was standing in front of a light-box studying an X-ray. His voice didn't sound familiar. Did they hire someone new? At this rate, they'd need a longer hallway.

"I don't mind saying I really *hate* these check-ups," Gordon said as he eased himself into the dental chair. "If it weren't part of the required police physical, I probably wouldn't come at all."

The dentist was washing his hands at the sink now. "Oh, come now, Commissioner—what in this world is more beautiful than a nice, big, pretty smile!" He spun around, holding a nasty-looking dental pick in one hand, grinning so hugely he showed every tooth in his evil, clown-white face.

"You!" Gordon tried to get out of the chair as the Joker brandished a large and decidedly un-dental drill. Something hit him the chest, exploded into a glittery cloud with a *POP!* and he found himself bound tightly to the chair.

"Naughty, naughty!" Harley Quinn posed cutely in front of the door. She was dressed in a white uniform that was at serious odds with her harlequin hat and clown-white face. "Don't wiggle around like that or doctor won't give you a sugar-free lollipop!"

Gordon opened his mouth to yell for help and she stuffed a large wad of cotton into it. The Joker looked Gordon over, shaking his head.

The Joker tutted. "My, my," he said, stroking his chin thoughtfully as he watched Gordon struggle. "This doesn't look good. This doesn't look good *at all.*"

"Your diagnosis, Doctah J?" Harley Quinn asked in that silly ditz-voice.

"Well," the Joker said, "I'm afraid *everything* will have to go." He turned on the power drill and advanced on Gordon as Harley Quinn reclined the chair. "Hold still now, Commissioner. This is going to hurt. *A lot.*" He knelt on Gordon's chest and aimed the point of the whirring drill at the center of his forehead.

Gordon squeezed his eyes shut. Over the decades, he had been shot, stabbed, beaten up, even tortured, and survived all of it, only to come to this—getting drilled to death by a couple of criminal clowns who had hijacked his dental check-up. If there was such a thing as fate, it had the Joker's sadistic sense of humor. Or maybe fate was the Joker's equally evil twin. That would explain a lot, Gordon thought, unable to breathe under the Joker's weight on his chest.

When he was sure he was dead suddenly there was another explosion and broken glass sprayed everywhere. The Joker got off his chest—*blessed relief!*—and laughed. "You're a little early for your appointment but I'll see you now anyway!"

Gordon opened his eyes. Maybe he was wrong about fate. Either way, he would never get tired of Batman showing up at exactly the right moment.

"It was an easy hint." Batman tossed something at the Joker, who let it fall to the floor. Gordon blinked—it was a pair of chattering false teeth with a tag saying, *To Batman, c/o GCPD.* "Sloppy," Batman said. "Predictable. You're losing your edge."

"'Scuse *me!*" Harley Quinn said huffily. "But the teeth were *my* idea—and so's *this!*" She turned a valve on a gas canister and aimed the hose directly at Batman's face.

Gordon could smell the nitrous oxide—laughing gas. Batman fell to his knees gasping and coughing. There was nothing funny about breathing in that much nitrous all at once. Except to Harley Quinn, who thought it was hilarious.

"Hey, that's a real gasser, ain't it, Mistah J?" she said between giggles.

In the next moment, Gordon thought the nitrous was making him hallucinate as events took a sharp turn into the surreal. The Joker grabbed the floppy points on Harley's hat, pulling her to him so they were nose to nose. "*I* deliver the punchlines around here!" he bellowed into her face. "Got that?"

"Yessir," Harley Quinn said, her voice tiny and fearful.

The Joker shoved her aside and the jolly Clown Prince of Crime persona was back. "Well, Batsie, it's been a hoot as always, but I really *must* run!" He paused at the door to add, "Keep flossing and watch those between-meals snacks!"

Gordon felt something drop into his lap again—a hand grenade, *sans* pin. Before he could panic, Batman swept it up and out the broken window, shielding him from the midair explosion with his cape.

His ears were ringing as Batman removed the wad of cotton from his mouth and cut him free of his bonds.

"Can you stand, Commissioner?" Batman asked, his voice sounding muffled.

Gordon got to his feet slowly, holding onto Batman's arm. "Thanks, old friend, I can stand *up*," he said. "What I can't stand is these damned check-ups."

27

The hideout *du jour* wasn't an abandoned warehouse, for a change. It was a warehouse in use, secretly owned by an organized crime don sympathetic to felons in need of a place to lie low that *wasn't* way out in the middle of nowhere. Besides paying rent, they had to abide by the rules: no body-dumping, no kidnapping, no drug dealing, no fencing stolen loot, or doing anything else that would attract cops. Also: no parties, no smelly cooking, and no fraternizing with warehouse employees.

Harley thought that was a lot of rules for a small space with a jerry-rigged shower and a toilet that took forever to fill after each flush. Not that she wanted to dump a body or throw a party with smelly hors d'oeuvres, but still.

On the upside, this hideout only had room for two. The henchmen had to find their own hideouts, and she had her puddin' all to herself. Although some of the Joker's strategy sessions went on so long, it was like the henchmen were there all the time anyway.

But there hadn't been any meetings for the last few nights. The dental fiasco had put the Joker in a foul disposition. Harley had gone along with ambushing Gordon at the dentist even though she'd been sure there was no chance of it going off the way the Joker imagined—if he *had* imagined anything. Her puddin' had figured out how to get into the dental practice but not how they'd get away afterward. She hadn't even been sure whether he was going to injure Gordon, kidnap him, or kill him. Not unusual—the Joker enjoyed improvising on the fly. Harley just wished he would tell her when they were winging it so she could be ready.

She hadn't dared ask him. The Joker didn't take being questioned or criticized well. And she should have known better than to appropriate a punchline—*he* was the Joker. She was only Harley Quinn.

Meanwhile, the henchmen were all walking on eggshells. The Joker could blow a guy's head off for one wrong word or a funny look. Or if they bored him. Or just because he felt like blowing someone's head off and didn't care whose. Those guys didn't know what it was like to have such a brilliant mind with so many ideas ricocheting around in it. There weren't enough hours in the day to think about all of them, so it was no wonder the Joker got tetchy sometimes. He was a complicated person and only Harley understood him.

As brilliant as he was, though, he was still very much a man, and Harley knew how to help a man unwind and put a smile on his face. She rummaged through her things and found her prettiest little red negligee. Yeah, this would definitely lift his spirits; she put it on, touched up her clown-white, straightened her harlequin hat, and pirouetted out of the screened-off area that served as their bedroom singing about how pretty she felt. The Joker liked her singing voice. (What he'd actually said was: her voice didn't make him want to drive ice picks into his ears. Close enough for jazz.)

Her puddin' was at his desk, which sat atop a raised platform under a light. She worried about him going up and down the stairs because there were no railings and he didn't have a gymnast's balance. But he liked watching her balance. She thought.

Harley danced up the steps to where the Joker was shuffling papers and scribbling notes. He had been at this for ages—time for a break! She cleared her throat. The Joker gave no sign he'd heard her. Sometimes he concentrated so hard, a bomb could go off right beside him and he'd never notice.

Harley climbed up onto the desk and struck the pose her gymnastics teacher had told her was graceful but just a bit too sexy for regular competition.

"Ahem," she said, low and throaty.

The Joker didn't look up. "Go 'way. I'm busy."

"Aw, c'mon, puddin'," she said. "Doncha wanna rev up your Harley? Vroom, vroom!" She gunned an invisible motorcycle. The Joker made a sharp gesture with one arm and she tumbled off the desk onto the floor.

"Oopsie!" she sang, popping up beside him. "C'mon, sweetie—I've got the whoopee cushion!"

The Joker gave a long, put-upon groan. "Listen, *cupcake*," he said, taking her chin in one hand. "Daddy's got a lot of work to do and you're not helping." His features twisted up with rage as he yelled into her face. "Just like you weren't helping with that *stupid teeth-chattering gag!*" He shoved her away as he got up and began pacing.

"Well, hey—" Harley got off the desk to follow him. "You don't like the teeth? Then *forget* the teeth! I can do better."

"Oh, no-no-no-no-*no*." The Joker glared at her. "I let you collaborate *once* and you *blew it*, little girl. That set-up was *corny*—old hat! Unworthy of my genius!"

"*I* thought it was funny," Harley mumbled. *And it got Batman to show up like he was supposed to*, she added silently.

The Joker shook his head. "It's time I capped off this running feud with a real corker," he said. "The ultimate humiliation of Batman. Followed by his deliciously delirious *death!*" He went back to the desk and began shuffling through the papers again. "There's got to be something in here I can use—something really funny!"

Harley shrugged. "Why doncha just *shoot* him and be done with it?"

The Joker slowly straightened up and turned to look at her through narrowed eyes. "'Just shoot him'? Is that what you said— '*Just shoot him*'?"

Me and my big mouth, Harley thought as the Joker stalked toward her.

"Know *this*, my sweet," he snarled, looming over her the way he always did when he was especially angry. "The death of Batman must be nothing less than a *masterpiece!*" Something squirted out of the flower in his lapel and Harley ducked just in time. It hit the dartboard with Batman's picture on it behind her and ate holes in it with a ghastly hissing noise.

"It must be *the triumph* of my comic genius over Batman's *ridiculous* mask and gadgets!" The Joker suddenly ran back to the desk and spread out a roll of paper. "Aha! The Death of a Hundred Smiles! Yes, it's perfect!"

Harley followed, hanging back so as not to get hit accidentally when he gesticulated. He was having another one of his energy surges. (She refused to call them manic episodes; her puddin' wasn't manic. He was a genius with higher-than-average energy levels.)

"I'll lure Batman to some remote, out-of-the-way place," the Joker was saying. "And when he least expects it—BANG!" He swung his fist, narrowly missing the side of Harley's head as she ducked. "A hidden trapdoor drops him into my specially prepared piranha tank!" He danced around, hugging the plans to his chest and laughing gleefully. "The last thing Batman will see is all those beautiful, hungry smiles as they tear into his flesh and—"

He cut off and all the joy drained out of his face. "Oh. Wait. *Now* I remember why I scrapped that one."

Harley peered at him anxiously, afraid to say something and afraid not to.

"Piranhas can't smile," he said, mournful and dispirited. "All those razor-sharp teeth are turned down in a permanent frown. Even my own Joker-toxin couldn't make them grin."

He tossed the plan away and sat down at the top of the steps. "Alas, bitter jest of fate!" he wailed, looking heavenward and shaking one fist dramatically. "My greatest death-trap shot to *squadoo*! All because I couldn't make those vicious little guppies smile." He lowered his head and slumped, the very picture of dejection.

Harley couldn't stand to see him that way. She cuddled up next to him and took him in her arms. "*I* know how to make some smiles, puddin'," she said in a playful, sultry voice.

His whole body stiffened under her touch.

"Puddin'?" But she knew it was hopeless; she'd done the wrong thing again.

A moment later, he was leading her down the stairs by her nose, pinching it so hard between his thumb and forefinger that she cried out on every step.

"Ow-ow-ow-ow-ow! That *hurts*! It really, really hurts! Please, puddin'—"

He pinched even harder as he led her to the door, opened it, then turned her around. "How many times do I have to tell you?" he roared, applying his foot to her backside. "*Don't call me puddin'!*"

Harley scrambled to her feet just as he slammed the door in her face. She started to beg him to let her in but suddenly all the fight went out of her and she sank down to sit cross-legged in front of the door. Thrown out again; how many times was this? She'd lost count.

No, she hadn't. This was the twenty-fifth time.

That averaged out at roughly three times a week for the past two months. She was lucky the weather was still warm. She'd better remember to wear her flannel onesie when it turned cold.

Who the hell *did* that? Who kicked a young blonde hottie out of bed before they even got into bed?

"Face it, Harl," she sighed. "This stinks out loud."

It did, too. She'd gone to college on a full gymnastics scholarship, and Gotham Med School had funded her with grants. She was the youngest psychiatrist ever hired at Arkham Asylum. And how had that worked out?

She was wanted by the law in two dozen states.

Okay, the career wasn't going so well. What about her personal life?

She was hopelessly in love with a murderous psychopathic clown. Who had just kicked her out—literally—for the twenty-fifth time.

"What happened to me?" she said aloud. "What made my life crazier than a—a freakin' March Harriet?"

Her throat tightened and tears began to well in her eyes as she looked up into the dark night overhead.

The dark night.

Abruptly the urge to cry was replaced by a much stronger urge to punch someone. Someone in particular: the dark knight. Batman.

Of course it was Batman—who else? It was *always* Batman, chasing her and her puddin', spoiling everything, ruining date night, making the Joker so crazy that he took everything out on her.

Batman, whose life was so empty he was obsessed with ruining theirs. Everyone kept saying her puddin' was psychotic. But what did you call a man who dressed up like a bat for the express purpose of harassing a couple in love—well-adjusted? Ready for primetime? *Not* crazy as a shithouse bat?

Yeah, that was how they rolled in Gotham City, the world's biggest cult, where everyone was brainwashed to worship Batman and hate anybody he hated. Anyone who didn't was declared criminal or crazy and ended up in Iron Heights or Arkham Asylum while Batman flitted around town, cosplaying and ego-tripping.

Harley sat for a while until she didn't hear any more movement from inside. Then she picked up a broken chunk of cement on her left; the spare key was right where she'd left it. Harley quietly let herself back in and tiptoed up the steps to where the Joker had fallen asleep at his desk with his head pillowed on his arms.

Poor puddin', she thought. He stirred, muttered "Batman" grumpily and subsided.

Harley shook her head. Crazy wasn't just contagious, it was also cumulative; she had to do something about Batman before he drove the Joker so far out of his mind he never found his way back.

She began picking up all the papers on the floor and came across the Death of a Hundred Smiles. Harley loved the name; it sounded significant, historical even, like something devised by an ancient master of execution.

She was about to roll it up when she saw she was holding it upside down.

◆

"This came in an hour ago." Commissioner Gordon held out a small square package in black-and-red gift wrap.

"Addressed to you," Harvey Bullock added.

Batman looked it over carefully. His gloves would protect him from any caustic or acidic substances, but if it released poison gas, the other two men would be at risk. Bullock would probably shake off any ill effects—the man was built like a tank. He didn't move fast but he could withstand a lot of punishment. Jim Gordon wasn't delicate but he was older, and it had only been a few days since the Joker had tried to kill him.

That had been only the latest of many attempts on Gordon's life. His friendship with Batman made him a target. A lesser man might have retired early and left town with no forwarding address. Jim Gordon refused to be intimidated by anyone, whether it was a homicidal maniac like the Joker; or a new mayor who wanted his own stooges in key positions in the city government; or the corrupt and wealthy families who were used to buying anyone they wanted.

After this last incident, Jim Gordon would merely be less inclined to get his teeth cleaned. But then, he would use any excuse to get out of going to the dentist, anyway.

Batman unwrapped the package to reveal a DVD in a plain white sleeve. "I guess it's movie night," he said. "Did anyone make popcorn?"

Harvey Bullock looked grumpy as he turned on the TV and DVD player. "You hadda say 'popcorn,' didn't you. Now I got a craving." Batman suppressed a smile. When it came to food, Bullock was the most suggestible person he knew.

Harley Quinn appeared on the TV screen in full costume and make-up. But she wasn't smiling.

"I hope this message reaches Batman before it's too late." She spoke not in her usual exaggerated Brooklyn accent but in what had to be her normal voice. It was shockingly un-ditsy. Batman and Gordon traded glances.

"I know you won't believe me," Harley went on, "but it's *no joke,* I *swear.* Mr. J's gone off his nut, and I mean *for real.*" She took a breath and leaned slightly closer to the camera. "After you stopped him from killing the commissioner, he swore he'd get even—not just with you but with the whole city. He's going to wipe out everybody! I've seen the plans. There are gas bombs, nerve agents—horrible things! At rush hour tomorrow morning, Gotham becomes one great, big, grinning ghost town!"

Bullock hit the pause button. "You think she's on the level?" he asked Gordon.

Gordon shrugged. "Let's hear the rest."

Bullock pressed play and all three men were shocked when Harley Quinn took off her harlequin hat, shook out her hair, and wiped her face clean of clown white. They'd all known who she really was, but it was shocking all the same. The last time Batman had seen her without make-up, she had been kneeling on the floor at Arkham Asylum, holding the Joker in her arms and glaring up at him with a mad, murderous rage more characteristic of a patient than a doctor.

After she had broken the Joker out of Arkham, Batman had talked to Joan Leland. At first Dr. Leland had been reluctant to say anything—the scandal was pretty embarrassing. No doubt she'd have lost her job if the Arkham board had been able to find anyone willing to take it.

When she did finally open up, Batman saw she was as bewildered as anyone else as to how such an intelligent young woman with so much promise could throw it away for a criminally insane murderer. Dr. Leland said it might well be paranoid schizophrenia; Harleen was at the upper end of the age range for women who usually develop it, but not too old to rule it out. In some cases, the onset was so slow and gradual, it wasn't caught for years, especially in a place like Arkham. Behavior that would raise flags anywhere else was business as usual there. Harleen's exposure to the Joker could have exacerbated any undiagnosed illness. But constant contact with him might have caused her to have a psychotic break even if she'd been perfectly sane. The Joker could have that effect on people.

If so, the effect seemed to have worn off, and not a moment too soon. "I finally realize this isn't funny anymore," Harleen Quinzel was saying, and her voice trembled. "No, I'm wrong—this was *never* funny. I feel like I've been—I don't know, stuck in some kind of weird place, some strange alternate dimension where everything was all warped and bent. But then suddenly I woke up back in the real world and now I can see clearly—I can see things as they really are. All the damage he'll do, all the people he'll kill. Unless you stop him, Batman."

She swallowed hard and closed her eyes for a second. Then she took a steadying breath and looked directly at the camera again. "I can help you get him but you have to promise to protect me. If you truly want to save this city, come alone to pier sixteen at the port of Gotham tonight at midnight. I'll hand over everything—complete details of the plot, the timetable, where to find the weapons—but only to you. It has to be you, Batman. You're the only one he's afraid of. You're the only one who can stop him. If you don't—" she shook her head. "It's too horrible to think about."

The screen went dark and, for a long moment, no one spoke.

"You heard her, Jim," Batman said finally. "I have to go alone. If she sees anyone else, she'll panic. The Joker's had her under his control. Somehow she's managed to snap herself out of it but she's shaky. If she sees cops, she's liable to fall back into her old state of mind."

"I don't see how she wised herself up after all that," Harvey Bullock said. "She don't look strong enough to argue about what's for dinner."

"Looks can be deceiving, Harvey," said Batman. "Maybe the Joker's plan for mass murder on such a grand scale was just too much for her and gave her the jolt she needed to come back to *this* planet. We have to treat her gently, cautiously. She's a lot like someone who's just escaped from a cult. If she gets spooked, she'll fall back into her old mindset."

"At least wear an earpiece so we can stay in touch," Gordon said.

Batman nodded. "Just make sure you stay out of sight."

28

At ten minutes to midnight, on the roof of the main building in the port of Gotham, Batman finally broke radio silence. "Jim," he said quietly, resisting the urge to touch his earpiece.

"Go ahead, Batman." Gordon sounded on edge.

"I've been here since ten thirty looking for hidden traps, henchmen, or any other nasty surprises," Batman told him. "So far, nothing."

"Any sign of her?" Gordon asked.

"Speak of the devil," Batman replied as a shadow moved out of the surrounding darkness to stand in a circle of dim yellow light in the middle of the pier—a slender young blonde woman wearing a raincoat and carrying a briefcase. "On time, all alone, and looking pretty scared. Going dark."

Which was a funny way to say he was going radio silent again, Batman thought; he was always dark.

◆

"You have some information for me?" Batman asked quietly.

Harleen Quinzel jumped and turned around, one hand pressed to her chest. "Oh, my!" she said breathily. "S-sure. It's all right here, just like I said." She held up the briefcase.

She really was tiny, Batman thought, just like a gymnast. "Open it," he told her.

She blinked up at him, momentarily baffled. "Oh! Of course! You're thinking booby trap, right?" She gave a small nervous laugh as she opened the case and showed him the papers inside. "I don't blame you, considering."

Batman took out a couple of papers. They looked like schematics for something but the light was too poor to see them clearly.

"So, is that okay?" she asked, her voice hopeful.

"I want Jim Gordon to take a look at these. If what you say is true, the police will have to mobili—"

"*TRAITOR!*" roared a familiar voice from somewhere out on the water.

"Oh, no—noooooo!" Harleen Quinzel wailed.

Even in the bad light, Batman could see the Joker standing up in the approaching motorboat. He was holding a machine gun.

"*Nobody* turns stoolie on me and lives, do you hear? *Nobody!*" The Joker laughed maniacally and began firing.

"*Down!*" Batman dived for the weather-beaten wooden planks, pulling Quinzel with him and shielding her with his body. In the back of his mind, he was wondering how the Joker could have gotten so close without his hearing a motor. Still shielding Quinzel, he slipped a batarang out of his utility belt and whipped it toward the Joker. It put a stop to both the laughter and the shooting by taking his head clean off.

Batman leaped to his feet and saw the Joker's head rolling around in the bottom of the boat as sparks sprayed from his neck. A *robot*? He was turning toward Harleen Quinzel when he felt a sudden sharp pain in the side of his neck and fell to his knees. Papers flew out of the open briefcase and scattered on the pier around him, magazine pages, takeout menus, flyers.

Fingers dug under the side of his cowl, found his earpiece, and yanked it out. "Sweet dreams, suckah," she said in her ditz-voice.

◆

The Brooklyn accent that had followed Batman down into darkness now led him up out of it.

"Lemme see, his arms are double-bound, ditto his legs—"

He tried to say something but could only produce a wordless groan.

"—took off the belt, triple checked all my knots and locks—"

There was something wrong with his head; all his weight seemed to be pressing against the very top of his skull. It was an effort to open his eyes, and when he did, nothing he saw made sense. Light fixtures stuck up from the floor and there was furniture on the ceiling. Barstools dangled around a bar where a tank was filling with water. There were some weird little shadows wiggling around in it. But the tank was hanging upside down from the ceiling—the water shouldn't have stayed in it.

A familiar, clown-white face floated into view, bells on two floppy points jingling cheerfully, also upside down.

"Harley... Quinn..." Batman groaned.

"Oh, you're awake!" she squealed. "Finally! Gee, that knockout drug really hit ya hard!" She stood back and gestured. "But you been hanging upside down for a while." She drank something purple from a bottle. Grape soda? "All that blood rushing to your head's gonna make you a little logy. Or a lot." She leaned back and gave him a long up-and-down look. Or a down-and-up look. "Yeah, you won't get outta this one."

Batman fixed his gaze on a spot on the opposite wall while his inner ear tried to decide which way was up. "The Joker," he managed after a bit. "Where—"

"Not this time, B-man," Harley Quinn said cheerfully. "No Joker, no gas-bombs, no city in peril—just you, that tank, and me."

The spot on the wall resolved itself into an upside-down, very distinctive swordfish. He was in Aquacade, Gotham City's premiere seafood restaurant. Reservations were hard to come by. Unless you didn't mind hanging from the ceiling after the place was closed.

"I want ya to know I went to a lot of trouble to pull this off," Harley was saying in her annoying put-on ditz-voice. "Not only did I have to drag your carcass up to this place all by myself, but—" She gestured at the tank. "I had to raid every fish collector and aquarium in town to get enough piranhas for this stunt. And I *hate* fish! *Ick!*"

Had she just said *piranhas*? "Then why bother?" Batman asked.

"To show Mr. J I could pull off one of his gags!" As if she were a Girl Scout going for a merit badge. "It's called 'The Death of a Hundred Smiles,' which has to be the best title for anything, *ever*. Mr. J gave up on it 'cause he couldn't get the piranhas to smile."

Yes, she'd said piranhas, all right, Batman thought. Unless he was dreaming, but that was entirely too much to hope for.

"But then, *I* had the bright idea of hanging the victim—which is to say, *you*, Batsie—upside down. That way, it'll look to you like they're all smiling! Pretty clever, huh?"

"Brilliant," Batman said flatly. "Genius."

Harley Quinn shrugged, laughing at him. "Okay, so you're less than thrilled. I don't blame ya. But for what it's worth, this ain't *poisonal*."

"You mean 'personal'?" He had to keep her talking, Batman thought.

"That's what I said: *poisonal*." Harley Quinn made a face at him. "Anyway, I actually enjoyed this little romp, ya know? But the time comes when a gal wants more from life. And what *this* gal wants now is to settle down with her puddin'." She sighed and Batman could practically see cartoon hearts and Cupids dancing in the air around her head.

"You mean you and the Joker?" Batman said.

"Right-a-rooney!" Harley Quinn sang gleefully.

It was too much. Batman burst out laughing, making his whole body shake and sway over the tank.

"I never heard you laugh before," Harley said uneasily, raising her voice to make herself heard. "I don't like it."

245

Batman laughed even harder.

"Cut it out!" she yelled. "Yer givin' me the creeps!"

After another fifteen seconds or so, Batman let himself wind down. "Harley, you're such a fool. The Joker doesn't love anyone or anything except himself."

"That's not true!" she snapped.

"Oh, please," Batman said. "The moment you set foot in Arkham, the Joker had you pegged as hired help."

"*No!*" she yelled. "You're a big fat liar. He told me things about himself—secret things, things he never told anyone else!"

"Like what?" Batman gave a short laugh. "His abusive father or his alcoholic mom? Or was it the runaway orphan routine—that's a tearjerker, very moving. He's gets a lot of sympathy with that one."

"Stop it!" Harley started to cry. "You're making me confused!"

"I'm trying to remember what he told that one parole officer years ago—oh, yeah. 'There was only one time I ever saw Dad *really* happy. He took me to the ice show when I was seven—'"

Tears ran down Harley Quinn's cheeks, leaving flesh-colored trails in the clown white. "He said it was the circus," she said in a small voice.

"Circus, ice show, carnival, puppet show—he's got a million of them, Harley," Batman said. "And like any other comedian, he tailors the material to his audience—he reads the room and goes with whatever he thinks will work best."

"No!" Harley screamed at him. "You're wrong! My puddin' loves me. *He loves me! You're* the problem! Always tryin' to come between us. We could be happy if it weren't for *you!* But now you're gonna *die* and we'll live *happily ever after!*"

"Oh, sure," Batman said. "Except he'll never believe *you* did it."

"He will so!" Harley Quinn squeaked with outrage. "I'm gettin' it on video!" She pointed at the video-camera set up on a tripod a few feet away.

"It's easy to fake a video these days—even a baby could do it," said Batman. *"Think*, Harley. How will the Joker know you *really* killed me? There won't be any hard evidence—the only things these fish'll leave are some scraps of cloth and a few bone shards. Those could have come from anything. Well, okay, you *do* have my belt—but that's not the same as my body. Sorry, but you'll *never* prove you killed me—not to *him*."

"We'll just see about that!" Harley Quinn told him and pulled out a cell phone. "I'll show *you*."

◆

Nothing on his desk looked good to him, and it was making the Joker question himself in a profound way. What if this were more than a creative dry spell—what if he'd really lost it?

Since his escape from Arkham, he should have been wreaking high-powered, big-league havoc on Gotham City, the kind that made all good citizens quake in their shoes and hide under their beds, freaking out over what might happen next. But he couldn't come up with a single new earth-shaking idea. And when he looked to his old ideas for inspiration, he saw nothing of his comic genius. It all looked lame and boring, clichéd. There was nothing that hadn't already been done. None of it was funny, it was all just crap that was too silly, too "Riddler"—that *hack*—or just plain unworthy of him.

How could this be? He used to dream up comic gems with every other breath. Being on the lam had never interfered with his creative process and this wasn't the first time he'd escaped—

Only he hadn't, he realized suddenly. *He* hadn't escaped from Arkham; Harley Quinn had broken him out. No wonder things were all wrong—she'd taken his mojo! *He* was supposed to call the shots but she'd turned him into her second banana.

Harley Quinn definitely had to go.

The phone rang, shattering his focus. He hated cell phones with a passion but Harley insisted they have them—another example of how she was calling the shots! He'd get rid of her and the phone, too. Just as soon as he found wherever it was hiding under the papers on his desk. When he finally got his hands on it, he was surprised to see what appeared on the screen.

♥ ♥ HARLEY ♥ ♥

Why would she call him when she was here? Or she was supposed to be—

"Harley, where the heck are you?" he asked impatiently.

Seconds later he was running for the car. He had a vague memory of Harley saying they couldn't use that car anymore because the cops had a BOLO on it. But she didn't tell him what to do anymore.

He could just imagine what the rest of the criminal world would say if this got out, the Joker thought as he roared through the empty nighttime streets. The Penguin: *There goes the Joker—you know, the guy whose girlfriend killed Batman!* And Two-Face: *I never thought he was that funny to begin with.* Worst of all, the Riddler would rub it in every time they met: *Well, hello, uh—what's your name again? Oh, right—Mr. Harley Quinn!*

That *hack.*

♦

"*Now* you'll see, Mr. Smarty-Bat," Harley said gleefully. "When I told Mr. J what I was doing, he was so thrilled, he couldn't even speak! He's on his way over right now to watch me feed you to the fish. And then—" She gave a long, happy sigh as her mind filled with joyful images of their happy-ever-after: wedding, explosions, children, holidays, more explosions, and then their golden years, when they would still be madly in love.

"HAAAAAAARRRRRRRLLLLLLLEEEEEEEY!"

She jumped up from where she'd been sitting in front of the piranha tank on the bar and ran toward the Joker with open arms. "Puddin'! You're just in time to see—"

Everything disappeared in a blast of blinding pain, as if a flashbang had hit her in the face. It hurt so much she was barely aware of hitting the floor.

After a moment, she sat up, holding the side of her face, which was now throbbing. Had Batman gotten loose and hit her? No, he was still hanging over the fish tank.

"Hello, Batman," the Joker said conversationally.

"Evening," said Batman, as if he weren't about to die the Death of a Hundred Smiles.

"'Scuse me," the Joker told him. "I'll just be a minute."

"Take your time. No hurry," Batman replied. "I'll wait here."

29

Harley watched in disbelief as the Joker stalked toward her in a full-on fury. She had run to hug him and he had backhanded her, she realized. Why would he do that? Tears welled up in her eyes.

"I don't understand, puddin'," she said. "Don't you *wanna* finally get rid of Batman?"

"Only if *I* do it, you idiot!" the Joker roared at her. "Batman is *mine*! You have *no right* to come between us!"

Harley had stashed the blueprints of the plan up her sleeve; she was shaking as she took it out and unrolled it. "B-b-but it's still y-y-your p-p-p-plan. Everything's j-j-just like y-you want!" The Joker snatched the paper away from her. "A-all I d-did was hang B-b-batman upside down so he'd see their little p-p-p-piranha frowns as little smiles! Now it works how it's supposed to—"

The Joker tore the plan to shreds in a frenzy, then jumped up and down on the pieces. "You had to *explain it!*" he railed at her. "If you have to explain the joke, *There! Is! No! Joke!*"

Harley scrambled backward as the Joker came at her. Veins were popping out in his neck, his forehead, everywhere.

"*My* jokes are elegant in their *simplicity!*" the Joker bellowed, reaching for her with his fingers bent like claws, like he was going to rip her to pieces, too. "You *see* them, you *get* them, you *laugh*— *End! Of! Joke!*"

Harley spotted a swordfish hanging on the nearest wall. She

pulled it down and held it in front of herself.

The Joker ignored it. "You should've remembered what I told you a long time ago," he raged. "One of the few real truths of comedy!"

"N-n-now, c-c-calm down, p-puddin'." She raised the swordfish in defense.

Instead of flinching, the Joker tore it out of her hands by the sword part and walloped her with the fish body. "You always take shots from people who *just don't get the joke!*"

Harley put her arms up to deflect the blows and staggered backward into a giant floor-to-ceiling window. Most windows in commercial buildings weren't easily broken; she fully expected to bounce off it. Then the Joker would probably skewer her with her own swordfish. God, she hated fish.

Unfortunately, this particular window shattered on impact. Harley found herself sailing out into the night before she could think to scream.

◆

The Joker grinned. Here he'd just been thinking Harley had to go and—*voila!*—she was gone. Sometimes things just worked themselves out.

He tossed the swordfish out the broken window after her. "And don't call me puddin'," he added, observing another cardinal rule of comedy: always get the last word.

◆

"I have to apologize for the kid," the Joker was saying as he lowered Batman to the bar in front of the fish tank. Batman could see it was a real struggle for him. He'd been locked up in Arkham for so long, he was badly out of shape. He wasn't getting any younger, either.

"She's like a lot of young people these days," the Joker went on. "No style, no sense of propriety. Tell you what, Batsie—let's just pretend tonight never happened. Sound good to you?"

"Sounds great," said Batman. The Joker finally managed to lay him out on the bar. Distant noises coming from outside indicated the cops had arrived. The Joker didn't seem to hear them; apparently he was also getting a little deaf in his old age. That was the downside of being a criminal: no health insurance, worker's comp, or retirement plan. Criminals never thought about that sort of thing. But then, as Alfred had noted, no sensible person was wanted in two dozen states.

"Okay, we're done here! See ya!" The Joker patted Batman's cheek affectionately and headed for the exit.

Batman had just managed to slide off the bar into a standing position when the Joker suddenly stopped and turned back to him, a nasty smile spreading slowly across his face. "On the other hand, this *is* a rather *rare* opportunity," he said, coming back toward him. "How does that old saying go—a bat in the hand is worth two in the belfry?"

The Joker pushed Batman down on the bar, bending him backward so his feet dangled inches above the floor. "Whaddaya know, Batsie!" Laughing maniacally, he whipped out a handgun and pressed the muzzle against the part of the cowl covering his nose. "Looks like you're going out on a laugh after all!"

Batman brought his legs up in a sudden sharp motion just as the Joker pulled the trigger. The shot missed Batman completely and hit the fish tank. The world's most dangerous waterfall cascaded down on both of them.

Free of the Joker, Batman made it to the nearby table where Harley had tossed his utility belt. He could hear the Joker cursing furiously as he slipped and fell amid the piranhas flapping around on the floor. Piranhas weren't quite as scary out of water but apparently some of them were determined to get a few last bites before their demise.

"Very funny, Batm—ow! OW!" The Joker tried to shake off a couple of piranhas that had clamped themselves onto his fingers. "Ow! Real friggin' funny, Batman. You must think *you're* a comedian—ow, ow *ow!*"

Batman freed himself from his last chain just as the Joker got to his feet and ran for the exit; Jim Gordon and Harvey Bullock were already there to meet him.

The Joker reached into his jacket. "Look out!" Bullock yelled. "He's going for his—fish?"

There was a piranha in the Joker's hand instead of a pistol. He slapped Bullock with it and ran.

♦

Knowing that cops were coming up the stairs and more cops had the building surrounded would have convinced most criminals to give up. The Joker took the stairs two at a time to the roof.

Batman burst through the access door to see him poised on the brick ledge, looking a bit like a diver on the high board. There was a storage building across the way and the distance was plainly impossible even for someone in top condition, but the Joker was going to try anyway. Batman took a step toward him and started to say it was suicide when he sprang off the ledge, his arms windmilling and his legs pedaling air.

Batman rushed to the ledge and was astonished to see the Joker hadn't missed by much—he was hanging from an iron railing on the edge of the storage building roof. Before he could even try to pull himself up, however, the railing broke off under his weight.

Laughing exuberantly, the Joker landed on the roof of a passing elevated train. "Made you look!" he jeered as it carried him away. Batman paid no attention; he was already heading for another part of the roof. He knew this section of track much better than the Joker did.

◆

The Joker was obviously having the time of his life. He put his thumbs in his ears and waggled his fingers, blew raspberries, thumbed his nose, and blew more raspberries. When he finally began to wind down, Batman spoke up from his position behind him: "She almost had me, you know," he said.

A mix of disbelief and fury twisted the Joker's features as he whirled to look at Batman.

"My arms and legs were chained," Batman went on conversationally, or as much as it was possible atop a moving train. "My belt was gone. I was dizzy from the blood rushing to my head—I was pretty helpless. I had no way out other than convincing her to call you."

The Joker swayed but kept his balance. All he needed was a little push.

"Your massive ego would never allow anyone else to have the 'honor' of killing me," said Batman, making air quotes. "Though I have to admit, *she* came a lot closer than *you* ever did." Pause. *"Puddin'."*

He practically saw the Joker's mind explode, vaporizing the last remnants of sanity. His wide, bloodshot eyes were wild as he leaped for Batman and closed his fists around his neck. Batman clapped both hands over the Joker's ears and the Joker threw an elbow at his face.

Batman let the momentum of the blow take him backward only far enough to give him room for a savate kick to the Joker's face. The Joker was so crazed now, he didn't seem to feel it. He threw several wild punches that Batman evaded easily, before he suddenly produced a knife.

Some idiot always brings a knife to a fistfight, Batman thought and slammed the Joker's wrist down on his knee. His fingers opened and the Joker tried to grab the knife with his other hand. It was a stupid move, and his last one of the night. Thrown off-balance, the Joker pitched over the side.

"*Noooooooooo!*" he screamed. "*Nooootttt aaaagggaaaaiiinnnnn!*"

He disappeared into thick clouds of black smoke from a factory chimney.

A few seconds later, Batman jumped to a different train going the other way. As he passed the factory again, he saw no sign of a body.

30

"...and although his body has not yet been found, in the chimney or anywhere else in or near the factory, it seems unlikely that Gotham's Clown Prince of Crime could have survived his latest brush with Batman."

Harley sat in the wheelchair, watching the flat-screen TV in Arkham's remodeled admissions waiting room through a fog of pain medication and regret. She'd never had so much of either.

The policewoman who had found her lying in a pile of trash seven stories below Aquacade had been so gentle, telling her not to move, help was on the way, and everything was going to be all right. Her soft voice had brought tears to Harley's eyes. She couldn't remember the last time anyone had treated her with such kindness.

Harley never got her name, never even saw her face clearly. She'd tried to explain it was her own fault for not getting the joke. But the woman told her not to worry about anything, they were going to help her.

"Still, the Joker has been known for resurfacing when least expected," the TV went on. "Time will tell."

Time will tell. One of those all-occasion clichés people used to sound like they were saying something while saying nothing. *Time will tell.* Harley closed her eyes.

How long had she been waiting for an orderly to take her to her room? Time would tell. And there weren't any rooms in Arkham, only cells. The people in them were called *patients* instead of *prisoners*. But they knew where they were, and what they were. They were crazy, not stupid.

How long would she occupy a cell here? Time would tell.

And vice versa, Harley thought. She could tell time, and the current time was Never Again.

No more obsession, no more craziness, no more Joker; Never Again. She could finally see that freakin' slime ball for what he was. It had taken a seven-story fall to knock some sense into her, but all her broken bones would heal and all her bruises would fade; that had been Better-Late-Than-Never O'Clock. Followed by Never Again.

The orderly finally arrived to wheel her to her cell and she opened her eyes. She didn't recognize him, which was a relief. Finally she saw the upside of the higher-than-average turnover among the orderlies. He was gentle as he helped her from the chair into the bed, and made sure she was comfortable.

I'll serve my time peacefully, she thought as he poured her a glass of water and put it on her tray table. *I'll heal myself and I'll get out of here to begin a new life, a better life. I will. I will.*

He left without closing her door. Harley wondered if he was coming back. Then Joan Leland appeared in the doorway.

"I really hope you've learned a lesson from all this," Dr. Leland said.

Where was a nice policewoman when you really needed one, Harley thought, her misery deepening.

"To think you were once so strong, so sure of yourself." Dr. Leland's expression was stern, and Harley supposed she couldn't blame her. She wanted to tell Dr. Leland that she knew what time it was—Never Again—but she was pretty sure the woman was too busy telling her off to appreciate her insights.

"Tell me," Dr. Leland went on, "how does it feel to have been so dependent on a man that you gave up everything for him and got nothing in return?"

She turned her face away so she wouldn't have to see her ex-boss scowling while she waited for Harley to admit she'd been so wrong and Dr. Leland was always right about everything. "It felt like—" she began.

And then she saw it, on the nightstand beside the bed: a single, perfect red rose in an elegant bud vase, with a note:

Feel better soon —J

In spite of everything, she welled up with tears of ineffable joy.

"It felt like a kiss," Harley murmured, smiling, unaware that Dr. Leland had left.

31

As lovely as a kiss may be, the memory will eventually fade. That's just how life is. Good, bad, or indifferent, nothing lasts forever and, in the end, memories are the most ephemeral things of all.

Although some memories do last a very long time. The memory of a seven-story fall, for example, will stay with a person a lot longer than the memory of a kiss.

Or, for that matter, the memory of something that felt like a kiss.

♦

Healing from trauma is a long, complex process. Three important parts of the process are: a) remembering, b) forgetting, and c) knowing what goes in column a and what goes in column b.

Another important part of healing is understanding the true meanings of things. For instance, take the word "asylum." Many people associate the word with an institution for the mentally ill or others requiring special care. But asylum-seekers are looking for a safe place, a refuge from privation, persecution, and fear—a haven, a sanctuary, a shelter. An asylum can be all these things, even Arkham Asylum, as Harleen Quinzel discovered during her time as a patient.

◆

Joan Leland insisted on treating Harley herself. Harley wasn't sure about that at first; having a former boss ask her every day if she'd learned her lesson wasn't terribly appealing. But it turned out to be nothing like that at all.

Harley asked Dr. Leland to take her off the heavy-duty pain meds right away but the doctor refused. She would wean Harley off the medication when she felt the time was right. A few days after her arrival at Arkham was not the right time.

She told Dr. Leland about treating the Joker with extra-strength ibuprofen. Dr. Leland had told her that a beating from Batman was a cake-walk next to a seven-story fall and suggested she try to think of it as falling out of love with the Joker. It wasn't a bad idea but Harley knew nothing was *that* straightforward.

Sometimes she woke up feeling self-possessed, strong, free of the Joker's influence and sure she'd stay that way. The feeling might last for days, long enough that she would begin to think, very cautiously, about the future. But then she'd be ambushed by the certainty that her life was empty and she'd spend the rest of it marking time until she died. She couldn't even turn to her memories for comfort because the happiest ones were of being in the Joker's sub-sub-sub-sub-basement cell, believing she was changing his life for the better with ground-breaking therapy.

They shouldn't have been her happiest memories, because they were all just a great big fat lie. The Joker had not merely deceived her; he had manipulated her into deceiving herself. What a dirty trick. Having to admit that, and accept why the Joker had done it, was a knife in her heart. And yet the feelings that came with those memories were the joy she'd felt in her work, of falling in love, not anger at his betrayal, or even shame at being the Joker's perfect mark.

How did a person recover from that?

It helped to remind herself that although she had broken the Joker out of Arkham, he was nowhere to be found now that she was inside and he was free. The news services were saying he was probably dead but Harley didn't believe it. It would take a lot more than falling off a train to put an end to the Joker.

But what *would* she do if a sudden explosion blew a hole in the wall and the Joker came striding in to take her away? Highly unlikely. But there was another scenario not nearly as far-fetched: what if Batman recaptured him and brought him back to Arkham?

They would put him back in isolation, of course. She wouldn't be allowed to see him, but he'd probably find some way to get a message to her. What would she do? Turn the message over to Dr. Leland, or keep quiet?

She hadn't turned over to Dr. Leland the message she'd found in her cell, which she supposed meant she hadn't learned her lesson.

And if he *didn't* send a message?

Would she feel him anyway, down in the cell where she had fallen in love with him, like a twisted variation of *The Princess and the Pea*? Would just knowing he was in Arkham undo her?

Her body continued to heal and her mind became stronger even if her emotions were shaky, and eventually Harley was able to talk to Dr. Leland about him. The Joker's narcissism had a profound connection to his obsession with Gotham City, Dr. Leland said. If he were still alive, he was there or close by. The Joker was convinced the city was rightfully his; if he could kill Batman in a sufficiently ostentatious and clever way, it would give him absolute power over Gotham and everyone in it.

"Delusional, yes," Dr. Leland said with a good-natured frankness that made Harley feel better about everything. "Stranger than Killer Croc or a flying, bulletproof alien? Not so much."

"If the Joker *were* recaptured and sent back here, would you tell me?" Harley asked suddenly.

"Immediately, if not sooner," Dr. Leland said with a half-smile.

"It would be no good trying to hide it. We could put that man in a cell at the center of the earth or on the dark side of the moon or in orbit around Neptune, and inside of two minutes, the whole world would know it."

◆

Months passed, and Harley continued to improve. Dr. Leland began to make noises about life after Arkham. Harley had known she wasn't serving a life sentence, but she didn't feel ready to think about getting out. It was still hard not to think of herself in terms of the Joker. Sometimes she wasn't sure she'd ever find her own separate identity again.

"I can still remember vividly what it was like to be—" Harley hesitated, trying to find the right words. "—to be under his control and believing beyond all doubt it was true love. And you're already talking about releasing me back into the wild."

"Your attachment to the Joker was the root of your problem," Dr. Leland told her. "You've broken that attachment and I've done what I can to reinforce your sense of yourself as an individual. But for your recovery to be real, you have to be 'in the wild,' as you put it." Pause. "Plus, we need the room for someone with more severe problems."

Doctor and patient laughed together. It made Harley feel good to hear how normal it sounded, a couple of friends sharing a laugh.

"But we aren't going to simply push you out the front gate and wish you luck," Dr. Leland went on. "You'll go to a halfway house for six months. Then you'll be evaluated and they'll decide whether you should stay longer or if you're ready for life 'in the wild.'"

"What's the halfway house like?" Harley wanted to know.

"I think you'll like it," Dr. Leland said. "I chose it because all the women there have been in some kind of toxic relationship that turned their lives upside down. Not all of them were love relationships. Some were enmeshed with so-called 'friends,' some were victimized by a parent, and a couple escaped from cults."

But not the cult of Batman, Harley said silently. She had to press her lips together to keep herself from speaking aloud. She hadn't talked about Batman in therapy; Batman was unfinished business, but Dr. Leland didn't need to know that. She already knew Dr. Leland's feelings on the matter: *You're not from around here.* And Harley couldn't do anything about that.

And although Dr. Leland might be prone to a little too much hero worship where Batman was concerned, *she* hadn't run off with him and committed a string of crimes. Nor had Batman smacked her around or thrown her out a seventh-floor window.

Some heroes had feet of clay; others were clay all the way up to their necks.

◆

Dr. Leland was sanguine about Harley's chances of finding work but said nothing about her getting her medical license back, and Harley knew better than to ask. All the women at the halfway house were employed, she told Harley. Harley wondered how many of them were working fryolators, washing cars, or cleaning places they'd never be allowed into otherwise. What kind of job opportunities were there for an ex-doctor with an Arkham diploma?

Of course, if she wanted to make real money, she could become a mob doctor. Someone who could take care of bullet wounds without calling the cops, and whose medical wasn't in veterinary medicine, was a real prize.

She was just kidding, Harley told herself: a private joke. But she filed the idea away at the back of her mind, in case Big Belly Burger couldn't get past the stigma of Arkham even just for drive-thru work.

32

At seven a.m. on the morning of Harley's discharge from Arkham Asylum, Dr. Leland gave her a shoulder bag, a small suitcase with a change of clothing, a little cash, a bus ticket, and a printout with a map and directions to the halfway house. She waited with Harley at the stop across from the gates; when the bus came, Dr. Leland hugged her, wished her the best, and pushed her up the steps.

Harley had thought returning to Gotham City would stir up a lot of emotions; instead, it was anti-climactic. Gotham wasn't a magical realm like Oz—it was just a city with people trying to get through every day as best they could.

Harley found her way from the Gotham City central station to the nearest elevated-train stop. The woman who sold her the day-pass told her which train to take and what station to get off at. From there, it was a brief bus-ride or a bit of a walk.

Harley decided to walk. The months she had spent with casts on her arms and legs had left her weak and out of shape. Walking was a good way to get back into exercise, a good way to get the lie of the land, too. It was a nice, residential neighborhood with a local train station and regular bus service—not the sort of place where super-villains hung out.

Harley saw toys in a lot of the front yards. That was nice, she supposed, but she was glad she'd grown up urban. She and her brothers hadn't needed a yard—all of Brooklyn had been their yard.

They'd played hopscotch on the sidewalk and teeter-tottered in the local playground. They hadn't needed to make play-dates; there were always kids around, and plenty of grown-ups, too, especially in summer when everyone sat outside on their front stoops.

She was still floating in a cloud of nostalgia when she came to the halfway house. It was a large Victorian, a bit shabby but solid, with a wrap-around front porch, a lawn that was more green than brown, and flowering plants lining the front walk. It looked very welcoming, but her stroll down memory lane had made her yearn to be back in the heart of the city, where traffic noise would wake her in the morning and lull her to sleep at night.

Maybe in six months, if she played her cards right.

Harley drew herself up tall and squared her shoulders, the way she used to before a difficult floor routine, and strode up the front walk. She trotted up the three slightly saggy porch steps and planted herself at the front door. (Perfect landing, without a wobble.) But before she could ring the bell, she heard an ear-splittingly loud *AA-OOO-GAH!*, followed by very familiar raucous laughter.

She turned around. The limo at the curb was a deep metallic purple; she knew that shade. Then the passenger door swung open.

His suit matched the limo, and that lime-green hair probably glowed in the dark. He gave her the smile that had always made her knees tremble and her heart pound. Even at that distance, she knew he was gazing into her eyes like he'd spent the last several months dreaming of this moment. Now it was finally here—he had come to pick her up so they could go do something outrageous.

When the Joker beckoned to her, Harley didn't hesitate. She dropped her suitcase, yelled "Puddin'!" sprinted down the walk, and dived into the front seat. The door closed behind her and the car pulled away from the curb.

What happened next was preserved for posterity on YouTube.

♦

Sixteen-year-old Betty Lemanski, who lived across the street and three doors down from the halfway house, saw the purple limo pull over and went outside with her cell phone. She was hoping to capture a candid video of an eccentric billionaire or celebrity. She hadn't been expecting a super-villain until she heard the laughter.

Betty didn't get a very good shot of the young blonde woman getting into the car but she hoped the driver's window would be down as it went past. It wasn't, but the car suddenly screeched to a stop right in front of her. The driver's side door flew open and the Joker ("The actual *Joker!*") tumbled out onto the street ("Ass over teakettle! I almost *died!*"). Betty watched flabbergasted as he scrambled up onto his knees and said, "But, cupcake, Daddy's *lost* without you!"

The woman behind the wheel laughed at him. *"I'm not your cupcake!"* she shouted, slammed the car door and drove away. The Joker got up and ran after her, still protesting his love. Betty Lemanski's footage ends as the Joker starts to give up the chase; at that point, Betty decided to go back inside, triple-lock the front door, and call the cops.

By the time they arrived, however, the Joker was nowhere to be found. Police canvassed door to door in a five-block radius, but the Joker had somehow slipped away unnoticed—no mean feat for a tall, skinny man in a purple suit, with green hair and a permanent evil grin.

The purple limo was eventually found at the bottom of the river by police working a different case. It was thought to be unrelated, but, in Gotham, you just couldn't be sure of anything.

33

Six months later...

When Dr. Irene Smith, MD, joined the midtown Manhattan branch
of New York Health Practitioners, she didn't have the thickest sheaf
of glowing letters of recommendation, but those she did have were
impressive, and from some of the most respected professionals in
the field of medicine. Dr. Smith herself was quiet, soft-spoken, and
demure, but very self-possessed. She didn't suffer from a lack of
confidence but she wasn't from the if-you've-got-it-flaunt-it school
of demeanor, which probably accounted for her rather surprising
patient list. Some were VIPs, some had a whiff of notoriety about
them, and some were actually a little scary. But obviously they all
trusted Dr. Smith, who seemed above reproach.

Dr. Smith had come to Manhattan from Gotham City, which
surprised her colleagues until she explained she was from Brooklyn
and she was actually coming back to her home town, if not her home
borough. That made more sense—everyone knew Gotham City was
one of those places unto itself. People from out of town seldom felt
completely at home there, while people from Gotham were never
at home anywhere else. They might travel far and wide but they
always went back, no matter how long they'd been away. It was just
something about the place—why else would a billionaire like Bruce
Wayne live there? He'd been all over the world and he could probably
buy his own country, but he called Gotham City home.

Hell, even criminals couldn't stay away. The Joker could have fled to some country that had no extradition treaty with the US and lived happily ever out-of-reach. But he always went straight back to Gotham City—if he ever actually left. And then there was that institution—Arkham Asylum. It had a pretty lurid history. What did Dr. Smith think about that, Dr. Eileen Thibodeau asked one night over drinks after work during a shameless attempt to pump her for information about Batman.

Dr. Thibodeau told Dr. Smith she saw Batman as the key to "that whole Gotham thing." She thought he had some kind of animal magnetism, maybe from something in the air or water that reacted with his biochemistry. It wasn't such a ridiculous idea—there were meta-humans with powers far more unlikely than the ability to fascinate and influence an entire city.

Dr. Smith only smiled and said her time in Gotham had been rather uneventful. She'd been part of a family practice and the most exciting thing she'd ever done was give flu shots to the offspring of the wealthy at Gotham Academy and Prep, and only to fill in for the school doctor who had gone down with the flu herself.

As for Batman's hypothetical charisma, Dr. Smith had no opinion. In the whole time she'd lived in Gotham City, she had never seen the hometown hero in person, only on the news or patched into funny cat videos on YouTube. Ditto Gotham's most flamboyant super-villains, who certainly seemed to be as crazy as everyone said—media-crazy. A lot of them had publicists as well as lawyers; reality TV had changed the world.

Gotham did have its own ambience, Dr. Smith said. How much Batman really had to do with it, however, was debatable. It could have been the other way around. Local historians said the area had always been a different kind of place, *sui generis*, even before the advent of the leotard.

Dr. Thibodeau would have pursued the subject further but Dr. Smith suddenly had a lot of appointments outside standard office hours and wasn't available for Happy Hour chitchat about Gotham City.

Then NYHP received a request from a wealthy businessman returning to New York after many years abroad, who wanted a personal physician. No one was surprised when management gave it to Irene Smith; she was already NYHP's fairest fair-haired girl.

◆

A car service took Dr. Smith to the Battery Park Esplanade, where there was a motorboat waiting at a slip to take her out to a yacht. "We've got a ways to go," said the woman who helped her on board with her large medical case. "I suggested picking you up at a pier in South Brooklyn but the boss wouldn't hear of it. I don't know what he's got against Brooklyn."

Dr. Smith smiled as she settled down on a cushioned seat. "You know what they say—the rich are different."

"Ain't they just," the woman said. "I hope you don't get seasick?"

"Not at all," Dr. Smith assured her. "I could live at sea."

"Good thing," the woman said, stuffing her curly brown hair into a woollen watch cap. "From what I understand, you'll be doing just that for a while. A couple weeks at least, maybe more. Comfy?"

Dr. Smith nodded. "And I went before I left."

Laughing, the woman nodded at a man on the slip to cast off. He tossed the rope to her and she coiled it and stuffed it under the seat in the stern before she started the motor and steered the boat out toward open water.

◆

Dr. Irene Smith took her tablet out of her bag and brought up the notes on her new patient. The combination of motor noise and wind made conversation impossible and she was pleased that her aquatic chauffeur didn't feel the need to try. She wanted to use the time to collect her thoughts before she met her eccentric, Brooklyn-averse patient.

She'd been told she'd be arriving in the middle of the patient's welcome-home party, which had made the news days ahead of time as *the* party of the year; anyone who was anyone would be there, and if you didn't get an invitation you were officially no one. Some claimed to have seen the guest list and said it was a mix of the usual suspects—Denzel, Krysten, Carrie-Ann, Keanu, Dwayne, Swoozie, and Pedro—along with some unusual suspects who were so important no one knew who they were. There were also a few Senators (but *no* Congressmen), two or three governors, and some representatives of the Mothers And Fathers Italian Association, all of them law-abiding children of law-abiding immigrants who had come to the US with nothing and made a fortune via hard work and ambition.

Dr. Irene Smith had never been to such a fancy shindig, nor had her alter ego, Harley Quinn. But neither persona felt particularly intimidated—a party was a party was a party. Harley figured it was too much to hope that the bar would be extensive enough to include grape soda. They'd probably have Orange Crush and Dr. Brown's Celery Soda, and all the fixings for egg creams so the guests could feel like they were having a taste of New York back in the day.

◆

Dr. Irene Smith, MD, had appeared right after Harleen Quinzel had disappeared following her discharge from Arkham Asylum. Dr. Joan Leland herself had pronounced her sane and healthy, and yet, scant minutes before Quinzel was supposed to have entered a halfway house to begin the next stage of her recovery, she had encountered the criminal who had abused her and ruined her life.

The sight of him in a ghastly purple limo had obviously triggered violent emotions; Quinzel had jacked the car and driven off without him. Not that the Joker had pressed charges.

Harleen Quinzel, aka Harley Quinn, vanished and became a folk hero, legend, and role model to aspiring young female criminals everywhere—the days when the best a girl could hope for was being a gun moll or some made guy's *goomar* were definitely over. (Poison Ivy's assertion that they should already have learned this from *her* never got any play on network news.)

♦

Dr. Irene Smith was perfect in every way. She did nothing to attract attention to herself or to make anyone ask questions. But as a doctor, she could access all sorts of sensitive information. Hospitals were teeming with it; all she had to do was put on a white coat and hang a stethoscope around her neck and she was practically invisible. And free to do as she liked.

The Joker's greatest desire was to be seen by everyone everywhere, all the time. But he was totally clueless. He'd never understood that you were most powerful when you went unnoticed.

What would Dr. Leland have made of that? She might have agreed but it was more likely she'd have asked Harley what did "power" mean to her, why was it so important, and did it really have to be? Which was missing the point, but Dr. Leland wasn't a criminal.

Batman would get it, though. He *was* a criminal, walking the fine line between fame and obscurity. In all the years—decades—he'd been Gotham City's favorite outlaw-hero, he had become a household name without ever being doxxed. To Harley, that was solid proof he was super-rich. For a while, she thought he might be several super-rich guys taking turns in the costume. But even if a group of men could have maintained the persona so consistently, Harley doubted they could have kept such a big secret for so long.

No matter how rich or well-paid they might have been, money was never enough. Harley was pretty sure that sooner or later, one of them would have gotten drunk in a bar and said, *Yeah, I'm Batman, baby, wanna ride in my Batmobile?*

Either way, it was crazy. And in Harley Quinn's professional opinion as an expert in human craziness, the Joker and Batman were two sides of the same crazy coin. Someday they would finally get a room and they'd never come out. What would become of Gotham City then?

Harley didn't know and didn't care.

34

The motorboat caught up with the yacht under the Verrazano-Narrows Bridge, just east of the Rockaway Ferry. Passengers rushed to the side facing the yacht, elbowing each other and the paparazzi; the latter would have been tipped off by someone on the yacht-owner's staff. Tomorrow the web would be full of telephoto shots of famous people dancing badly. There was no point in throwing a fancy party without any little people to gaze longingly at what was out of their reach.

Two men in tuxedos helped Harley board the yacht from the stern. Their shoulder-holsters bulged slightly under their jackets—the idea was to discourage misbehavior without being too obvious. Harley chuckled inwardly; when you knew the tricks, you wondered why they weren't obvious to everyone.

"Glad you could join us, Dr. Smith," one of the men said. "I'm Thomas, Mr. Dell's executive assistant. My compliments on your choice of footwear." He looked down at her non-slip white canvas boat-shoes. "Have you spent much time on the water?"

"Only in quantities small enough to fit in a glass with ice cubes," she replied.

Thomas laughed politely. "Mr. Dell is waiting for you on the upper deck. Follow me. Joseph will take your medical bag for you."

They went up two ladders, passing the DJ on the middle deck. He nodded at them, grinning from ear to ear as he hovered over his equipment. Harley nodded back, amused; he probably thought this was the gig of a lifetime. He had no idea.

"Are you sure this is a yacht?" Harley asked Thomas as they reached the top deck and entered an enclosed area. "It seems more like a scaled-down cruise ship."

"Actually, my dear, it's a mega-yacht," said an elderly man in a reclining chair. "Or so I've been told. It doesn't sound like an official classification to me. Young people these days, they're all mega-this and mega-that."

Two more men in tuxedos stood behind him, their faces expressionless as their boss touched a button on a control in his hand and the chair cushion rose, standing him up on his feet. "So lovely to meet you, Dr. Smith." He took her hand and kissed it. "I'm glad you're able to join the party."

The years had not been kind to him. It took all of Harley's self-control not to wipe her hand on her trousers. When he smiled, the old man looked like a slightly more human version of Killer Croc. She hadn't noticed that the last time she'd seen him, but he hadn't been smiling at the time.

"Not to be a party-pooper, but I'd like to examine you. Nothing too extensive or invasive," Harley added, as the old man's expression turned apprehensive. "Just get your vitals, ask a few questions. A quick and dirty once-over."

He was grinning again as the chair lowered him back down to a sitting position. No doubt he had an endless supply of playing-doctor jokes he couldn't wait to use.

"So if you executive assistant types wouldn't mind giving us some privacy?" Harley said, looking from Thomas to the other men.

No one moved.

"Sorry, my dear," Mr. Dell sighed, "but it's no use trying to get me alone. They won't let me out of their sight. Garbo would die of frustration."

Thomas appeared to be the only one with the ability to

change expression; he looked politely puzzled.

"I *vant* to be *alone*," Harley said, mimicking Greta Garbo. Thomas only looked more bewildered. Harley turned to the old man. "Young people these days."

He threw back his head and laughed himself into a coughing fit. "Oh, my dear," he panted when he could speak. "I love beautiful young women who don't need references older than last week explained to them. What did you say your first name is?"

"Doctor," Harley said cheerfully, which set him off again. She already had her stethoscope out and was undoing the buttons of his shirt. His cough sounded like textbook congestive heart failure. No doubt a doctor had already told him that; Harley imagined his response had been to order a thirty-two-ounce prime rib and sprinkle an inch of salt on it before popping some Viagra.

"Please try to be a little quieter," she said after a bit. "I need to hear if your heart's still beating."

"Oh, I'm pretty sure it is now that you're here, my dear doctor," he chuckled.

Harley's hackles went up; she covered it with a five-hundred-watt smile. "Your pacemaker isn't set on disco, is it?"

More laughter; Harley had to wait to listen to his chest. Then she took his blood pressure with a wrist cuff instead of the more accurate upper-arm wrap. He wouldn't have to worry about his blood pressure for much longer.

Harley took three readings, then turned to Thomas. "Are you sure your assistants can't wait outside till we're done here?" she asked him. "The numbers I'm getting here are dangerously high. This usually happens when there are too many people in the room—the patient's attention is all over the place and it's impossible to get an accurate reading."

Thomas looked slightly apologetic. "Mr. Dell's safety has to be our primary concern. A man as successful as he is has a lot of enemies—"

"And one of them is high blood pressure, 'the silent killer,'"

Harley said impatiently. "It's like this: I'm going to take his blood pressure again, and if I get numbers as high as before, I'll call the Air Ambulance for emergency transport to the nearest urgent care facility. From here, that would be the new clinic at Norton Point."

Threatening him with Brooklyn finally did the trick. The old man gestured at the men and growled, "Get. *Out.*"

"But Mr. Dell—" said Thomas.

"I'd be a sitting duck in Norton Point," he said in a low, dangerous voice. "If that happens, you're all fired and you won't like your *severance.*"

Harley made her face assume the same expressionless look the men wore as they left. She wondered if they noticed the resemblance. Probably not; they didn't look like detail guys.

"Alone at last!" The old man practically licked his chops. "Now, what did you have in mind, my dear?"

"First, let's get you nice and comfy," Harley said, slipping the chair control out of his hand and reclining the chair fully. He wasn't lying as flat as on a proper examination table but this was good enough. "I need you to relax before I take your blood pressure again."

"You wouldn't *really* send me to North Point, would you?" He sounded playful but Harley heard a plaintive undertone. Poor baby.

"I'd only want to make sure you got to the closest facility." Harley moved behind the chair and began gently massaging his temples. "But never mind. Try to relax now."

"That feels so good," he sighed. "Would you mind doing that just a bit longer?"

"Not at all," she purred, keeping her touch gentle. "We need to get that blood pressure down out of the stratosphere."

"I think you're just what the doctor ordered." The old crocodile chuckled. "The doctor that the doctor ordered."

"Good one," she sneered. He didn't notice.

"You know, I've been doing business for a very long time," he went on. "When I started out, you probably weren't even a twinkle in your father's eye."

Harley made herself go on rubbing his temples instead of stabbing her fingers into them.

"I've still got plenty of deals left to make," he said. "But I find now I'm in need of a personal physician to help me through the day. And my days can be pretty long. I won't bore you with the details."

"Oh, I know all about *your* monkey business, Mr. *Dell—vecchio.*" The tough Brooklyn cookie crashed the party. Harley vaulted over the chair and landed astride his chest. "How ya doin'? Remembah me?" she asked as he stared up at her, dumbfounded. "Harleen Quinzel, of the Brooklyn Quinzels. Ya tried to sell me to one o' yer poivoit friends. Ring any bells now?" She squeezed his torso between her knees, hard enough to make him gasp.

Delvecchio fumbled at the arm of the chair. Harley knocked his hand away, lifted the panel on the arm and found the pistol he'd been going for, just in time to shoot his "assistants" as they came back in. Even without the silencer, she doubted anyone could have heard anything over the music, which wasn't disco but breakbeat. She'd always loved breakbeat. The Joker had hated it, but he'd hated all music.

Delvecchio tried to grab at her but he was too feeble to do anything more than annoy her. Still straddling his chest, she hit his solar plexus with the heel of her free hand, knocking the wind out of him.

"Uh-uh-uh!" Harley said. "Finders keepers!" She wrinkled her nose cutely at him. "Know what else I found? This nice big boat. An' I'm keepin' that, too!" She climbed off him, took him by the front of his shirt and yanked him out of the chair. He stumbled but she held him up easily as she dragged him outside to the part of the deck overlooking the party below.

"But just to show you I ain't mean," she said, "I'm gonna let you swim home! That's gonna be quite a ways since you got something against Brooklyn—I would, too, if I tried to sell the sweet little Quinzel girl from round the way to a poivoit—so I guess you better get started!"

Delvecchio cringed in terror as she dragged him around to the side directly over the water so he could see all the foam churned up by the engines.

"*Bon voyage*, Mr. Delvecchio, and don't get caught—" Harley pitched him over the railing. "—in the engine propellers under the—" The foam turned red. "Oops." She wiped the gun off and tossed it after him.

Harley went back inside, stepping over the assistants' bodies, and removed several components from her medical bag. It didn't take her long to put them together. This was her favorite toy. The Joker had hated it because he was terrible at assembling anything. It was that instant gratification thing—he always wanted stuff to pop into his hand fully formed and ready to go, which was why he had turned his nose up at the lightest, most portable machine gun ever made. She hadn't.

Sticking extra clips in the waistband of her neat trousers, Harley stepped outside again and looked around. She should probably handle the DJ next, she thought and slung the machine gun over her shoulder to climb down to the next deck.

"Turn it off!" she shouted. He shook his head, putting a hand to his ear. Harley mimed turning a knob. "*OFF!*"

The DJ gave her an incredulous look. "Say what, baby?"

Harley shrugged. "I tried," she said and killed his equipment with the machine gun.

The DJ screamed and backed away.

"Don't call me baby," she said, and motioned toward the rail with the gun's still smoking muzzle. "Now swim home."

He went over the side without another word.

Harley turned to look at the rest of the partygoers, who were gaping up at her with shocked, terrified faces. None of them looked like they could have been named Denzel, Keanu, or Swoozie.

"From where we are right now," Harley announced loudly, "you can swim to Coney Island and get some Nathan's hot dogs. So everyone who *wants* to survive this party should jump right now. And anyone who doesn't—" She fired into the air.

The screams were louder than the music had been. But the boat was clear in barely a minute.

"Okay!' she said aloud, slinging the machine gun over her shoulder again. "Now where's the steering wheel on this thing?" In fact, she had looked up information on the yacht ahead of time. The control room or bridge or whatever they called it was right where the map had said it would be.

The radio crackled suddenly. "This is the Coast Guard calling recreational vessel *King's Throne*. We have received calls of an emergency and people in the water. Please advise, over."

"It's all good in the hood, CG," Harley replied. "Buncha folks decided they wanted to go night-swimming. You know rich people—they're different. Pick 'em up if you want, it's no skin off my nose. Over."

"Ah, who am I speaking with?" asked a different male voice. "Please identify yourself. Over."

"Oh, sure," Harley said. "I'm None of Your Business, Stay Outta My Way," Harley said cheerfully. "Maybe you hoid o' me. Ovah!"

"Is this Harley Quinn, the Joker's girlfriend?" demanded the man on the radio. "Respond immediately, over!"

"Hey, pal, I ain't *nobody's* girlfriend," Harley informed him. "Now step *off* or get stepped *on*." That didn't really work when you weren't on land, she thought, but what the hell. "Ovah an' *out!*"

"You're making a big mistake—"

Harley snapped off the radio. Sooner or later, they always started with the you're-making-a-big-mistake routine. Maybe she was. But if so, it wasn't one she'd already made.

She changed course and put the lights of Coney Island behind her.

ACKNOWLEDGMENTS

Very special thanks to:

My wonderful son, Robert Fenner. We used to watch *Batman: The Animated Series* together when he was a little boy. I had no idea at the time that having fun with my kid would be so advantageous professionally.

Thanks also to Steve Saffel for inviting me to the party and to Ella Chappell, super-editor with nerves of steel.

And to Paul Dini, for giving us this very intriguing, very dangerous woman.

...and always to my husband The Original Chris Fowler, who is the complete and utter opposite of Mr Wrong.

—*Pat Cadigan*

Mad thanks to:

Steve Saffel, host, editor, sanity preserver and mentor on this wonderful journey.

A terrific collection of collaborators including Alan Burnett, Eric Radomski, Bruce Timm, Tom Ruegger, Dustin Nguyen, Paul Levitz and so many others I've been fortunate to work with on Bat-related animation and comics through the years.

Just about everyone at DC.

Jimmy Palmiotti and Amanda Conner, for Coney Island.

And most important, to my dearest Misty Lee—my toughest critic, my eternal inspiration, my love forever.

—*Paul Dini*

ABOUT THE AUTHORS

PAUL DINI is an American writer and producer who works in the television and comic book industries. He is best known as a producer and writer for several Warner Bros. Animation and DC Comics animated series, including *Tiny Toon Adventures, Batman: The Animated Series, Superman: The Animated Series, The New Batman/Superman Adventures, Batman Beyond*, and *Duck Dodgers*. Dini went on to write and story edit the popular ABC adventure series *Lost*. He has written a number of comic books for DC Comics, including *Harley Quinn, Superman: Peace on Earth*, and *Dark Night: A True Batman Story*.

PAT CADIGAN is a science fiction, fantasy and horror writer, three-time winner of the Locus Award, twice winner of the Arthur C. Clarke Award and one-time winner of the Hugo Award. She wrote the novelization of *Alita: Battle Angel*, and a prequel novel to the highly anticipated film, *Iron City*. She also wrote *Lost in Space: Promised Land*, novelizations of two episodes of *The Twilight Zone*, the *Cellular* novelization, and the novelization and sequel to *Jason X*.